RIVER RUNS DEEP

River Runs Deep

by Jennifer Bradbury

A Caitlyn Dlouhy Book

Atheneum Books for Young Readers
NEW YORK LONDON TORONTO SYDNEY NEW DELHI

ATHENEUM BOOKS FOR YOUNG READERS ★ An imprint of Simon & Schuster Children's Publishing Division ★ 1230 Avenue of the Americas, New York, New York 10020 ★ This book is a work of fiction. Any references to historical events, real people, or real places are used fictitiously. Other names, characters, places, and events are products of the author's imagination, and any resemblance to actual events or places or persons, living or dead, is entirely coincidental. ★ Text copyright © 2015 by Jennifer Bradbury ★ Cover illustration copyright © 2015 by Grady McFerrin ★ Map on pages vi–vii by Rick Britton ★ All rights reserved, including the right of reproduction in whole or in part in any form. ★ ATHENEUM BOOKS FOR YOUNG READERS is a registered trademark of Simon & Schuster, Inc. ★ Atheneum logo is a trademark of Simon & Schuster, Inc. ★ For information about special discounts for bulk purchases, please contact Simon & Schuster Special Sales at 1-866-506-1949 or business@ simonandschuster.com. ★ The Simon & Schuster Speakers Bureau can bring authors to your live event. For more information or to book an event, contact the Simon & Schuster Speakers Bureau at 1-866-248-3049 or visit our website at www.simonspeakers.com. ★ Also available in an Atheneum Books for Young Readers hardcover edition ★ The text for this book is set in Dante MT. ★ Manufactured in the United States of America ★ 0616 MTN ★ First Atheneum Books for Young Readers paperback edition July 2016 ★ 10 9 8 7 6 5 4 3 2 1 ★ The Library of Congress has cataloged the hardcover edition as follows: ★ Bradbury, Jennifer. ★ River runs deep / Jennifer Bradbury. — First edition. ★ pages cm ★ Summary: Twelve-year-old Elias is sent to Mammoth Cave in Kentucky to fight a case of consumption—and ends up fighting for the lives of a secret community of escaped slaves traveling along the Underground Railroad. ★ ISBN 978-1-4424-6824-5 (hc) ★ ISBN 978-1-4424-6825-2 (pbk) ISBN 978-1-4424-6826-9 (eBook) ★ 1. Mammoth Cave (Ky.)—Juvenile fiction. [1. Mammoth Cave (Ky.)—Fiction. 2. Tuberculosis—Fiction. 3. Slavery—Fiction. 4. Fugitive slaves—Fiction. 5. Underground Railroad—Fiction. 6. African Americans—Fiction.] I. Title. ★ PZ7.B71643Ri 2015 ★ [Fic]—dc23 ★ 2014049034

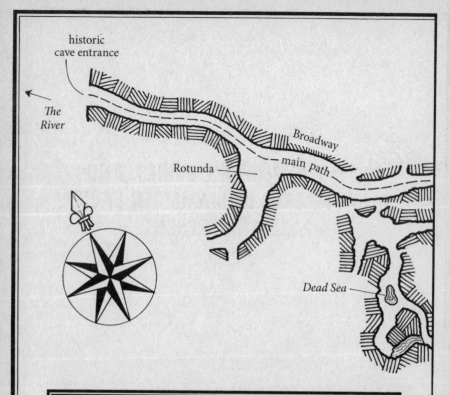

historic cave entrance

The River

Broadway

main Path

Rotunda

Dead Sea

MAMMOTH CAVE

Mammoth Cave entrance & Elias's tree

Elias's hut (on the left)

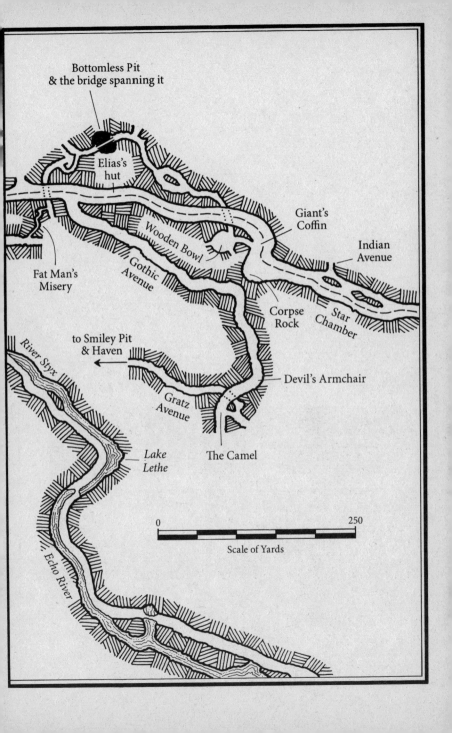

Bottomless Pit
& the bridge spanning it

Elias's
hut

Giant's
Coffin

Indian
Avenue

Wooden
Bowl

Fat Man's
Misery

Gothic
Avenue

Corpse
Rock

Star
Chamber

to Smiley Pit
& Haven

Devil's Armchair

River Styx

Gratz
Avenue

Lake
Lethe

The Camel

Echo River

0   250

Scale of Yards

RIVER RUNS DEEP

★　★　★　★　★　★　★　★　★
　★　★　★　★　★　★　★　★
★　★　★　★　★　★　★　★　★
　★　★　★　★　★　★　★　★
★　★　★　★　★　★　★　★　★

From the history of the patient
Elias Jefferson Harrigan,
age twelve years

December 30, 1842

Have agreed to admit my youngest patient yet. Though I resisted his mother's first three appeals to send him to me, like the widow in scripture she persisted, and I relented. His age is most concerning. How a lad from the open spaces of the Virginia coastline will tolerate the rigor of confinement underground . . . I cannot tell. Nonetheless, we have a hut that has recently been vacated, and an empty bed is a great drain on the spirits of my other charges. Further, if I am to find a cure for the blasted disease, I must have as many patients as possible to help me discover the right course of treatment. But perhaps his arrival will lift spirits all around. And perhaps his youth will prove a boon to his recovery.

Perhaps.

January 10, 1843

The boy arrived yesterday. He is frightfully small for his age, and had he not come so far—a week's journey all told down rivers and by stagecoach from Norfolk to our doorstep—I might have sent him home immediately. I suspected his mother had deceived me regarding his age, but inspection of his teeth and the eruption of his large molars convinced me otherwise. How his stature might bear out on his treatment remains to be seen. I suppose the phthisis has already taken its toll, slowing or even reversing his growth.

His size is not my only concern. My man Stephen Bishop has remarked on the boy's low spirits. Upon arrival, my other patients seemed to forget briefly why they came. The first glimpse of the gaping entrance of Mammoth Cave seems to crowd out the worry—the worry of carrying so virulent a disease, the worry of subjecting oneself to so dark and alien an environment. But Stephen reported that the boy remained stony-faced, steadfast in his gloom despite my best guide's attempts to impress him with the grand peculiarity of our extraordinary cave.

This report worries me even more. If the boy is so resigned as to be unmoved by the beauty and mystery of this place, is he beyond the reach of my science?

January 15, 1843

Elias has no trouble resting, though it may be that he is still recovering from his journey. He has little appetite, though whether a symptom of the disease or a response to his prescribed diet, I cannot yet determine. Hope to see slight improvements in his respirations and coloring within a week. Am less hopeful regarding his temperament. He endures his treatments so listlessly. The nurses report he spends most all his days lying abed, fiddling with ropes, reading the same books over and over, or writing letters home. He has made minimal effort to befriend Nedra or Mr. Pennyrile in the huts nearest his.

I fear I have made a grave error. The cave vapors can restore the flesh, but the boy's spirit remains weak. The spirit is ever the battleground.

Chapter One

MONKEY'S FIST

The fire popped behind the grate of the little stove, startling Elias awake. He reached over to scratch Charger's neck, but of course, not finding the dog there, opened his eyes and remembered where he was. The room was similar enough to his own back in Norfolk. There was a bed topped with a faded patchwork quilt. A braided rag rug covered most of the floor. A table and chair sat tucked into another corner, Elias's writing paper stacked on top, edges curling in the damp air. On the opposite wall hung a set of rough shelves holding a framed portrait of his family, his extra clothes and boots, as well as the razor and strap he'd brought along but would never need.

Above his bed was the window, just like his room at home. In Virginia the sun would stream in each morning with the call of shorebirds to tell Elias the day had begun.

But not here.

The sun never shone through this window.

How could it, when it was underground?

He sat up, tried to clear his throat, but fell to coughing instead. The spell was a short one, but all the same he was almost tired enough by the end that he was tempted to lie back down. Instead, he forced a swallow from the cup of water by his bed and grabbed the pencil off the table. He turned to the flat section of the wall above his bed and counted the hash marks there before adding one more. Nineteen. Had it been only nineteen days? He couldn't be certain without the rhythms of a day to confirm it.

Still, nearly three weeks he'd been inside the cave. Three weeks of nothing but rest and waiting and reading and thinking inside this little hut, with its walls made of puzzled-together stone, its curtain hung across the doorway for privacy, the roof open to the ceiling of the cave, vaulting another twenty feet up.

One of the slaves had left Elias's breakfast. Or maybe it was supper after all. There were no clues there, either. The doctor had put him on a strict diet straightaway.

"Eggs and tea," Dr. Croghan had announced after Elias's first examination, explaining that simplifying the diet would allow the body to concentrate on fighting the disease. Eggs, according to Croghan, were the perfect food, and he boasted that the horehound-dill tea was his own special concoction. The doctor seemed so pleased about it that Elias hadn't the heart to tell him the tea tasted like sucking on a pickle boiled in honey.

It was harder to take than the eggs, but even those grew tiresome shortly. Still, he knew he should be glad. The treatments could be worse. They'd tried all kinds of remedies on his father back in Norfolk before the end. Elias had worried then that the treatments meant to cure his father's lungs might only kill him quicker.

So if Croghan's tea tasted foul and the eggs got old, at least he hadn't worried about the doctor's methods killing him. Yet.

No, the remedies he endured easily enough.

But the boredom he did not.

It was the stillness and the dark and the sameness of it all. Nothing to do but rest, no one to talk to but the slaves who tended him or the doctor who saw him every day. The doctor had encouraged him to visit with his nearest neighbors. The section of the cave where his hut sat was a good-size chamber, though not so big as some of the rooms he'd passed through on the way down. Two huts sat on the other side of a little courtyard, some forty yards away from his. Between them sat a sort of nurses' station—a large fire ring, kettles, boxes of supplies, and provisions arrayed around whatever slave was on duty at the moment.

At first Elias had been keen to know the pretty lady with the golden hair in one of the far huts. Nedra. But not anymore. He visited with her once in a while, but the way he might have with a shut-in back home, or an old relation he was obliged to call on but couldn't wait to leave as soon as he'd arrived.

And that made him feel even worse.

The hut next to hers was more of a mystery. Elias spent a fair amount of time watching Pennyrile's cabin. He'd glimpsed the man only rarely and never saw him clearly or for long, as Pennyrile shut the curtain quick if Elias looked his way. He kept silent in there, not speaking even to Dr. Croghan or the slaves. But there were noises from inside, noises that spooked Elias. Cooing and warbling and flapping. The sounds of pigeons.

Pigeons. Down in a cave of all places.

Elias's curiosity still hadn't gotten ahold of him enough to find out why Pennyrile kept birds, or why Pennyrile was so secretive.

He'd written two letters home, filled with the kinds of things he felt he ought to say—that he was obeying the doctor, that the cave was interesting, that he missed his mother, grandmother, and sister. He'd received three letters from Virginia that he'd read until the pages had worn thin.

But there had been no new letter for a week, and the silence made it easy to slip into a sort of gloom, the kind where he almost let himself believe Mama and Granny and Tillie had given up on him, had sent him away to get rid of him. That *that* was the reason he didn't hear from them more.

He'd felt it at home some, when his friends stopped coming. Before sending him to Kentucky, his mother laid him up on the sleeping porch where Gideon and Harold would stop by once in a while, lingering on the steps, biding a few minutes with him. But eventually they took to only waving as they passed the hedgerow, and not long after, they quit passing by the house at all.

Elias tried not to hate them for forgetting him before he'd even died. But it was hard.

Tying knots helped some; reading helped less. The book of poetry he'd borrowed from Nedra was a disappointment. The knights were barely in any of the poems, and there were no battles or magic, at least not in any he'd discovered yet. But he'd gone and swapped with her for his copy of *The Death of Arthur*, so it was all he had for now.

He reread a longish poem that Nedra had dog-eared. At least this one had Lancelot. None of the rest made much sense to him, though he liked the way the words felt when he whispered them to himself as he read, keeping time like bells on a horse's harness.

> But in her web she still delights
> To weave the mirror's magic sights,
> For often thro' the silent nights
> A funeral, with plumes and lights
>   And music, went to Camelot:
> Or when the moon was overhead,
> Came two young lovers lately wed;
> "I am half-sick of shadows," said
>   The Lady of Shalott.

That part—the bit about being sick of shadows—he understood fine. He was sick of weak candlelight, too. Not to mention eggs without bacon or a hunk of bread.

No halves about it.

Tossing the book aside, he took the coiled rope off the bedpost and set to work on a monkey's fist, twisting the ropes and tucking the end through, over and over until he had a tight ball of a knot stopping up the end of the rope. Perfect for throwing. It was such a good knot, he hated to see it go to waste. Nedra across the way knit, and when she finished, she had something to show for it. But Elias could only undo his work and start anew. It was nearly enough to drive him to take up knitting. Nearly.

"What's that 'posed to be for?" a voice whispered.

"Who's there?" Elias jerked his head up and looked to the window. Empty. "I said, 'Who's there?'" Elias repeated. He had heard a voice, hadn't he? Or had his fever climbed again? Sometimes when it rose, he worried that he saw things . . . heard things.

"I ain't nobody," the whisper came again, even softer. "Jus' wondered about that tying you do."

Nobody? Elias thought. Had to be somebody. But it didn't sound like anybody he could name. Living in the dark taught a body to listen. He could tell the doctor coming just by his walk, and a voice was even easier to recognize. But he couldn't place it on account of the whispering. He reached for the lamp, began to pull it closer—"Far 'nough," the voice whispered.

Who on earth was it? he wondered. Not the doctor, of course. Not one of the other patients who wouldn't have reason or the energy to spy on Elias anyhow. That left only the slaves.

But this voice wasn't Stephen's. Stephen Bishop wouldn't have lurked at a window for anything in the world. The man was squat and strong, with glossy black hair that curled out from underneath the edges of his slouch cap. When he'd brought Elias down from the entrance the first day, he'd proudly pointed out all the wonders of the cave, his voice carrying as smoothly as that of an actor aiming to be heard up in the cheap seats. He took too much care with his appearance to hide in the dark and liked the sound of his own voice too much to whisper. He'd been bossy to boot, telling Elias not to go wandering, no matter what.

And it wasn't Nick's voice either. Nick, who often brought his meals and more fuel for the stove, wore an old felt parson's hat, shirt buttoned all the way up to his neck. His voice, when he cared to use it, rolled deep and rich, punctuated by pauses so he could spit short streams of tobacco off into the shadows. He was kind to Elias in both his few words and his manner, and was far too forthright to sneak around.

And though the voice was high and quiet, it wasn't Lillian or Hannah or any of the other young women who served as nurses in the ward.

No, the voice was young, and it was certainly one Elias had not heard before.

But the eyes—he'd seen those eyes before.

He'd noticed them his second day, staring in as he read, but they disappeared before he could even call out. And he'd seen them twice since, both times appearing in his darkened window, far enough out of the circle of light thrown by his lamp. And there were countless times Elias had *felt* someone watching, but when he checked, saw nothing in the window.

They were back now, looming a few inches above the sill.

"Who are you?" Elias asked, clenching the knot in his fist.

The eyes blinked, hovered, like they had no face to belong to. "What you do all that tying on those ropes for?"

Elias swallowed once. "This one's for throwing."

The eyes blinked again as the voice made a sort of *hmph* sound.

"Who are you?" Elias asked again.

"Don't matter."

Elias nearly asked the voice if it were really there at all, or if he were only imagining it, his bored brain inventing a strange visitor. Maybe his fever had spiked after all. But if the presence at the window were the product of his imagination, he couldn't very well expect it to confess. Elias chose his next words with care. "Are you a—" He cut himself off, tried again. "Nick said this place has haints."

The voice laughed quietly. "You askin' if I'm a ghost?"

"Are you?" Elias persisted. He'd pushed himself all the way up against the head of the bed, his spine pressing hard into the frame.

"Maybe I am," the voice said. "What about you?"

"Well, naw, I ain't a ghost."

"You sure?" the voice asked. "You just like the rest of 'em. All y'all do is sit around and do nothing all day. Cain't leave. And you're so peaked, you might as well be one."

"I'm sick," Elias protested. "I ain't dead. Not yet, anyhow."

At that moment Nedra set to coughing, a fit that came on as sudden as a squall. Elias heard Lillian rush across from where she sat by the fire. And when he looked back at the window, the eyes had vanished. In a flash of courage, Elias leaped to his knees and poked his head out the window.

No one there.

But he listened closely, and in the ebb between Nedra's racket, he heard feet running—bare, he reckoned by the soft slapping sounds—moving off down the slope, heading away from the huts.

He knew precious little about ghosts or haints, but he figured they floated more than walked. And in the light cast by the fire on the far wall, he could make out a shadow of movement, the faintest outline of a pair of arms extending for balance.

Ghosts wouldn't make shadows, would they?

Chapter Two

WATER KNOT

Elias fetched up the lamp and took off in the direction he'd seen the shadow fleeing.

He was lucky the nurse was busy. He was unlucky, however, in that his lamp didn't want to stay lit. He had to slow himself several times, cupping a hand in front of the flame to keep it from snuffing out, watching anxiously as it pulled dangerously thin.

The flame wasn't the only thing gasping. Elias's lungs protested the quick walk, that familiar feeling of iron bands wrapping around his chest returning. He heard his own breath whistle in and out. But he would not cough, he promised himself. *Just breathe shallow,* he thought, *you can cough when you've caught him up. . . .*

He was in a new part of the cave, an area just past the ward, down the path from the way he had been brought in. And then he realized that whoever—or *whatever*—he was following wasn't carrying any light. How could he not be carrying a light?

Elias heard movement far off at the end of the passage, then footsteps once again. He walked on, sure he'd found his ghost-who-was-not-a-ghost. "Go back!" came the voice, the same voice that he'd heard at his window, but this time harsher, a whisper-shout like the cry of some banshee.

In all the stories Elias had heard about faeries or spirits that led knights astray to trap them, he never once heard of those spirits telling the knights to go back. He reckoned maybe, somehow, that might be a good sign.

So he continued picking his way through the chamber and down to the tunnel he'd heard the voice shouting from. At last, he saw light ahead of him. His heart thudded, and he worried he might commence to wheezing or coughing, but he had to keep up. To his surprise, the light ahead wasn't moving. It was fixed in one spot, just beyond a bend to the right. He slowed as he drew closer, craning his neck around the corner to see his ghost for the first time.

But it wasn't a ghost at all. It was Stephen Bishop.

Stephen wasn't wearing the fancy getup he'd been in that first day when he guided Elias in: just a pair of ragged old pants, cotton shirt, and thin wool coat. He appeared younger out of his finer clothes, and Elias guessed he couldn't be much past twenty, the mustache over his lip still filling in.

Stephen sat cross-legged, writing in a little book with a nub of a pencil, the lamp perched up high on a rock. Elias noticed his printing was as neat as a pin, square and even as he wrote on a page already half filled up.

"Stephen?" Elias said, looking around the low tunnel.

"You should be in bed, Elias." Stephen didn't even look up.

"But—" Elias began before his cough finally caught up to him. He braced his hands on his knees, rode out his bucking lungs, and searched the tunnel ahead and behind him to make sure that he hadn't passed his ghost by mistake. Finally his cough died and he could finish. "But I was following . . ."

Stephen tilted his head. "What?"

Elias shrugged. "There was something at my window the morning after I got here. I could only see the eyes, and then just now they were back, and he talked to me. . . . Said he weren't a ghost—"

"Ghost?" Stephen was incredulous.

Elias felt foolish now. "He was there!" he insisted, "I

followed him. Whoever it was, he was running ahead of me without a light."

Stephen blew out his breath quick and sharp. "Only ones who know the cave well enough to go without a light for any length are me and Nick and Mat, and we do that only up by the entrance. And it sure wasn't Nick or Mat, and it wasn't me, was it?"

"Which one's Mat?"

Stephen almost laughed. "You'd have known if it were Mat. Trust me."

"But—"

"I think you maybe just got a touch of cabin fever."

This was true ten ways from Sunday, but to Elias's ear, it sounded as if maybe Stephen was trying a little too hard. He stayed quiet. "You figure on finding yourself a ghost, is that it?" Stephen asked. "Mercy. All you're going to do is make yourself into one, running off in the cave alone."

"I—"

"Never you mind about chasing haints." Stephen patted the cave floor. "Now sit down and catch your breath."

Elias sat, shamed and annoyed, certain none of the Knights of the Round Table ever got such a scolding. From the likes of a slave, no less.

Yet the truth of it was, Elias was more worn out from the chase than he liked to admit. He began fiddling with the end of a rope he found dangling from Stephen's pack.

"You can read?" Elias asked. "And write?" To hear Granny tell it, Kentucky was hard on its slaves, worse than Virginia even, on account of they didn't have so many and what they did have kept running off North to get free. Plus, it was against the law anywhere to teach a slave or a colored person to read.

Stephen's lip became a hard line. "I read," he said evenly. "That all right with you?"

Elias understood he'd offended him. He felt at once sorry for having done so and troubled for caring. Back home they owned a house girl and an outside man, and his mother and granny were nothing but kind to them. His own daddy had hired freedmen to work the docks and even to sail for him at times. Daddy'd said a man who didn't look after his property didn't deserve to have it in the first place; whether that property were a boat or a Negro, he didn't see the difference.

So Elias didn't see any cause for Stephen Bishop to bristle at the question of his reading or not.

Stephen flipped forward in his book, to a drawing with a series of notes next to it. "See that hole?" he asked, pointing at a trickle of water in the wall in front of him at eye level. Elias did. "That one opened up about three years back, or at least that's when we noticed it first. So I've been watching it. Along with others."

"Others?"

Stephen gestured around him, at the cave beyond. "Little places where the water starts to weep through. This one's grown nearly a quarter inch since I started keeping track of it."

A measly quarter of an inch after three years. Then again, caves were patient things after all. Too bad Elias couldn't be.

"Where's the water come from?"

Stephen pointed. "Up there. Dropping from somewhere else."

"From the river, maybe?" Elias asked, starting over on a water knot. He missed the sound and smell of water almost as much as he missed his family. He'd lived by the ocean his entire twelve and a half years; the marshy area where the James met the sea was his whole world. And he'd seen no rivers to rival the James as they came inland following the Wilderness Road. The last one they'd passed had been slow and skinny and muddy green, flat-bottomed barges squeezing up it like eggs passing through a chicken snake.

He'd not mind seeing a river down here.

Stephen bent back over his work. "Rivers are both farther in and below where we are now." He flipped briefly to the beginning of the book, the first drawing looking like nothing if it wasn't a map. It reminded Elias of the nautical charts his father used, various lines showing shipping routes or navigable rivers.

"Hey!" Stephen said, noticing at last the knot Elias was working in the cord. He snatched it from him. "A piece of rope isn't a thing to tangle up for fun. Not down here. You got no notion how many times I've been glad to have a rope—"

"I didn't tangle it," Elias protested, adding, "yank on them ends." Stephen did, and the knot came out clean and simple. "Water knot's a sort of trick knot, but serves useful on ship." Stephen looked at him curiously. "My daddy had ships," Elias offered.

Stephen coiled the rope slowly. "You know all kind of knots then, do you?"

"Reckon I do."

Stephen's eyes flicked from the rope to Elias to the rope again. He was clearly considering something. "What would you say to helping me and the boys one night? Out here?"

Elias sat up tall. Bother the ghost. A chance to do something, and with Stephen no less. Though he was prouder than a slave maybe ought to be, Elias liked him well enough. And now that he'd finally left his room, he thought he'd like to get out again. "When? Now?"

"Not tonight. Later. Only you don't go telling about

it. Or about chasing haints off in the cave, you hear?"
Stephen stood, tucked the book and pencil into his bag,
and flung one end of the rope at Elias. "Hold on to this.
I'll keep the other end. Last thing we need is you wandering off again."

"Now see here—"

"Just take it." Stephen was firm. "If you want to come
out with me, you'll learn to do what I say."

Elias huffed. He wasn't used to being spoken to this
way by colored men, slave or free. Still, the promise of a
chance to go exploring was worth a little wounded pride.
"Fine." They walked back up the little slope of the tunnel,
Elias feeling like a dumb cow being led back to the barn.

"You haven't been this far before, have you?" Stephen
asked him as they entered the big room Elias had passed
through a few minutes back.

"Only just now. When I was following . . . well . . ."
Elias trailed off.

"Watch this." Stephen walked to the wall of the
chamber, stuck the handle of his lantern in his mouth,
and climbed up a pile of loose rock. He set the lantern on
top and came back down. "Look up there." He swept his
arm at the ceiling. For a second, Elias forgot to breathe.

There were stars. Hundreds of them. Twinkling up in
the black. "How?" he whispered. How indeed? How had

they managed to poke a hole in the cave all the way to the sky?

"Something, isn't it?" Stephen asked, bending down and picking up a rock. "Some kind of shiny rock up there in the ceiling. Not gold or anything valuable. But it glints in the light. The smoke's blackened it up so you see it only in patches."

"Like stars," Elias said. He gave a tiny little sputter of a cough, but it didn't catch.

"Exactly. That's why we call this the Star Chamber."

Elias just gaped, wishing it wasn't what Stephen had described. That it was instead an actual window to the outside.

"You much at throwing?" Stephen asked.

"Huh?"

"Here"—Stephen placed the rock in Elias's palm—"heave it up there good—if you chip off some soot, you'll make a new place." Elias tested the rock's weight in his palm and tried to gauge the distance to the stars. He had no idea how far it really was, but he wound up and hurled the stone hard and fast at a steep angle. It clinked against the ceiling immediately.

"Good throw," Stephen said, grabbing the lantern. "I charge fellas on my tour a quarter to do that."

"A whole quarter? Just to throw a rock?"

"Not just to throw a rock. To make a *star*. And name it for their sweetheart. And if that sweetheart happens to be right there with them, you bet they pony up that quarter right quick."

Elias grinned. He couldn't help but picture his daddy hucking a stone up there for his mama. He once saw him skip one nine times. He'd have made a whole constellation.

Stephen slowly led Elias back up to the ward, pointing out things as they went. Elias expected the pace was on account of Stephen having slipped into the role of tour guide. That, or he was aware of how winded Elias had been on the trip down. Even now the air whistled and scraped over his throat as he drew breath.

It was clear Stephen was proud of the cave, loved it even, and couldn't help talking about it because of that. And Elias liked listening to him, but he kept thinking about the voice at his window, how it had warned him to go back, how it must have passed right by Stephen Bishop. Stephen had been awfully quick to decide that the voice and the footsteps Elias had heard were merely his imagination. Wouldn't anybody else have asked more questions? Tried to explain away what Elias thought he saw and heard?

"You sure you didn't see nobody sneaking by you in

that tunnel?" Elias interrupted Stephen as he was explaining how the old Indians used to light their way in the cave.

Once again Stephen's reply was almost too quick. "I told you to forget about that," he said, sounding for a moment as if he didn't disbelieve Elias so much as he didn't want to talk about it. Stephen caught himself, checked his tone. "Look, you got turned around, and your imagination ran off with you. But if you keep thinking on it, you're likely to get the doctor worried the sickness is creeping into your mind—"

"I ain't crazy!"

Stephen's voice dropped lower. "I didn't say you were. But then again, I'm not the doctor."

"I ain't," Elias repeated.

"I know," Stephen said, apologetic now. "So just forget about it, all right?"

They walked on a ways before Elias understood that they weren't returning to the ward. "Where we goin' now?" he asked as they rounded a huge chunk of rock that lay to the side of the main path.

"Something you ought to see," Stephen said.

"What is it?" Not that Elias really cared. He was just glad that Stephen wasn't taking him back yet.

"Something," Stephen said simply. They walked in silence, the path clean and smooth, so Elias reckoned this was at least part of the way Stephen and the others led their tours. It emptied into a little rounded chamber with other paths branching off.

"Where're we?" Elias asked, looking around at the different tunnels. He could imagine a knight standing there where he stood, hunting a dragon hiding up in any of these passages.

"Wooden Bowl," Stephen said. "C'mon." Elias followed him to one of the tunnels, and they began to climb back up.

After they'd gone a few dozen yards, Stephen held up a hand. "Shh!"

Elias stood stock-still.

"You hear something?" Stephen whispered.

Elias listened. At first he heard only the sound of his own breath, the faint hiss of the lamp burning up the oil. But then he heard the warbling, cooing noise he'd been hearing from Pennyrile's hut the last few weeks.

"Pigeons!" Elias said.

Stephen followed the sound.

What was a pigeon doing down here? Elias wondered.

When they finally found the bird, he saw why.

It huddled up against the wall of the cave, perched on a tiny shelf of rock. As the light found it, the pigeon craned its neck outward, and Elias saw the iridescent flashes of green and purple as the pigeon twisted its head to look at them.

"Hey, fella." Elias inched a hand toward the bird. The pigeon didn't peck at him, but it rumbled a little and made as if it would beat his hand away with its wings. But only one wing opened, the other trying but giving out halfway.

"It's lame," Stephen said.

Elias made soft cooing noises, ventured closer with his hand, and waited there until the bird lowered the good wing. "You think it got free of that Pennyrile man's hut?"

Stephen pointed to a scroll of paper wound tightly around the bird's leg, tied off with a piece of twine and a neat square knot. "Looks to me like he sent it out and it got lost."

"They carry messages?" Elias asked, beginning to understand. Stephen nodded.

"He used to walk them up nearer the entrance to let them go. But he can't manage it anymore. We offered to do it for him, but he seems disinclined to trusting. I found a dead one even farther in, and told him so, but he still sends them out."

Elias edged his hand closer. Soon he found the bird would let him stroke its gray breast with the back of his finger. "Got lost, didja?" he asked, gently cupping the bird in his palms. It answered with a trilling coo.

"You plan to carry him like that?"

Elias could imagine no other means to carry the bird. And he ought to take it back to Pennyrile. Even if the man were a spook, it didn't mean the bird ought to starve down there in the dark. "I can tie the rope around my wrist if that's what you want—"

Stephen sighed, but he looped the rope over his shoulder. "I won't make you. Just keep up."

Elias had spent his whole life carrying animals—turtles, bullfrogs, geese, Charger as a pup—and the bird seemed used to being handled, seemed to know staying with Elias was better than staying alone in the dark.

It wasn't long before they reached another chamber. "Wait here," Stephen ordered.

Elias stopped and stroked the pigeon's back with his thumb. He liked the feeling of the bird in his hands, the tiny heart hammering against his palm.

The feel of something warm and alive was blessedly familiar.

Stephen walked ahead to where another lantern hung and lit it with the flame of the one he carried. The light caught and burned bright as the room came into focus.

Elias saw the bridge first, a rickety-looking thing. It was little more than a narrow walkway, maybe the width of both of his feet together, with rails rising up and flaring out.

It looked more like the skeleton of a ship back in dry dock, stripped down to the ribs, than it did a bridge. But it was a bridge, spanning a dark sea of nothingness, still and deep and deadly. He found his heart racing in time with the bird's.

"That's Bottomless Pit, ain't it?" Elias asked. The pit was famous. The nearer Elias got on his journey from Virginia, the more often he'd meet a body who'd been to the cave, or heard tell of its wonders. And this was one Elias had heard spoken of often.

"Yep." Stephen motioned Elias over. Elias joined him and peered down, holding the pigeon off to the side.

He studied the bolts that anchored the bridge to the rock, mainly to avoid looking into the pit itself. It made him dizzy, that drop. "Drilled those myself," Stephen said, pointing at the bolts.

"With what?"

Stephen slung his pack around and withdrew a hand drill. "This. Bit's goin' dull, but it does the work. Rock's pretty soft anyhow. My first way over was a couple of ladders lashed together in the middle, but we couldn't bring folk across it, so we worked this one up." He stepped onto the bridge. "C'mon."

"I can see good—"

"Get on out here," Stephen insisted. Elias riled against the order, but he didn't want Stephen to think he wouldn't be helpful, or that he was yellow. All the same, he found it impossible to not look down as he placed his feet one in front of the other, wishing he had his hands free to grip the railing on either side. Stephen faced Elias when they came to the middle. "That's sixty feet to the bottom down there," he said.

Elias felt his insides drop, and the pigeon gave an alarmed coo as Elias's grip tightened. Sixty feet. He'd climbed the rigging on his father's ships, but that wasn't nearly so tall. And even that had given him fits when it was time to come back down. "Mercy," Elias said.

"And not the only one like it," Stephen said. "There're pits and falls all over the place out here. No bridges on most of them." Elias was beginning to see why Stephen had brought him here.

"You remember what I said when I first fetched you into the cave?" he asked.

Elias did. He recited Stephen's first warning. "'Don't go wanderin'.'"

Stephen's voice was stern. "You think you can heed that now?"

Elias barely managed to whisper, "Yes, sir."

At the ward, Lillian stood up quickly when she saw Elias climbing the slope with Stephen. She tightened up the shawl she wore over her trim shoulders like she was adjusting her armor, long cotton skirts churning around her ankles as she bore down on Elias. "What are you doing out of your hut?" She felt his forehead, leaned in and listened to his breath. "Clammy head and soundin' like a rusty gate."

"Easy, Lillian," Stephen said. "I was just showing him something. He's all right. And he won't tell Doc Croghan about you letting him sneak out."

She planted a hand on her hip and made her eyes so wide that her brows disappeared beneath the hem of the gray cloth she wore wrapped around her hair. "You know he sick, Stephen Bishop. Find somebody your own age to run about with."

Stephen took a step closer to Lillian and smiled, teeth flashing bright in the firelight. "I plan to, ma'am."

Elias suddenly started to feel out of place, wondering if maybe Stephen had ever thrown a rock at the ceiling for Lillian. Luckily, he had a good reason to slip aside.

He walked to Pennyrile's hut and used the toe of his boot to knock on the doorframe. "Sir?"

At first there was no reply. Then Elias heard a shuffling within, the other pigeons stirring and cooing. And then the man appeared, pushing back the curtain across the door. His eyes were dark, all pupils in the low light. A heavy mustache bristled over his lip, like a squirrel had left its tail parked there. A bright red scarf was tied up at his neck, the bulk of it bulging out oddly to one side. Other than the scarf, he wore only a dressing gown and a pair of heavy woolen socks. An oily, fishy smell hung about him.

Elias tried and failed not to stare at the bulge on the man's neck, and in his failure couldn't help noticing that the wrap was topped off with a neatly done lighterman's hitch and finished with a pair of half hitches. It was a tricky knot, one the men used to moor a boat up to the dock and then cast off easily.

Then Elias remembered himself, remembered how much he was always told not to stare, and he managed to tear his eyes away from the knot and the bulge it covered. "I . . . uh . . . I found your bird." He held the pigeon out.

Pennyrile scowled, then his eyes grew wider as he roughly took the bird from Elias. He palmed the body of the bird upside down in one hand and checked its legs. For fingers so meaty, he deftly untied the message, freeing the roll of paper and tossing it onto the bed behind him.

"I think his wing is—"

But Pennyrile had already righted the pigeon and was testing the wings. Working at the left one set the bird grunting and cooing.

"That's the one." Elias winced. "He doesn't seem to be able to fly, but—"

The rest of his words caught in his mouth as he recognized what Pennyrile was about to do. He'd changed his grip, holding the bird by his head in one hand and by the body with the other. He'd seen the house girl back home hold chickens that way right before they ended up on the table.

"Stop!" Elias hollered as Pennyrile began to twist the pigeon's neck. "Please!"

The man waited, silently watching Elias, hands still ready to snap the beautiful green-and-purple neck. The bird didn't move but to blink once at Elias.

"If it's all the same to you," Elias said, forcing the words to slow down, "I can look after him. Get him flying again."

Pennyrile leaned forward slightly and narrowed his eyes.

Why won't he say anything? Elias wondered.

"Please," Elias added. The memory of the pigeon's heart beating against his hand was still so fresh.

Pennyrile sucked at the inside of his cheek, still eyeing Elias, still with his hands poised to snap the neck. But just as suddenly as he'd prepared to end the bird's life, he righted the pigeon and returned it to Elias.

"Thank you!" Elias gathered the bird to his chest. "Thank you!"

He backed away quickly and ran to his own hut. He was too relieved to have saved the bird a second time to take note of Stephen's and Lillian's looks of concern. And he was far too happy to pay much mind to the uneasy feeling he got when he glimpsed Pennyrile still watching as he pulled the curtain across his own door.

Chapter Three

HALTER HITCH

Your lungs sound slightly improved, I believe," Dr. Croghan said as he tucked the tube he used to listen to Elias's chest back into his leather bag. He glanced at the pigeon. "Though your new friend's chatter makes it somewhat difficult to hear."

"His name's Bedivere." Elias rapped a knuckle on the tabletop. The pigeon strutted closer, twisting his head this way and that. Bedivere was a good name. The name of King Arthur's best friend, the one who he trusted to throw Excalibur back into the lake.

Croghan started to pet the bird, but Bedivere threw up his good wing and squawked.

"I think I'd prefer that he be caged like the rest of

Pennyrile's birds," Croghan said, eying a brass watch as he held Elias's wrist to count out the heartbeats. In the silence, Elias studied the doctor. He wasn't so old that he'd begun to go gray, but his hair needed a trim and he hadn't shaved. He wore a gentleman's clothes, but he'd missed a button on his waistcoat, and his trousers sported a patch poorly stitched.

"Oh no, Doctor," Elias said. "He can't fly. We're pals, see?" Elias rapped his knuckle once more on the tabletop, and Bedivere hopped into his palm.

"Fine," Croghan agreed. "But if you begin to decline, I'm afraid the bird will have to go."

"I been drinking your tea and eating all the eggs," Elias protested as he drew the bird closer. "Bedivere won't make me sicker."

"We aren't just after your not wasting away further. Our objective is to make you *well*." He paused. "Are you feeling better?"

Elias considered. Maybe? He was at least pleased about last night's adventure and rescuing Bedivere. So yes, he felt better in that way, even if not in the way the doctor meant. "Some," he said. "A little. I promise if I feel worse I'll tell you."

"We'll see," the doctor mused. "But, at any rate, it's time we added something to your regimen."

"I thought the cave air was meant to be enough," Elias said, worried.

"The vapors in the cave are powerful," Croghan began, "but they primarily arrest the march of the wasting disease."

Elias recalled the mining operation that sat up near the entrance to the cave. The timbers from the Revolutionary War were still in perfect condition, owing to those magical cave vapors, which was how Croghan landed on bringing sick folks down there to heal. "So while the vapors do their work, we must do ours, pioneering the very latest in curatives."

Elias wasn't sure about curatives, but he liked the bit about pioneers. "I read a book about Lewis and Clark and their push to the Pacific," he offered.

Dr. Croghan brightened. "Did you know that I have for an uncle Mr. William Clark? And that I trained for surgery under the same physician as Meriwether Lewis?"

"No foolin'?"

"Indeed. The new frontier is here." He gestured around the hut, to the cave beyond. "This place holds secrets and discoveries to rival those of the great expedition."

The doctor had a way about him, all hope and optimism, that Elias liked. Still, new treatments worried him.

Croghan tapped his lip in contemplation, staring at

Elias. Elias stared back, took in the dark circles under the man's eyes, the bony fingers. And he wondered if maybe he weren't like Merlin just a bit. Merlin was said to have retreated to a cave after Arthur died. And if the doctor did manage to cure him, it would be magic to rival that of the old stories. Magic to no longer hear the crackling in his lungs, feel the frequent pain in his side, or be seized by coughing spells, or bouts of fever. Magic to not feel so spent all the time, to want to eat the food put in front of him instead of forcing it down.

"A poultice twice a day, I think," the doctor announced finally. "Wild ramps fried in goose fat."

Elias's shoulders relaxed with relief. Granny put poultices on him all the time. They weren't any bother except for making him a little greasy.

"You haven't been out in the cave much, the Negroes tell me," Dr. Croghan said.

Elias bit his lip but said nothing. If the others hadn't told about Elias wandering into the cave last night, he wasn't about to.

"I think I'll take you with me on my rounds next week," the doctor said. "That way I can observe you and see how you do with the increased activity. I wonder if inhaling more of the cave air might incite a more rapid healing. A brisk walk should get you respirating at a more rapid pace."

"Why aren't Nedra and the others going for walks, then?"

Croghan exhaled loud and slow. "Many of my patients arrived here already too weak for the activity, Nedra included. Pennyrile used to be more active, walking his birds up toward the entrance to release them, but with the scrofula at his neck and not so much in his lungs, the more vigorous breathing may be less effective."

"Scrofula?" Elias asked. "That's why he keeps his neck wrapped up?"

"Yes," Croghan said. "Sometimes they call it the King's Evil. In Europe in the Middle Ages they believed it could be cured by the touch of a king or a queen. Ridiculous, but it became the custom. Nothing at all to do with real medicine, of course. At any rate, poor Pennyrile is losing weight rapidly and his spirits seem low. I'm encouraged he gave you the bird, to be honest. Perhaps making a friend will do you both good."

Elias chose not to explain how he came to be Bedivere's protector. Doing so would have required him to reveal how he'd found him in the first place. "So what do you do for scrofula?" he asked instead.

Croghan seemed eager to be off. "The bear fat and whale oil compound on his neck attacks the growth from without, but the silence cure is the first line—"

"Silence!" Elias said. "*That's* why he don't say nothing!"

"Yes, Elias, that is why he doesn't say *anything.*"

Elias thought on how a lost voice was one more thing added to the pile of the many already taken away in the name of healing.

"Eat your eggs." Dr. Croghan snapped shut his leather bag. "You need to keep up your strength."

Though he wasn't the least bit hungry—he never really was anymore—Elias forced himself to eat half of his eggs. Bedivere seemed even less inclined to eating, but Elias reasoned it less to do with appetite: He needed feed for the bird.

"Be right back, fella," he said, worrying—and maybe hoping—that the bird might try to follow him like Charger would have. But Bedivere, roosting on the back of the wooden chair, just stared blankly, cooed once, and let Elias go.

Elias dashed across the clearing, glancing at Nedra's window. She was bent over her knitting, the lamp drawn close.

At Pennyrile's hut, he tapped on the doorframe. "Mr. Pennyrile?" he called out softly. Now that he knew the man was not meant to speak, it made his silence a little less unnerving, but still, Elias wasn't sure how to talk with a man who couldn't talk back.

"I don't mean to trouble you, sir," Elias went on. "But if you could spare some feed for that pigeon you give me, or at least tell me what he eats, I'd—"

The curtain whipped open.

Pennyrile stood there, not quite smiling, but not looking entirely displeased to find Elias at his door. In his hands he held a slate and a nub of chalk. He was bundled up in a long wool coat, the collar revealing a new wrap at his neck, this one finished off with the same elaborate knot as before. But as he moved, the fabric shifted, revealing a lumpy edge of bluish purple, like an old bruise, glinting beneath a layer of ointment. *Bear fat and whale oil,* Elias recalled the doctor saying, the odor suddenly recognizable to him. Whale oil they burned at home, and on board his father's ships. Elias forced himself to look the man in the eye. Despite his size, Elias could see that Pennyrile was indeed losing weight like the doctor said. His face, deeply lined and spotted all over by the sun, had begun to hollow out, the cheeks caving in.

"I . . . good morning, um . . ." Elias had almost forgotten the reason for his errand.

And then he heard a sound that made him remember a different life. One where he'd have been right then if he weren't so sick. Pennyrile began writing across the slate. It was just like the one Elias had used in school back in Norfolk, the same kind Horace Peters had cracked over Merriman Oakes's head when Merriman had called Horace a Yankee. Pennyrile wrote quickly, the chalk scratching and shrieking. After a second he turned the slate around and tapped the words he'd written there.

Victor Pennyrile. The printing was spindly, all lowercase letters.

He tapped his chest.

"I know," Elias said. "I'm Elias. Elias Harrigan. Pleased to meet you."

Pennyrile pointed at his neck, at the kerchief he had knotted there.

"Doc Croghan told me. I'm sorry for you."

Pennyrile shrugged, like it couldn't be helped. Then he pointed at Elias's chest, almost touching it. Elias flinched, but he understood the question in the gesture.

"Yes, sir," he said. "My lungs're bad."

Pennyrile kept his black eyes fixed on Elias as he scratched something more onto the slate, the rasp of the chalk more whisper than screech this time.

So young, the slate said when he held it out, and he looked at Elias like he was a horse that needed putting down.

Elias bristled, suddenly recalling how quickly Pennyrile'd been ready to snap Bedivere's neck. "I don't want to keep you, but could you maybe spare some feed?"

Pennyrile motioned Elias to follow him inside.

It was much the same as Elias's hut, with its narrow bed and table and stove and shelves. But pushed up against one wall was a great tin washtub. Elias shuddered, glad no one had brought up the notion of a proper bath yet. He searched for some other place to put his eyes. Right inside the door, half filling the window, was a set of wooden cages.

The pigeon loft.

Elias didn't know much about keeping birds, but a quick glance told him that the enclosure had been built for more birds than the two it held now. They seemed almost lonesome in there.

"Why's it so empty?"

Pennyrile wrote again. *Had lots more. Sent them out already.*

"You gonna have whoever's been getting the messages send 'em back?"

Pennyrile swiped the slate clean with a scrap of red cloth and wrote again. *Too much bother.* He paused, then wrote more. *Didn't figure on being here this long.*

"You can always send out messages with the regular post, can't you?"

Pennyrile shook his head, acted as if he would not elaborate, but then wrote: *This way better.*

Elias wasn't sure how he figured that, what with the

birds getting lost and injured and not taking the messages all the way out. But he didn't ask, deciding that maybe the less he knew about Pennyrile's reasons, the better. "About that feed?"

Pennyrile's eyes brightened. He set the slate on the table and hefted a cotton sack off the shelf. Rummaging around in his breakfast dishes, he found an empty cup. The two pigeons remaining in the loft began to coo and flap in anticipation. Pennyrile rapped sharply on the cage. The birds quieted.

He then scooped out a measure of dried corn and handed it to Elias. "I'm obliged," Elias said, taking the cup.

Pennyrile held up a finger and pointed at a dish of water settled in the bottom of the pigeon loft.

Elias understood. "Give him fresh every day?"

Pennyrile nodded once.

"How often with the grain?"

Pennyrile held up two fingers.

"Morning and night, then?"

Pennyrile tapped his nose, pleased to have been understood.

He stayed that way, grinning at Elias long enough to make him uncomfortable. With nothing left to discuss, and the notion of small talk seeming cruel with one for whom communicating was hard, Elias thanked the man again and made to go. But Pennyrile caught him by the arm, held up a finger, and then fetched up his slate. He swiped it clean, then wrote quickly.

You went off in the cave last night.

No question mark there. Like there wasn't any point arguing what it said.

"That's where I found the bird—" Elias began before Pennyrile cut him short.

Doc doesn't know?

Elias felt something pricking at the back of his neck. Why would Pennyrile care?

"No, but—"

More scratching at the slate. *Just saw you. Jealous.*

Jealous? Elias relaxed a fraction. Maybe Pennyrile was as bored as Elias.

Pennyrile was writing again. *Won't tell.*

That settled, Elias thanked him and took a step back toward his own hut, but Pennyrile rapped the slate sharply again. Elias waited as Pennyrile wiped off his slate and scrawled something new. This time the letters were more jagged, written faster, less sure of themselves.

Sending out a pigeon later. Want to watch?

Elias looked at the two remaining in the cage. "But what if it gets lost too?"

Pennyrile shrugged, then scribbled: *Needs must.*

Elias couldn't stomach it. He didn't like the thought of more poor birds getting hurt or killed trying to find their way to the entrance. "I could maybe carry the bird out for you, if you wanted? So it had a better chance of making it home?"

Pennyrile made a face to show he was surprised and pleased at the offer.

"I wouldn't mind," Elias continued. "Doctor wants me to come walking with him soon, anyhow."

Pennyrile considered. Then he erupted into a frenzied scratching at the slate. *On second thought, best reserve birds. And have another way.*

"Another way?" Elias asked as Pennyrile swiped the slate and wrote even more.

Tree at entrance where I used to walk when stronger. My friend leaves letters there for me. You could leave my note for him there instead of sending out bird.

"If he's near enough to leave a note for you outside, then why doesn't he just come the rest of the way in?"

Pennyrile's smile faltered just a step, like he wasn't pleased to have Elias questioning him. But then he wrote. *We value privacy.*

Still puzzled, Elias looked toward the loft and the two birds still within. Pennyrile might send them out. They'd only get lost in the cave like the others. And no wonder.

They weren't made to fly around in the dark, and he'd seen enough of the cave to know it was an easy thing to lose one's sense of direction. It had to be even trickier for a bird used to flying in the daylight. "I don't know, sir," Elias began. "Seems a heap of bother when you could just use the regular post. Or Croghan's hands to go back and forth to your tree."

Pennyrile shook his head, clearly losing patience now. He flipped the slate and wrote on the other side. *Can't trust. Some of them read. Don't like it. Only you.*

"But—" Elias began before Pennyrile held up the other side of the slate, pointing a stubby finger at the word *privacy.*

Even though Elias was standing perfectly still, he felt the wheeze begin to grow from that tiny whistle that was almost always there to the rusty gate Lillian had described. The cough would come on soon if he wasn't careful. "I don't know—"

Pennyrile wrote again. *You carry for me. I give you feed for the bird.*

Elias thought Pennyrile's expression would not have been out of place carved into a jack-o'-lantern sneering from a fence post. And those words written on the slate sounded more like an order than a request. He was beginning to get an odd feeling about the whole business when Pennyrile added: *A friendly arrangement?*

Elias hesitated, but he didn't have much choice, did he? Besides, what harm could it do in the end? "All I have to do is carry a letter?"

Pennyrile lifted one shoulder as a yes.

Elias heard voices coming up the path. Pennyrile jutted his chin toward the sound and held a finger to his lips.

"All right," Elias whispered, the cough in his lungs like a boat straining against its mooring lines. It would escape him soon. "But I don't know when I can do it."

Pennyrile wrote. *Will have letter ready by time you need more grain for bird. Take then.*

"I won't do nothing wrong," Elias backed away as the voices outside drew nearer.

Pennyrile waved a hand at Elias like it was the silliest notion in the world. But it didn't make Elias feel any better. "I'm going now," he said, sliding out the door.

The dried corn rattled in the cup as Elias ducked into his room just as Nick came over the rise with another man, carrying a big kettle between them.

Elias nearly fell against the wall as the cough erupted, shuddering through him in weak waves. Despite how weak the strength of his cough was, it still was almost too much for Elias. He sank to the bed and held a handkerchief to his mouth. When he finished, he pulled the fabric away. Nothing in it, at least. Bedivere cooed at him.

"I know," Elias said, pinching out a measure of the corn and dropping it onto the floor. Bedivere hop-flapped from the back of the chair to the seat and then to the floor and began pecking up the feast. Elias collapsed in the chair, listening to the sound of Nick and the other slave talking and working, and the sound of Bedivere's beak snapping greedily around each kernel of corn. But somehow the sound of that chalk on the slate, that scratching, still echoed in his head.

Chapter Four

FIGURE EIGHT

The sharp tangy smell of onions lingered hours after the day's poultice grew cold and was taken away. It was still there after supper when Elias heard footsteps coming up the path. He didn't recognize the gait, but as it drew closer to his door, Lillian called out, "Evening, Mat."

"Elias in there?" a man growled, tugging the curtain across the door without waiting for an answer. The man was lighter skinned than either Nick or Stephen, the hair poking out from underneath his cap nearly straight. He was tall, too, narrow in the shoulders, with a pair of braces holding up pants that gapped at his waist.

"You Elias?" he asked, lips hardly moving inside his beard. "Get your gear. Stephen said to fetch you."

Elias didn't have any gear—any that might be useful, anyway. But he pocketed his length of rope and tightened the laces of his boots. "Who're you?"

"Mat Bransford. C'mon, we ain't got all night."

Elias grabbed the cup of corn and scattered some for Bedivere.

"What in blazes is that?" Mat asked, jabbing a finger at the bird.

Elias hesitated. "It's a . . . a pigeon?"

Mat seethed. "I know it's a pigeon. You don't need to get fresh! But what are you doing with it?"

Elias stroked the top of Bedivere's beak. "Mr. Pennyrile give him to me. He's got a lame wing, so I figured on—"

Mat glared at the bird like it was a snake he might crush if he met it in the road. "You best be careful about the friends you make." Then he ducked out the door, not bothering to hold the quilt aside for Elias. Lillian intercepted them.

"Where you taking that boy?" she whispered as she tucked herself between Mat and Elias.

Mat groaned. "Stephen took a notion he'd be useful. We won't hurt him," he said, adding, "much."

"The doctor wants him resting." Lillian crossed her arms. "He won't be pleased if you wearing him out tonight."

"Naw, I expect he won't, but he ain't gonna hear it from

me," Mat said, giving Lillian a look. If Elias weren't so eager to get out of his room, he might have been afraid to go with him.

"Hop to," Mat said to Elias. Lillian threw up her hands and waved them off, muttering to herself.

Elias had to work to keep up with Mat, but he actually felt a little better. Winded, sure. Legs weak, yes. But not wheezy, and a coughing spell seemed wonderfully distant. Maybe the poultice had helped after all.

"I never seen you before," Elias said when he trusted his breathing to let him speak.

Mat only grunted.

"You new here too?" Elias wanted to show that he was friendly, to show this Mat fellow he had plenty of good reasons to trust Elias, just like Stephen did.

"I been here five years. You been here a month, but you're asking if I'm new?" He stalked off quick again down the path.

"I just haven't seen you, like the others, that's all."

Mat walked faster. Elias knew he ought to save his breath; Mat seemed to like making him walk too fast. But he couldn't help it.

"You and Nick are brothers?"

"Why'd you ask a thing like that?" Mat said, squeezing through a narrow cut of rock.

"Y'all both got Bransford for last names," Elias explained as he squeezed after him.

Mat humphed. "Called Bransford 'cause our old master was Bransford. He leased us up here to the man owned the cave afore Doc Croghan."

"You're better off here, I reckon," Elias offered quietly.

Mat laughed bitterly. "Could be worse."

Elias was sure it could. Croghan seemed kind. And he seemed permissive enough, letting Stephen and Nick and Mat roam around exploring the cave when they weren't working. He couldn't see what Mat had to be so growly about, why he seemed so resentful toward Elias, why he was so put out with Pennyrile.

"Why'd you say that about Mr. Pennyrile before?" Elias asked.

"Trouble a mile off, that one."

"But he's dying," Elias pointed out. "How much trouble can he be?"

Mat stopped, held the lamp up, and waited until Elias met his eyes. Elias noted their unusual color—a pale green—and how they caught the light like a possum's.

"Had a fellow on a tour once. He told me about going over out west to the territory. Hunted some of those great grizzly bears. Said when they finally got near enough to shoot at the thing, it took a dozen rounds of shot to bring it down. And said every time they hit it, the bear got tougher and madder and meaner. Killed one of the horses before it gave out."

Elias sure would've liked to talk to *that* man.

"Sometimes animals is most dangerous when they're right at the end," Mat finished.

Elias wondered if that could be true, recalling how helpless his father had been in his last days. As he was thinking on this, he saw lights in the distance. Moments later they came upon Nick and Stephen looking into a cleft nine feet up near the low ceiling.

"There he is," Stephen said, looking over at Elias, sniffing the air. "You smell like onions."

Elias's hand wandered to his shirt. "Doc's been having 'em do poultices on me. Ramps and goose fat."

Nick made a sound that might have been a chuckle, and he spat a stream of tobacco over his shoulder. "Be good and greased up for it, any road."

"Greased for what?" Elias asked.

Stephen patted the rock wall. "We've been at this spot for a while now. Trying to figure out what might be over there. Trouble is," he said with a frown, "none of us can fit through."

Elias looked at the spot again. It might have been sixteen, eighteen inches across at its widest. He swallowed hard but kept his voice steady. "How far you get?"

"Stephen got farthest, not quite up to his hips," Mat offered. "So he thought maybe you might try."

Stephen had half a foot on Elias in height, but was broader by more. Part of Elias couldn't wait to try. But the other part was hollering that he could die right there in that hole in the wall.

"You willing?" Nick asked, holding up a loop of rope knotted in something terribly like a noose.

"After I get through . . . what then?"

Stephen took over. "We fetch up a light for you. And then you go as far as you can before the rope gives out. If you still can go farther, we splice another rope on. That way you can find your way back out."

"Or if you fall in a pit, we might be able to catch you," Mat added, eyes flashing wickedly.

"Might?" Elias took a step backward.

"We'll hold fast on it," Stephen said, shaking his head as Mat lowered the loop over Elias's head, then shoulders, finally securing it around his waist.

"You mind if I retie this?" Elias asked, looking at the almost-noose. It might hold fine, but a bowline would be better, less likely to snag on something.

"Go on then," Mat said, crossing his arms and rocking back on his heels.

Elias steadied his hands, took one end of the rope,

measured out an arm's length, and twisted a bight to tie a bowline. His daddy's words echoed in his head. *Send the rabbit up the hole, then around the tree, and then back down the hole.* Satisfied, he tightened and dressed the knot.

"Is it pretty enough for you, or you want me to find some flowers to stick in there too?" Mat asked, annoyed, but Elias could tell by the way his eyes stayed locked on the knot that he was admiring it. Figuring out how to do it himself.

"Here," Stephen said, handing Elias a lighter weight of rope, "fix this to your waist rope. Then if you need something, we can tie it on and send it up to you."

"What am I going to need?" Elias asked, his voice breaking on the last word. Stephen leaned down to catch Elias's eye.

"More light or a pry bar or something. That's all."

"Okay, then." Elias studied the cut in the rock he was meant to shimmy through. It looked smaller suddenly. "I suppose I'm ready."

"You want to climb it, or you want we should boost you?" Stephen asked.

"I can get up there." Elias reached for the rock. It was cold beneath his hands, but it was dry, and that was something. He gripped a couple of the biggest knobs and then lifted one foot onto a good solid chunk jutting out of the wall, testing it to be sure. Then he stood himself up, his left foot still floating in the air till he found another good edge up near where his knee was before. He balanced, then brought that other foot higher and reached up with his left hand at the same time. Before he could say "Jack Robinson," he was looking into the edge of a black hole.

"There's a good little seam in there," Stephen said from below. The rope at Elias's waist felt heavier than before. But he ignored its weight, and soon his hands scrambled in and found the spot Stephen described. Elias slid his fingers in to the second knuckles and heaved himself up. His head scraped the side of the passage as he got his shoulders inside, and his knot dug in at his waist as he began to crawl.

Stephen called out, "Good, now," and Elias could tell he'd made it farther than Stephen had. The space grew tighter and Elias had to lie down, arms in front of him, in order to squeeze through. He used his knees and toes to push forward, staying on his belly, bumping now and again against the walls of the passage. But he didn't feel any rock above him yet.

"You solid there?" Stephen hollered up.

"Yeah," Elias said, breathless.

"Get ahold of the little rope!"

Elias inched forward a little more and found that the chamber widened. He gathered his knees under his chest and crouched, jiggling the rope at his waist.

"We going to send you a light," Stephen said.

Elias felt the rope dance in his hand, then heard Stephen call, "Haul it up. Slowly!"

The light came clanking along the rock behind him, tipping sideways as Elias pulled it into the passage. It nearly went out, but somehow the flame held. He inched it along, the tin shrieking against the stone until he could grab the handle.

He brought it in front of him, ready to see the wonders of the cave, and at first he thought he did. A smoothed wall surrounded him, solid floor beneath his knees. But then he saw that it ended a few feet away, a narrow shaft no wider than a sapling shooting into the rock above him.

A dead end.

"Nothing here," he called back to Stephen. "Just a chamber and then a hole in the ceiling."

"How big a hole?" Mat asked.

"Four or five inches!" Elias shouted back.

Elias heard Mat swear. Stephen groaned. "You sure?" Mat asked. "You check the whole space? Sometimes the path dips down. No way under the walls?"

Elias crawled to the edges of the little dome. They were uneven, deeper in some spots than others, but solid enough. He hated the feeling of having let them down, but there was nothing for it. "Nah," he said. "You want me to come on back?"

"Hold on," Stephen called up. *Hold on?* Elias began to feel the closeness of the space press in on him. He strained to make out the conversation below, but after a minute got tired of waiting and became itchy with the nearness of the walls. He was beginning to crawl out when Stephen shouted up, "Can you write your name?"

Elias screwed up his face. Write his name? "'Course!"

Then Elias heard the three of them arguing in earnest.

"He's no visitor!" Stephen snapped.

"He ain't one of us, neither!" Mat hissed. "Don't you let him."

"Not like anyone gonna see it in there, anyhow," Elias heard Nick mumble, but he couldn't tell from his tone whose side he was arguing for. Still, it seemed to win the day.

"Never mind," Stephen called to Elias, "come on back out."

Elias sent the light back first, then reversed himself through the passage. His feet dangled out in the air until he felt hands on his ankles, guiding them onto secure spots on the wall.

"You all right?" Stephen untied the knot at Elias's waist. Elias was breathing a little fast, and there was a scrape near his spine that stung like a yellow jacket, but he was fine. Better than fine. He was excited.

"Need me to go someplace else?" he asked, forcing his breathing to slow down. But still only a hint of a wheeze, and not even the ghost of a cough. Maybe it was the goose fat in the poultice, he thought. Granny always used bacon grease. "I mean, you got any other tight spots you need a runt like me to squeeze into?" Nick laughed softly and started coiling the rope. Mat groaned.

"We got a couple of places," Stephen said, "where we could use a body with a smaller frame."

Elias grinned. "Let's go!"

Stephen shook his head. "Not tonight. We got business elsewhere."

"Can I come?"

"I've got to get home," Mat said. "Soon, I reckon, if we've been here as long I expect we have."

"And I best get some sleep before I have to get the breakfast on," Nick added. Until that moment, Elias had almost forgotten that squeezing through crannies and exploring was only part of their work in the cave. They were, he reluctantly reminded himself, slaves, after all. So he shrugged and tried not to let on how badly he didn't want to return to his hut.

Nick passed Elias a waterskin with a stopper tied to the neck. "Drink up," he said. Elias did exactly that, thirsty from the hustle down there and from shimmying himself through the hole. The water was cool and slid down his throat like chipped ice, leaving a hint of a taste in his mouth that reminded him of sucking on a penny.

He took another drink and offered the bag back to Nick. "Tastes funny," he said.

Mat shot Nick a look. "Nick?"

Nick spat. "Maybe the bag needs rinsed."

"Bishop?" Mat was anxious.

"It's all right, Mat," Stephen said, though he was watching Elias with interest as well. "It won't hurt anything."

Stephen squatted and opened his pack. Elias saw another coil of rope, another jar of water, the drill he'd shown him that day at the pit, and an extra little phial of fuel for the lantern.

But under all those things were books.

Books.

Three that Elias could see. Three tattered primers, like ones he might have read when he first started learning how.

It didn't figure to Elias. Stephen could read. He'd even heard him talking with Nedra about the Lancelot poem, and it sounded like he understood it better than Elias did by a country mile. For Nick or Mat maybe? But why haul them all the way down into the cave? Why weigh down a pack? It didn't figure at all.

Elias started to ask about it, but Stephen drew out that notebook Elias saw him with the other night. He flipped to the middle, where a map covered both pages. "You said it ends just inside?"

"About six feet across on the floor"—Elias gestured with his hands—"like a little dugout."

Stephen moved his finger expertly across a route that resembled a stream branching off the main path that Elias guessed marked the passageway where his hut sat. Stephen traced the tip of his pencil down the line to a mark so small, it looked like a mistake on the page, a stray stroke that wasn't meant to be there at all. He wrote a tiny number 77 next to the spot.

"What's the number for?" Elias asked. Stephen thumbed ahead in the book, and Elias saw all the pages were numbered. Seventy-seven was blank. "Reference," Stephen said, holding the notebook up, where Elias saw a likeness of the wall he'd just climbed represented in considerable detail. The cleft he'd shimmied through was a black hole of hash marks. Stephen wrote in careful letters: *passage ends six feet from opening. Dome.* He flipped back to the map in the center of the book and studied it for a few seconds, tracing his finger south along the path they were on.

Elias found it more and more like staring at the charts his daddy used to figure out which routes to send his loads of cargo. On those, the lanes would bend around shoals or islands, wide berths to keep the ships from grounding themselves on the shallows. Elias noticed that this map had something like that too. A space near the southeast corner where the routes seemed to bend around something impassable.

"What's that?" he asked, pointing at the spot on the map.

Stephen looked up at him sharply. "What?"

"That spot," Elias said, "where nothing goes through. Is that the pit?"

Stephen smiled, but it wasn't a friendly smile this time. "Just a piece we haven't been in much yet." He moved his hand along the map to the north. "Pit's right here."

Elias scratched his head. "Why ain't you been in there?" He wondered if maybe they'd paint sea monsters and leviathans on there, like the old sailors used to on places they hadn't been.

Nick and Mat exchanged looks over Stephen's head. "You want me to take him back now when I go?" Mat said, his voice louder than necessary.

"I want to stay. I ain't tired, I swear. Been lying around that hut all day. And I'm not even wheezing much—"

Nick sucked on his teeth. "I got to git," he said.

"I have the tour tomorrow and something to do before then," Stephen said.

"C'mon, just show me some—" Elias began, desperate not to go back to the quiet of his hut.

"No," Stephen said firmly. "Now go on back with Mat, and don't bother me about it or we won't bring you out again."

Elias started to argue. How dare they talk to him like that! But the threat of not getting out with them tomorrow was enough to make him hold his tongue.

Chapter Five

LAPP KNOT

Y ou need anything?" Lillian asked.

Elias shook his head and tapped the paper with a pencil.

"I'll be back before too long," she said. "Just going over to Hannah's to fetch some soap." Lillian had just changed the turban she wore, two braids thick as cables trailing down her shoulders.

"I'll stay put," Elias promised.

"If Miss Nedra need something—"

"I'll run over," Elias said.

Lillian hesitated. "You sure you won't wander off?"

Elias held up the paper. "This'll keep me anchored."

Satisfied, Lillian went, leaving Elias to his letter.

He found he didn't have the right words. He wanted to write about his adventures of a few nights back, scaling the wall, cramming himself into the hole. Or about Nick's kindness, how his tobacco smelled like Daddy's had, or even Mat's surliness. Most of all, he wanted to write about how unusual Stephen Bishop was, about his maps and his writing and reading, how Elias found him a bit too proud for his own good, but at the same time found the man had plenty to be proud of. He admired him. But Mother and Granny wouldn't have understood, may have even been alarmed at it. Maybe if he wrote and just didn't tell them Stephen was black, he thought? But to what end? And why did it matter to him?

He settled on telling them he'd taken on Bedivere as a pet, leaving out all but the most necessary details on how he came to have him. *An interesting fellow here keeps birds and gave me one to look after.* If it left a lot out, he reckoned it was for his family's own good. Even a pigeon alone might give Granny cause to complain. Then he filled a page with a description of the doctor's poultice, and added a paragraph regarding the news that Croghan was kin to William Clark. He was just beginning to assure them he was getting better, working up to suggesting that they might bring him home soon, when he felt himself being watched again.

"Hey," he heard a voice whisper from the window.

Not a voice. *The* voice.

Elias glanced up. His heartbeat kicked into a canter, but he wouldn't be made a fool of again. Not this time. "I ain't talking to you."

"Are so," the voice came back. "You jes' did."

Elias glared at the window, tried to make out the eyes, but couldn't see them there this time. "I mean, I'm done with you. Not gonna chase you or talk to you or think on you no more."

"Why not?"

"'Cause you got me in trouble with Stephen is why. I don't know who you are, or how you go round the cave like that, but he didn't believe me I was following anybody. And they took me out not long ago and I aim to get a chance to go out again, but something tells me you'll muck that up if I let you. So, whoever you are, if I don't pay you any mind, you'll leave me alone."

Just when it was quiet enough for Elias to wonder if the voice were gone, came this: "I brought you something." A hand emerged from the darkness. Elias saw it for only a second as it dropped something through the window. But he saw enough to tell that whoever was on the other side was a Negro.

In spite of his promise to ignore the voice, Elias

abandoned his letter and picked up the dropped something. Bedivere hopped over to inspect the offering.

Elias unwrapped a scrap of blue cloth to find a cube of
salt pork, about two inches square. It was already cooked,
the grease of it spotting the fabric, the edges crisped brown.
Elias's mouth watered just at the sight of it. He lifted it to
his nose, smelled the salty, fatty deliciousness of it, and
his stomach flipped itself over in expectation. He couldn't
remember the last time he'd truly felt hungry, truly wanted
to eat something. Maybe it was because it wasn't what
he'd been forcing himself to eat for weeks. Or maybe the
hint of his appetite returning meant he was getting better.

"Thought you might be liking something besides eggs
and tea," the voice said.

Elias would have liked nothing better, but he forced
himself to wrap the food back up and place it on the windowsill. "Can't eat it," Elias said firmly, returning to his
letter. "Doctor's orders." Oh, how he wanted to gulp it
down. In truth, it was only half out of fidelity to the doctor's remedy that he didn't. The other half couldn't let
this voice, this pest, make amends just by giving Elias a
treat and making him forget how he'd led him off in the
dark and made him look a fool.

The gift disappeared back into the darkness. "How
come you ain't tell the doctor about me?"

"Who says I didn't?" Elias scribbled in the margin of the letter.

"'Cause you didn't."

Elias wondered how often this person was listening at his window. "Look, if you want to sneak about and get yourself whipped for bothering me and snitching food, that's your hide. But I don't fink on nobody, no matter who they are."

"That's big of you."

Elias didn't care if it was or not. He concentrated on his letter. *I am stronger, the doctor thinks,* he wrote. *Maybe in a few more weeks I can—*

"Who you writin' at?"

Elias fumed but answered anyway. "My family."

"They near?"

"Virginia," Elias said. "Clear to the coast."

The voice whistled softly. "Your folk sent you all the way over here? Just to eat some eggs and lie round and get some doctoring?"

"It weren't like that!" Elias hissed, but he was having a harder and harder time convincing himself that it wasn't. He pretended to be keen to come, keen to see some of the wilds of Kentucky, to see a cave so big and ancient it was named after the mammoths that died out long ago.

But it had been Granny's notion. All their attempts to save Daddy had failed. When Elias fell sick, Granny learned about Dr. Croghan and his grand experiment. *I'd cotton he's onto something,* she'd said.

His mother had seized on the hope of a cure. Elias went along with it to make her happy, but he missed his family more than he ever thought he would. Many times he'd recalled that last glimpse of them waving from the landing back in Norfolk, the tears on his mother's cheeks, the ones Granny blinked back. Tillie holding fast to Charger's collar, wrestling with the big dog to keep him from jumping into the river and following the boat.

He'd figured that even if the doctor's cures didn't work—and he hoped, oh how he hoped, they would—at least he could spare his mother the sorrow of watching him die the way Daddy had.

Still, it was hard to be so distant, hard not to resent them a little for sending him away.

"It ain't like that," Elias said more softly.

"I barely 'member my mama," the voice whispered. "She was long gone 'fore I left."

Left? Elias perked up at the word.

"And I ain't never seen me an ocean. But I traveled all the way up the Mississippi afore I ended up here. You seen the Mississippi? Lawd, that's a river, that is—"

"Just go 'way," Elias said, shifting to the bed, sliding Nedra's book out from under Bedivere, who had climbed up on it and was working loose a thread in the binding. "Shoo," he said to both the bird and the voice on the other side of the window.

"You don't want me to go," the voice said.

Elias snorted and flipped the pages noisily.

"You readin' now," the voice said. "I see how it be. Rather read some old book than visit with a pal who brung you a gift."

Pal?

To keep from having to listen to such nonsense, Elias read the words out, starting at random in the middle of the poem.

> *On either side the river lie*
> *Long fields of barley and of rye,*
> *That clothe the wold and meet the sky;*
> *And thro' the field the road runs by*
> *To many-tower'd Camelot;*
> *And up and down the people go,*
> *Gazing where the lilies blow*
> *Round an island there below,*
> *The island of Shalott.*

He read the first stanza at a racing clip, loud and steady, so that by the time he'd finished it, he had to pause and gulp air. It was enough time for the voice to break in.

"What's 'clothe the wold'? That don't make a lick of sense."

Elias ignored the question and charged through the second stanza, louder this time. As he finished, he held his breath, waited for the voice to say something, but didn't hear it. What he did hear was Nedra calling.

Nedra. His heart sank a little. It wasn't her fault she was nearly the spookiest thing about the whole place. Still, at least it gave him an excuse to get away from the voice.

"Elias?" she called again.

He threw the book on the table, sending poor Bedivere hopping sideways to avoid being hit, and bolted out the door. Once outside, he couldn't help looking round to the side of the hut. Nothing there but darkness.

"Elias?"

"Coming!" But he hadn't made two strides before a stone rolled out from the shadows and right past Elias's feet.

Elias froze as the stone came to a stop.

Pest. He set his jaw and walked over to Nedra's. Dr. Croghan had told him about her. That she had a fiancé who had visited often at first. That she taught French to the daughters of fine families down in Memphis where she lived before she came here. Elias had not had the courage to ask how long it took her to reach her current state. He didn't want to know. Didn't want to know how quickly he might end up like her.

"Yes, ma'am?"

"You were shouting out *Shalott*." If there was such a thing as a ghost in the cave, Nedra had to be the closest. She was still beautiful; that was easy enough to see. But her long golden hair had grown matted and frizzy, like a pony left wild. Her skin was pale enough to seem transparent, save for the blushed spots in her cheeks. Her blue eyes were sunken deep into her face, and she had the stink of fevers about her that Elias remembered from his father's battle. And the fever gave her over to broken conversation, so Elias had to work twice as hard to puzzle out what she was saying.

Nedra sat in her straight-backed chair in front of her little stove, a small bundle on her lap. He thought quickly to come up with a story to cover why he was hollering. "I . . ." he began. "Sometimes it's just a fair bit too quiet in here."

Nedra stared past him, like she wasn't seeing him at all. "You have a new friend."

Elias startled.

"You heard him?" Elias asked carefully, wanting, surprisingly, to protect the pest's secret.

Nedra smiled, almost wickedly. "Such a clamor, always a clamor, though no worse than before."

But the voice always whispered so quietly, almost so Elias could barely hear him. *How could she have heard?*

"Did you name him?"

"Name—" Elias caught himself. Why would he name the boy?

"Everything should have a name. Even a bird—"

Bedivere! She meant the pigeon!

"He's called Bedivere," Elias managed. "After Arthur's knight. And he's eating good at least. Gobbled up most of the corn I got off Pennyrile already. He's a pig, that one."

"A pig and a pigeon," she muttered.

Elias thought she appeared more strung out, drawn thinner than she had a couple of days before. Daddy had done that toward the end. Every day when Elias went in to see him in the morning, he'd look different, like a little more of him had forgotten to wake up, gotten lost in the night.

"Here," she said, holding out the bundle.

"What's this?"

"It's green," she said nonsensically. "Like Gawain's knight. Like the sash."

Elias was almost more worried that he *could* follow

her thoughts. He let the scarf's length drape to the floor, felt the soft scratchiness of the wool, recognized the yarn she'd been working with when he first met her the day after he arrived.

"It's nice," he said, holding it up to the light, admiring the way the little stitches acted as much like perfect little knots as anything else.

"Wear it," she commanded. "It's so cold."

Elias wrapped it around his neck loosely. "Thank you, miss."

"Take care on your quests, squire," she whispered, leaning forward. And the way she said it, Elias was sure she'd seen him leave with Mat three nights ago, maybe even seen him chase the ghost last week.

"Yes, ma'am. Thanks for the scarf."

She didn't reply but took up her needles and some blue yarn, and began to knit again. Elias decided he had been dismissed.

When he reached his room, he found Bedivere pecking at something on the table.

It was the fraying end of the little cloth tied around the piece of salt pork.

Pest. Or friend. Elias was so out of practice in having friends that he'd forgotten how hard it could be to tell the difference.

"Boo," the voice whispered as Elias settled back on the bed.

"I know you ain't no ghost," Elias said, but he couldn't help but smile. "And stay outta my room."

"You don't know nuthin'! Can't even get eyes on me when you try—"

"I know ghosts don't make shadows. And they don't leave chunks of bacon for folk they haunt."

"You worried I was, though."

"Did not." Even this Elias had missed. The bickering. If people did get near enough to him to talk when he'd gotten sick, they never argued with him. Even Tillie gave up fighting with him. Elias picked up his book.

"Don't you get tired of reading all the time?"

"Don't you get tired of lurking round windows?"

"I do more'n talk to you," the voice said, adding, "I get myself all over."

Bedivere hopped across the tabletop, stretched his neck out to the window, and warbled.

"You don't like that streak o' lean, you might want to know them birds' not bad to eat," the voice pointed out. "A job to pluck but taste all right if you know what you're about."

"He ain't for eating!" Elias looked with horror at poor Bedivere.

"Not for you, anyway," the voice said. "Think the doc would let you eat pigeon eggs?"

"Only chicken I reckon, but I don't figure this fella's gonna go laying anytime soon."

"What's yer book about?"

Elias narrowed his eyes at the window. Why wouldn't he show himself? Why was he hiding? Not just from Elias, it would seem, but also from everyone else?

"I don't read," the pest went on. "Never took to it."

"You ain't supposed to be talking to me, are you?" Elias asked.

The voice made a sort of clicking noise, like he was sucking the inside of his cheek. Bedivere stretched up tall and cocked his head. "Naw, I reckon I'm not."

"How come?"

"Can't say."

Elias could hear plain enough that *can't* meant *won't*.

"Look, if you're gonna get into trouble, and if you getting into trouble is gonna give Stephen or the doctor or anybody else a reason to get sideways with me, maybe you ought to just go. Not like we're friends anyhow, seeing as I don't even know your name."

An injured sort of silence settled before the voice whispered, "M'name's Jonah."

"Jonah," Elias repeated, adding, "like in the bible. That one went courtin' trouble too." Of course his name was Jonah. He heard tales from his father about men aboard ship who seemed to bring bad luck—storms, poor winds, trouble with supplies—how they were called Jonahs on account of the Jonah in the Old Testament who got himself thrown overboard during a storm and swallowed up by a great fish.

"Tell you what," Jonah whispered, "now that we're friends, I'll tell you somethin' else."

"Like what?"

"Like what Croghan do to the others." Jonah's voice dropped lower.

"Why would I care about that?"

Jonah made a noise. "You got it easier'n some, I tell you that. But maybe you too afraid of hearing—"

"Can't be that bad," Elias interrupted, though he remembered from watching his father suffer that it could.

"Worse than you imagine," Jonah said. "But first you gotta tell me something."

"What?" Elias asked.

"Tell me about that Gawain you and the miss was talkin' 'bout."

Elias worked the hem of the scarf. Of course Jonah had been eavesdropping on his conversation with Nedra.

He might have even managed to sneak across to listen at her window.

"How come I have to go first?"

"Just tell!" Jonah whispered fiercely.

Elias bristled at being told what to do, but he couldn't afford to be choosy where his friends were concerned. So he told the story of Gawain from memory, the way his father used to tell it, emphasizing the parts about the green giant riding in astride a massive green horse to challenge Arthur's knights. He told how Gawain accepted the challenge to trade blows with the ax, how later he came by the magic green sash that both saved his life and cost him a measure of his honor.

Jonah was silent for a long while after Elias had finished. "All that in that book?"

"Not this one," he said. "The one Miss Nedra borrowed off me."

"I liked that bit where the Green Knight turned back into a man at the end."

Elias had too. "Called a 'glamour,'" explained Elias. "Merlin used 'em all the time. Making somebody look like somebody else."

"A *glamour*," Jonah said, trying the word.

"Now you."

Elias heard the sound of stones shifting outside the

window. Jonah dropped his voice lower. "That Pennyrile over there? Doc has him taking these baths."

Elias remembered the tub. "Cold ones, I guess."

"That ain't the worst of it."

Elias waited.

"It ain't regular old bathwater he has him washing in. Croghan has Pennyrile taking him a bath in a tub of horse piss—"

"He never!" Elias gasped.

"He did," Jonah confirmed. "And he'd been feeding them horses on nothing but cabbage and carrots for three whole days 'fore he collected it."

Elias was stunned. His eggs and tea and poultice seemed nothing now.

"And there're others he blisters—a big old mustard plaster he puts on 'em, raises up sores. Supposed to draw out the infection."

Elias winced.

"And Miss Nedra over there, she weren't half so crazy when she first come. I reckon it's being down here and all them weird—"

Jonah stopped abruptly. Elias couldn't help himself. "Weird what?"

But Jonah didn't reply. And a moment later Elias knew why.

Lillian edged the curtain aside. "Elias?"

Guilty, Elias palmed the cube of salt pork. "Hey, Lill."

"I'm back," she said softly, scanning the inside of Elias's hut.

"Okay," Elias said. "I walked over and saw Nedra. She was all right when I left. Give me this scarf."

He raised the tail to show her the scarf, but she barely took it in before resuming her scan of the room. "Get some rest," she said, adding, "Doc's got a big morning planned for you tomorrow."

"All right."

She lingered, eyes hanging on the window a second too long. "Night."

Elias scooted down the bed and trimmed the lamp. It wasn't until he was nearly asleep that he arrived at how queer it was that Lillian never asked who Elias had been talking to. He recalled her eyes scanning the room, the distracted way she spoke to him, but all the time, she never asked him why he'd been whispering.

Chapter Six

THIEF KNOT

You're quiet this morning, young man," Dr. Croghan noted as he took Elias's pulse.

Elias said nothing. He was always prone to saying little when he felt guilty.

He'd eaten the salt pork.

Sometime in the night he'd woken up famished. He'd retrieved the little wrapped chunk of meat and had only meant to smell it. But his belly was so hollow and the bacon smelled so good and one tiny bite couldn't hurt, he reckoned. And even though it was cold and starting to dry out, it was delicious. That first bite was so good, he figured if he'd undone the doctor's remedy, one more little bite wouldn't matter, would it?

And then there was really only enough to make up one last tiny taste.

So he'd eaten the whole piece. He felt awful about possibly messing up his healing.

But he also knew if he had another piece, he'd have eaten it on the spot, maybe in a single bite.

So with his stomach slightly fuller but his conscience heavy, he tried to sleep. But between the guilt and the puzzle of what Stephen had been doing with those books in his pack, and wondering who Jonah really was, and wondering what Pennyrile needed him to carry letters for . . . well, he spent more time thinking than he did sleeping.

"I'll perk up," Elias said. "Just takes me a while to get my oars in the water."

Croghan seemed satisfied enough with the explanation. "You've had your breakfast?"

"Three boiled," Elias said. "Drunk my tea."

Croghan slapped his knee. "Good. Then I expect we're ready."

"Hold on." Elias scattered the last few kernels of corn on the tabletop, slung the pan of water out his window, and filled it with fresh from his jug. "Ready."

Outside, Lillian was at the fire, waiting expectantly for Doctor Croghan to emerge.

She intercepted them halfway across. "Doctor, I can't

get Miss Nedra to swallow that stuff you brung down. She just gets to retching—"

Croghan held up a hand. "I'll be right there," he said to Lillian, then to Elias, "We'll be off in a moment. Check in with Mr. Pennyrile—get a little more grain for that bird."

Elias had been hoping to put off getting more feed longer. Not that it would have mattered: Pennyrile was watching them from his window.

"A few minutes, no more," Croghan said, following Lillian into Nedra's room.

Elias sighed, ducked back into his hut, and grabbed the little cup. When he emerged, Pennyrile was holding back the curtain, waiting for Elias to come in.

Pennyrile let the curtain fall shut behind Elias and shuffled over to the bed, breathing hard and whistling a little with each exhale. The birds ruffled in the loft.

Pennyrile immediately handed Elias a thick fold of paper, done up with a wax seal.

"Mr. Pennyrile . . . ," Elias began. "I feel funny about this. If it's all the same to you, I reckon maybe we ought to just let the doctor or the slaves carry your letters. I won't put you out anymore getting feed—the others can bring it in for me, so—"

Pennyrile snatched up the slate and wrote in quick, jagged little letters.

Bargain is a bargain.

"Yes, but—"

Pennyrile was already writing again. *Take the letter.*

"But, sir, I—"

Again the man wrote. When he flipped it back around, it read: *Think doc would like to hear the liberties his hands are taking with one of his patients?*

Elias tensed. "What's that mean?"

Pennyrile wrote. *Hate for your new pets to get themselves whipped for overstepping.*

And suddenly the whole thing had turned around on Elias. He'd suspected before that this was more than a favor, that he was getting roped into something he wanted no part of. And now he knew it.

This was an order. And if he refused, Pennyrile would make trouble for Stephen, Nick, and Mat.

"What am I supposed to do with this?" Elias asked through clenched teeth. He dared a look up as Pennyrile erased the message and began writing more. He'd changed the scarf and knot covering the scrofula. The thief knot was one of Elias's favorites. Anybody who didn't know would think it was just a plain square knot, but if you looked close enough, the ends of the rope ended up on the same side of the knot—not opposites like a square. People used it to tie up important things they didn't want seen, because they'd be able to tell if they had been snooped at. A thief might go to the trouble to tie the square knot back, but they likely wouldn't have noticed it wasn't a square knot in the first place.

Pennyrile knew his knots. Now he turned the slate around. *Outside the entrance. Tree. Jar buried at roots. Symbol on tree.*

"Fine. But what symbol?"

Pennyrile indicated the letter in Elias's hands. Elias lifted it into the light, inspecting the great glob of wax that sealed it up, the color like the purple wine stains bubbling out from underneath Pennyrile's scarf. Stamped in the wax was a perfect circle containing two letter *P*s that slanted away, back-to-back, stems crossed at the bottom, like twin branches of a forked tree trunk.

"Just look for this?"

Pennyrile held up a finger and wrote more. *Bring back correspondence inside.*

"How d'you know you got mail waiting up there?" Elias asked, skeptical.

Pennyrile wrote underneath his last message. *Haven't checked in while. Will be one.*

What a lot of trouble, Elias reckoned. A bird when you could just mail a letter. A tree when whoever was delivering it in the first place could have just walked in easily enough. Pennyrile had said they valued privacy, but what did that signify? Unless he really had something to hide.

That might account for using the birds—maybe they were flying someplace secret, someplace the post wouldn't carry.

Elias thought it through one more time. Pennryile sent the pigeons out with messages tied on. Homing pigeons were trained to fly in only one direction, so whoever wrote back would have to send their letter a different way, which was why Pennyrile picked up his own letters at the tree.

But what was Pennyrile hiding? What did he have to be so private about? Maybe it was all a big lark, Elias thought. Something to pass the time. There was fun in it, Elias admitted. Messenger pigeons, sneaking about, a secret tree. Maybe the whole thing was an amusement, a means to occupy Pennyrile, like Nedra's knitting or Elias's knots. There was a touch of fun in it, wasn't there?

But the notion of fun and Pennyrile didn't seem to get along.

Something still didn't figure.

"I ain't one to pry, sir," Elias began, "but if you could walk up there before to fetch your mail, why don't you just leave your notes for your friend in the same spot? Why'd you have to go through all them birds?"

Pennyrile narrowed his eyes, acted like he wouldn't reply, but then he wrote. *Speedier.*

Elias considered. Provided the bird made it out of the cave, it would be quicker to deliver the message than the post, quicker than waiting for someone to come and look in the jar to see if there were a message waiting. But what was urgent enough to go to all the bother?

"If your friend's near enough to drop the letters, wouldn't it be a whole lot faster—"

Pennyrile's face went as purple as the blotches on his neck. *Enough questions.* He wrote the words slowly, underlined them twice.

Elias knew he'd been dismissed. He didn't like the feeling, but he tucked the letter in his pocket. "Suit yourself," he said, going to the grain bag and scooping out a cupful. "But I don't know when I'll get it done."

Pennyrile's eyes seemed to burn as he kept them fixed on Elias, all the while writing on the slate. When he finished, he held it up. *Sooner the better.* Elias didn't have to ask if he was being warned, and when Pennyrile broke his stare and wrote again, Elias wasn't surprised by the words that appeared. *Hate to have any more birds die just because you can't be counted on.*

Elias drew himself up taller. "I'm good for it," he

said just as Croghan called out for him. Elias left without another word to Pennyrile.

"Miss Nedra's all right?" Elias asked as he and Croghan began to walk.

Croghan made a sympathetic noise. "Bit of a fever blew up in the night. But the draught should help," he said. "She is a dear girl. Excellent chances."

Elias thought he sounded unsure.

"How do you find Mr. Pennyrile?" Croghan asked as they headed for the Star Chamber that Stephen had shown him the other night. Elias saw the hut that served as Croghan's office tucked in next to the wall.

"All right, I suppose."

"He's a fascinating fellow," the doctor said. "Quite the waterman—like you, you know."

"I wondered," Elias said, thinking of the knots.

"When he wrote to me, he introduced himself as an accomplished river pilot. Seems he's been up and down all the big rivers of the East and West."

"Never said boo about it to me."

Croghan's foot slipped on a wet spot. "He was kind enough to let you keep one of his pigeons, so he must have taken something of a shine to you."

Elias didn't want to spoil Croghan's notion of Pennyrile's niceness. "I like the pigeon," Elias said noncommittally.

They walked under the twinkling heaven of those fake stars, past what Elias thought might have been the tunnel where he'd followed Jonah and found Stephen. Then they were in a new area of the cave. Around the bend he saw the lights from two other huts, smelled the smoke from their fires.

Croghan dropped his voice. "Mr. Sarneybrook is in the one on the right, Pastor Tincher on the left. Tincher's a good sort, a preacher. But we'll start with Sarneybrook. I think you'll like him, and the stillness cure can be lonesome, so he'll be awfully glad of a visitor."

A young woman perched on a stool before the fire. "Good morning, Hannah," Croghan said. "Have your patients been fed?"

"Yes, sir," the girl squeaked.

"Anything to report?"

"No, sir."

"The pots emptied?"

"Yes, sir. Nick come round and took 'em out."

Elias studied his boots. He was embarrassed enough about the pot he had to keep under his bed, which the slaves were meant to empty for him. He'd have given anything for a privy.

"The water is hot?" Croghan gestured to the kettle. Elias could see the steam wisping from the spout.

"Yes, sir."

"Prepare the compresses," he ordered. "And bring them in as soon as they're ready."

Hannah fetched a bundle of rags and got to work.

Croghan stalked toward the hut on the right and paused briefly at the door. "Mr. Sarneybrook? I've brought you a caller. May we come in?"

Without waiting for a response, Croghan led Elias through the door.

"Doc," said the man lying on the bed. He was sunk into the mattress, like he'd begun to melt into it.

"How are you this morning, Sarney?" Croghan asked, pulling the chair up by the man's bedside.

Elias hung back, wondering what he was meant to do, where he should stand.

"Who's that you got with you?" Sarneybrook asked, raising his head to try to get a look at Elias.

Croghan gestured to Elias, coaxing him forward. "This is our newest patient."

"Elias Harrigan, sir." Elias started to offer his hand but stopped. Was the man allowed to move even that much? Elias figured he'd better be safe than sorry. "Very pleased to meet you."

"Come closer so I can get eyes on you, son."

Elias didn't want to. The stink of Sarneybrook's night

sweats was sharp in the close hut—the same awful smell had hung around his father, no matter how often they changed his nightshirt or his sheets.

The smell was bad enough, but knowing *he'd* reek that way one day only made it worse.

Still, Elias came alongside Croghan at the bedside and awkwardly leaned over so Sarneybrook could get a look at him.

"Where d'you hail from, Elias Harrigan?" Sarneybrook seemed ill used to speaking, seemed to have barely enough energy for the words.

"Norfolk, Virginia, sir," he said.

"M'wife's people come through from Virginia," the man said. "Always meant to visit. Wanted to swim in the sea."

Elias wasn't sure the man would ever see anything beyond this cave again in his lifetime. While he was no expert on the disease, he could tell that the light was dimming in Sarneybrook's eyes, the way it had with his father at the end. Pity and grief leaped up in his chest.

Croghan lifted the blankets and gently rolled Mr. Sarneybrook on his side. The man sort of flopped over. "I miss moving my own self about. I used to love tramping up the mountains. Went up and down Black Mountain in the same day, just for sport. Now look at me."

"Makes it worse that Doc's got cold hands," Elias offered.

Sarneybrook laughed softly, but the laugh withered to a weak cough. "Boy's not wrong," he said when Croghan laid him back down. He lifted his eyes to Elias, then flicked them toward the table, where there sat a pail covered by a red cloth. "Have one of them sorghum cakes. Blanche—my wife—she was over yesterday morning. Brung me more'n I can eat," he said. Elias lifted a corner, and the smell of molasses and cinnamon nearly knocked him down.

"Elias is on a careful diet," the doctor said, leaning close to listen to Sarneybrook's breathing. "I'm afraid sweets aren't part of it."

Elias said thanks to the man anyway, who seemed disappointed. "I wish somebody'd enjoy 'em. I can't bring myself to want to eat anything no more. I think it'd do my wife good to see somebody had one," Sarneybrook said, something like a smile playing at his mouth.

Croghan was bent over Sarneybrook's chest, eyes closed listening. Sarneybrook winked.

And Elias had already eaten the salt pork anyway.

And the cakes were small.

He rescued one from beneath the cloth, tucking it into his pocket before the doctor sat up.

"Better today, I think," Croghan said to Sarneybrook. "How are you feeling otherwise?"

"Right enough," Sarneybrook admitted.

"Any more . . . Well, have you heard any more—"

The old man looked at Elias. "The doctor reckons I'm working up a good case of cabin fever," he explained. "All this lying around in the dark making my mind play tricks on me—"

"It's happened before—"

"I don't care if you think I'm off my nut, Doc," Sarneybrook said. "Or the boy, neither. And to answer your question, Jonah and me had us a nice visit last ni—"

"Jonah?" Elias erupted. *Jonah!*

Croghan spoke over his shoulder. "Keep your voice down, please."

"Did you say Jonah?" Elias asked, fighting to rein in his excitement.

"It's not uncommon for the mind to play tricks on a body, particularly one that used to be so active. And while the imagined—"

"He ain't imagined," Sarneybrook insisted. "Got my own personal haint. The cave's lousy with 'em, at least it was years ago when I did the tour. Besides, who else is going to keep company with a fella three quarters of the way dead like me?"

"You'll beat this yet," Croghan said, though he didn't sound as cheerful about it as Elias thought he might. "And now that you've met Elias, I'm sure he can have one of the hands show him down here to visit some other time. You'd both enjoy that, wouldn't you?"

Elias, too taken with the news that Jonah was friendly with others like Sarneybrook, did not reply. Maybe Jonah had even nicked that chunk of meat for Elias from Sarneybrook's plate when he wasn't looking.

"I think he and Jonah'd get on fine," Sarneybrook joked, though the doctor's smile seemed forced.

The doctor patted Sarneybrook's shoulder. "I'll have Stephen come down and read to you when he gets time," he said. "But now I'm afraid I need to continue my rounds." He stood. "Elias?"

Elias wanted more'n anything to tell Sarneybrook that he'd been visited by Jonah as well. Wanted more than anything to tell him he hadn't imagined it. And he would, he decided, when he came down next time. Soon.

"I read, too," he told Sarneybrook in a rush. "I can bring a book and read to you when I come again."

Sarneybrook smiled. "That'd be fine. Or you can just tell me about the ocean. I think I'd like that even better."

Elias promised that he would.

In the next hut, Pastor Tincher greeted them warmly, but soon was putting the screws to Elias about how the Baptists had it right and how Elias better get his house in order.

Soon they moved on, heading back toward the main cave, Elias only half listening to Croghan telling him about the next set of patients. He was too busy thinking about what he'd just learned about Jonah, trying to decide how he felt about it. And then he landed on it—he felt a touch jealous! How many other patients did Jonah call on?

But at the next little grouping of huts, no one mentioned Jonah or visitors of any kind, really. There was a woman about the same age as his mother called Mozelle, who seemed nice enough and slipped him a withered apple when Croghan stepped out of the room for a moment.

Next door to her lived a circuit lawyer Doctor Croghan kept referring to as the Honorable Mr. Cherry. He offered Elias a wedge of good-smelling cheese, which Elias refused as the doctor looked on approvingly.

But at the third hut, Croghan placed a hand on Elias's arm. "You'd best let me see the widow Patton alone," he said. "She's quite unwell."

Weren't they all unwell? Weren't they all here because they were unwell? But there was something in Croghan's look that made Elias understand. It wasn't that he didn't want her to be bothered by Elias. It was that he didn't want Elias to see *her*. See someone dying quite as obviously as she apparently was.

So he waited out in the clearing with Dorothy, one of the nurses who sat in for Lillian now and then.

"You want something?" she asked him, not unkindly.

Elias thought of the treats he'd collected. They seemed silly to him suddenly. Silly to care about an apple or a sweet—things he'd have cared about before he fell ill. He realized he'd almost forgotten why he'd come. Forgotten that he was going to die, and that if he didn't want to, he ought not go sneaking food the doctor thought he shouldn't have. He'd already given in with the salt pork. "No, thanks."

Mr. Cherry called out for Dorothy. When she disappeared, Elias tossed the apple and the sorghum cake into the fire.

Not long after, Croghan came back out, looking grim, but as soon as he saw Elias watching, forced a smile. "One more to go," he said, motioning for Elias to follow.

They made quick work of the short walk up to the last hut.

A figure stood in front of the hut, snapping twigs off a shrub that someone had planted outside the door. The man abandoned his little garden when he saw the doctor approaching with the lamp.

"Good morning, Shem," Doctor Croghan called. "How are—"

"Bring him near . . . ," Shem said, shuffling barefoot

toward Elias. The man was gaunt and pale, sweat beading his brow. Before Elias knew what was happening, Shem buried his nose in the fabric of Elias's coat, right at his chest, and inhaled. Long, deep sniffs.

"That's enough, Shem," the doctor said gently, prying the old man's fingers from Elias's coat. "Let Elias be."

The man's eyes met Elias's, full of disappointment. "You're not new," he said accusingly.

"Elias has been here for weeks," the doctor explained. "He's come to heal up as well."

"I can't smell the sunshine on you." Shem let go of Elias's coat and let the doctor guide him back inside his hut.

"Mat's got a tour coming in later. Perhaps they can visit with you a spell. You can see if they have the scent about them." He whispered to Elias, "Wait here, son?"

Elias was happy to wait outside. He knelt and scooped up some of the soil from the little garden patch, wondering if they'd had to bring it in along with the plant.

Inside, Shem whimpered as Croghan spoke to him. He heard the clinking of glass against glass, the sound of a dropper against the neck of a bottle. *Laudanum,* Elias guessed. They'd used the powerful drug with Daddy to help him sleep. And by the silence that descended on the hut a minute later, he figured he'd been right.

Croghan stepped out. "Well," he said. To Elias's ear,

that *well* sounded fairly full of things he wasn't saying. But it was fine, as Elias didn't feel much like talking.

"Shall we head back?" Croghan asked.

Elias was ready. If he'd brought the other visitors any cheer, he felt depleted himself, like it had been sucked straight out of him. Croghan seemed worried too, that the benefit of the physical activity might be undercut by low spirits. "I'm eager to see how your lungs have responded to the exertion."

Elias just trudged on.

"Perhaps your next walk could have you join Stephen or Mat for part of a tour instead of just visiting with me."

"Whatever you say, Doc."

As they walked, his mind drifted back to Jonah.

He was trying to work out how to ask Croghan if any of the other patients had ever mentioned a ghost or spirit or visitor called Jonah when it hit him.

Croghan hadn't recognized Jonah's name. When Sarneybrook had said it, when Elias had blurted it out in response, Croghan had only seemed concerned for Sarneybrook.

If Croghan did have a boy called that, wouldn't he have said something?

And if Jonah wasn't a slave shirking work to haunt folks, well . . . who was he?

Elias recalled all he had heard about Jonah so far.

Jonah had left someplace.

Jonah was black.

Jonah was inside the cave, without Croghan knowing, maybe without a lot of people knowing. The facts slotted into place, like the bights of rope in a difficult knot.

Jonah was, Elias realized, a runaway.

Chapter Seven

DOUBLE FISHERMAN'S KNOT

A week slunk by. A week in which Elias grew sicker still of eggs and foul tea and his little hut. A week in which he stewed on his discovery that Jonah must be a runaway, a fugitive slave. He'd heard Stephen and Mat pass by often enough, their voices echoing as they guided tours, but they'd not collected Elias to go exploring with them again. Nick had been around some, hauling water or firewood for Lillian, and he sat with Elias a little, learning a couple of knots when he had time.

Elias filled his days tying knots and reading—having at last swapped books back with Miss Nedra—and trying to stay awake in case Jonah came by. He'd missed him at least once, awakening to find another of Sarneybrook's sorghum cakes sitting on his windowsill. As good as it smelled, he didn't eat it; instead he broke it into crumbs and let Bedivere peck the bits up from his palm.

He began to wonder if, since the bird was clever enough to be trained to fly home, could he be taught to do other things? He'd taught Charger to fetch, stay, and shake hands. He didn't reckon he'd ever get Bedivere to roll over, but maybe he could get him to do something else.

So he spent hours trying to teach Bedivere to come when he called. He used the crumbs of the sorghum cake, whistling and saying his name softly, imploring the bird to come closer. But Bedivere just cooed and warbled and occasionally hopped over to see what Elias had. He thought wistfully of how easy it had been to call out for Charger, how the big dog would come bounding to him.

After a while, he gave up and slipped Pennyrile's letter from his pocket.

He'd had it too long. Pennyrile had asked him twice if he'd delivered the note, but Elias had not had a chance to get up to the entrance since accepting it. Elias had promised he'd take it as soon as he could, and were it not for the fact that the pigeons were even less reliable, he was sure Pennyrile would have asked him to give it back.

But he hadn't. So for the hundredth time, Elias studied the symbol stamped into the wax seal over the fold. He'd grown more worried over the week about the message it might contain, and he'd tried to lift the edges of the paper, tried to see what might be written there. But they were folded neatly enough to keep him from learning anything. He returned the letter to his pocket.

It didn't matter. He was under Pennyrile's thumb for certain. He'd take the letter. If he didn't, he knew Pennyrile would surely send those other birds out to die in the cave.

Though he told himself there were worse things he could deal with (Sarneybrook's perfect stillness, for instance), he didn't like the feeling of being owned by the man. He kept seeing Pennyrile's words on the slate, kept hearing the scratch of the chalk. And he marveled at how a fella who was near enough to being mute could be so loud inside his own head.

Then he had the strangest thought: he wondered how Stephen and Nick and Mat and all the rest of them stood it. Doctor Croghan seemed kind enough, but even so . . . being ordered around, not being in charge of your own self. Was this what it felt like? Was this what the house girl and their outside man back home felt like?

He shook the thought off and reasoned that it had to be different.

But even so. Another thought came to him.

What about Jonah? Maybe if a slave wasn't treated right, maybe it meant he didn't have to stay. Like his daddy had said, a man who couldn't be bothered to scrape the hull of his ship free of barnacles didn't deserve to have the ship. Maybe an owner who didn't look after his slaves deserved to have them run off.

They were good to their hands back at home, and Croghan was good to his, as far as Elias could see. It could be worse. Mat had even said so.

But for the first time, he admitted that just because something could be worse, it didn't mean it also couldn't be *better*. Didn't mean that a body got used to being treated like a boat, steered and directed and told where to go. Didn't mean that a body gave up, no matter how much it appeared to be satisfied with what life had become.

He thought about the man back home. George? It was George, wasn't it? Or was that his boy who he brought with him to work the gardens sometimes? Did George feel that? Or what about Sally? Did she get tired of cooking and cleaning and answering the door?

His wondering didn't help him a whit with the matter of Pennyrile, though. In the end, there was nothing for it. He'd deliver his letter.

All in all, it was a fine mess.

He was still stewing on it, still trying to get Bedivere to

respond to his name, when Nick called softly at the door.

Elias sprang off the bed and burst through the quilt. "Yeah, Nick?"

If Nick was startled by Elias's eagerness, he didn't let on. "You feel like coming out with me?"

Elias brightened. "You bet!"

Nick grinned. "You fancy fishin'?"

Elias figured he was pulling his leg. "Sure. Fishing."

"You gonna bring that bird?"

"He'll be all right," Elias said, dropping to a knee and tightening his bootlaces.

"C'mon, then," Nick said, spitting toward the shadowy side of the hut. Elias sure hoped Jonah wasn't hiding there.

Lillian came to the door. "Y'all can't be turning this boy into some sort of pet—"

"I'll have him back 'fore supper," Nick said.

"See you do," Lillian said to Nick, before addressing Elias. "Wear your hat."

Elias obeyed and followed them out of the hut, smiling at the thought of a new adventure. But the smile faltered when he saw Pennyrile watching from his window. He checked his pocket to make sure the letter was still there.

"Um, Nick?" Elias said when they were out of earshot.

"Hmm?"

"I was wondering," Elias said. "I mean, I was hoping, that is . . ." He hemmed and fussed with his words, but Nick stayed patient. "I was wondering if I could take a peek up top," Elias said finally.

Nick slowed. "Up top?"

"I ain't seen the sun or anything in over a month. And I promise, it won't have to be long, just a single second, and Croghan won't have to know—"

"Croghan gone over to Cave City," Nick said. "But he wouldn't like it. Naw, I should—"

"Please," Elias begged. "I just need to see light that don't come from a candle! To sniff some fresh air."

Nick bit the inside of his lip. "Only for a minute," he decided. "And we best hurry if I'm to check the traps and get you back on time."

Elias almost hugged him with relief. If Nick could take him this one time, Elias would be sure of the way out. And then he could do the other letters by himself. "Thanks, Nick. I promise to be quick."

Nick was quick too, setting a relentless pace toward the entrance. Elias took stock of the landmarks, mapping the route in his mind so he could find his way back by himself if he needed to. He was so busy making his mental map and so busy trying to keep up with Nick that he didn't even notice how good he was feeling. How strong his lungs felt. But when he caught Nick staring, he asked him, "What?"

"You lookin' better," Nick said. "Ain't got that ashy look you had when you first come."

"Eggs and tea and cave air, I guess." Elias took a deep breath, feeling his lungs expand and collapse again without cracking or popping or experiencing the bits of needlelike pains that he'd gotten sometimes when he tried to draw in too much air. Nick was right. He *was* better.

"Sump's workin'," Nick agreed. The breeze kicked up around them as they passed through an opening about the size of a barn door.

"Why's it blow like that?" Elias asked, remembering how the wind had been at his back when he'd first come in with Stephen. Now it was stiff enough that he had to lean into it. Nick left the lamp behind, sheltered from the breeze.

"Cave's Breath," Nick explained. "Indians called it so. Blows in like this when it's cold outside, out just as quick when it's warm."

"But how?" Elias asked, wondering at a cave big enough to make its own weather.

"Just do," Nick said. "No 'countin' for it."

Soft gray light made him forget the wind. It took everything Elias had not to run toward it.

The sun was high, the air clear and cold. He hadn't noticed before how beautiful it was here in these woods, the canopy vaulting impossibly high above the cave entrance, bare branches like fancy brocade against the sky. He whipped off his hat, let the light soak his hair and face, shut his eyes, and tilted his chin up toward the treetops, the rim of the cave.

"Nice day," Nick offered, biting off a fresh plug of tobacco and settling it between his cheek and his gum.

Elias laughed just for the joy of it. "Perfect."

"I knew it'd be a good one when I walked over this mornin'," Nick said.

Elias opened his eyes. "You live out here," he said, realizing he'd sort of imagined him living somewhere in the cave. But why would he when he wasn't sick? When he could be out here with sunshine and blue skies?

Nick pointed out to the east. "Not far."

"All by yourself?"

Nick spat, staining a rock a good six feet away. "Naw. Got me a little room halfway 'tween the hotel up there and the place Mat share with his wife—"

"Mat's married?" Elias was incredulous.

"Met Parthena not long after me and him came up here. Got some little 'uns, too."

"You never met a girl?" Elias asked. Nick seemed more

the type, he reasoned. He couldn't imagine Mat sweet on anybody or putting up with children.

"Someday," Nick offered.

There was a lot in that "someday," Elias guessed. A lot he didn't understand, but he heard one thing he did recognize: hope.

Elias walked farther away from the overhang forming the arch of the cave. "We got traps to check," Nick said. He wasn't often in a hurry, but Elias sensed he was now. Then he remembered the letter he was meant to deliver, the reason he'd begged Nick to bring him out here in the first place.

But not even the letter in his pocket could curb his joy. He didn't know if it was the sunshine or the sneaking about or if Croghan's treatments really were working, but he felt good. Strong. Really strong. He eyed the slope that rose up sharply from where they stood to the ridge above them. He remembered coming down that slope, leaning heavily on the rope handrail to keep his balance. It had worn him out then. He couldn't wait to try it now.

"Please, Nick . . . ," he began. "Let me get up and down the hill. Just once, just to see if my lungs'll hold up." He meant it. He really did want to see what he could do.

Nick took a deep breath. "Go on then," he said at last. Elias didn't wait for him to reconsider. He ran to the rope handrail and began hauling himself up quick. The rope flew through his hands, his feet striding out, taking great big bites out of the hillside. He was up top in no time at all. Elias whooped when he gained the ridge, then he leaned over, hands on his knees, panting.

He glanced behind him at the entrance.

The cave gaped wide. He thought of the story of Jonah from the Bible, being swallowed by the great fish. From here the mouth of the cave looked exactly that: a mouth set to swallow up the whole woods and the world beyond. Loose rock of all sizes made a fencerow of crooked teeth. Ferns—still green most of them—fringed the entrance like whiskers.

Nick hollered from below. "Don't you go that fast coming down," he warned. "You're liable to tumble and snap your own neck. Then the doc'll have mine!"

Elias waved him off and wandered a few steps until he was out of sight. The ground was drier than it had been the day he'd arrived, wagon ruts starting to crumble at the peaks. He fished the letter from his pocket, studied the symbol printed on the wax, and began to search.

Nick called up for him to hurry, and as he shouted back that he'd be right down, he spied the tree. The beech's silvery trunk was stout at the bottom, but about two feet from the soil it forked, sending two trees growing off in opposite directions. And right where they split, at the base of the V, he saw the emblem from Pennyrile's letter cut neatly into the bark, small enough you wouldn't notice if you weren't looking for it, big enough to make out all the detail and know it had been put there on purpose if you were.

Elias rushed to the tree and brushed the dried leaves at the base out of the way. Someone had hollowed out the space between two of the roots, and in it was an old glass jar. Elias fished it out and popped off the rusty tin lid.

Just as Pennyrile said, there was something inside.

Elias unscrewed the lid of the jar and removed the letter. It was sealed the same way Pennyrile's was, with the same symbol, only this time done up in green wax. He peeled the corner back a hair and saw the top part of the first page.

Dear Brother,

Brother? Pennyrile had a brother? Pennyrile had a brother to whom he couldn't send a proper letter out in the post with the rest of the mail? A brother who was near enough to correspond with him this way? But had Pennyrile ever had a visitor? Maybe he had a brother he didn't want anyone to know about? Or maybe he was party to one of those churches where they all called one another brother even though they weren't any relation at all?

"Elias!" Nick called up again, his voice insistent. Elias swapped the notes and stowed the jar back in its place, covering it up with leaves again. He studied the symbol carved on the tree one last time. What was Pennyrile up to? He'd work it out later. Right now he had fish to catch. And Nick had waited long enough.

Back on the path inside the cave, Elias matched Nick's strides. They took a jog without warning off to the left of the main path into a passage Elias had never been in before. They found themselves in a low-ceilinged room, the rock above them smooth and nearly flat. A cairn of loose stones had been built up in the middle like some sort of pillar, though Elias expected it was just for show and didn't really hold anything up. But on the ceiling, all over the room, he saw names, dozens and dozens of them.

Some were written in black soot, others in chalk. Names and dates, too. Some of them more than fifty or sixty years old. Elias scanned them as they walked. Even noticed an advertisement for a miracle tonic cure scratched in among them.

"Tourists like to write they names in here."

"Like you and Stephen and Mat do when you go exploring," Elias said, reading all the while.

Nick's head see-sawed as if to say they weren't the same, but he didn't explain.

"But why are some of them backward?"

"Lots of 'em use a candle tied on the end of a stick. They hold the flame up close to the rock to blacken it, bit by bit. But they don't want the wax dripping in they faces, so we put a mirror on the floor. They look in that, make the name by looking in the reflection, and sometimes they forget to switch the letters round to make 'em look proper." It seemed right to Elias, somehow, that the images were reversed. His mind leaped to Nedra's poem, the lady weaving, her mirror.

"You want to write your name?" Nick asked. Ladies' names crowded up next to fancy ones with words like *Honorable* before them, or *Esquire* after them. Elias wanted to. Something about putting your name up on a wall was irresistible, sort of like you couldn't stand long in front of a river or a pond without eventually tossing rocks out into it.

But when he looked at Nick, he found him watching expectantly. And something about the way he stared told Elias he wanted him to say no.

"Nah," Elias said. "Thanks anyway." Nick smiled like

Elias had said something right, and he started walking back down to the main cave. Elias couldn't help but glow a little, feeling like he'd passed some kind of test.

"Stephen showed me this," Elias said a few minutes later as they reached the Star Chamber. Croghan's office was empty and dark.

"Star Chamber's good for more than just gawking. Got half a dozen tunnels that take us where we need to go." He led them across the room as Elias lifted the light higher, trying to set some of the stars twinkling. He felt lucky indeed to see stars and sunshine within the span of a few minutes.

They tucked into another tunnel where the floor sloped down sharp. They descended rapidly.

"We going fishing now?"

"If they any left to catch," Nick said, and Elias could almost hear him smiling as he said it.

"Why you want to fish down here?" Elias asked. "Best part of fishing is sitting on the pier or out in a boat. Can't nothing that grows underground taste good, can it?"

"Fish ain't for eating," Nick said. They dropped farther, and here and there Elias had to use the sides of the walls to steady himself. His foot splashed in a puddle, and he heard the sound of water lapping against stone for the first time. Nick offered Elias a hand now and then, or told him where to step to avoid a hole or a puddle. Elias was fairly certain they weren't on the tour.

"What are they for, then?" Elias asked once the walking became easier again.

"Sellin'."

"Sellin'?"

"You'll see." And a moment later he did. A fine vein of water cut through the floor. Elias figured it must have been deep, it ran so smooth, but he could straddle its width with ease. Downstream, it collected in a little basin before it tipped slowly over a wash of rock and into a seam in the wall. Nick hung his lantern off a spur of rock.

"See that?" Nick pointed to a basket sort of thing, a few inches of it poking out above the water. The reed was woven tight and true, and when Nick lifted the trap out of the pool, the water drained from it slow like seawater through sailcloth. The trap was bigger than Elias expected it to be based on what poked up through the surface of the stream. By the time Nick had cleared it from the water, it stood nearly as tall as Elias, and about two feet wide. Nick had made it specially to fit. There was a slot cut into the side that yawned like a mouth.

"Yessir," Nick said as he laid the trap on its side. Elias heard a sound that could only be a fish flopping. Nick unhinged the bottom and three lily-white fish flipped out.

Three lily-white fish that didn't have any eyes.

"Frogs and stars," Elias whispered.

It was . . . it was . . . Why, it was like the time he went to the sideshow with his father down at the parade grounds. They had seen a bearded lady, a two-headed calf, and all sorts of things that defied imagination. That was what these fish did—defied imagination.

"Cave fish," Nick said, holding one up carefully. Its fins were like lace, or fairy wings, hardly anything there at all. Its snout angled sharply up, but there was nothing like an eye anywhere on its head. Elias could see right through its skin, the heart pumping away.

"I sell 'em to the tourists on the sly."

Elias watched Nick open the waterskin—the very one he'd had Elias drinking from the first time he came out—and slide the fish inside. "Why?" Elias asked, though he wasn't sure if he meant why did Nick sell them or why did people want them.

"Folk pay a whole dollar for 'em," Nick said.

"A *dollar*?" Elias asked, stunned. Nick scooped up the other two fish.

"I mean to buy my freedom with these fish."

"How many you need?"

Nick hesitated. "Not sure, really. They don't go round telling us what we're worth. But once a man tried to buy me offa Bransford, offered four hunerd fifty. And Croghan leasing me and Mat for near a hundred dollars a year."

It was a small fortune, Elias knew that much.

"So I reckon," Nick went on, "I save up as much as I can, sell me about a thousand of these fish, and then I ought to be able to buy myself out. Then maybe I set up some-place with a wife."

Elias had no idea how long it would take Nick to gather that many fish. He knew enough about Nick to know he was the patient sort, but it would take years. Years of nab-bing up these little fish, years of leading people around on tours.

"Why'nt you just run?" Elias asked suddenly, thinking of Jonah.

"Running ain't no good." Nick did the clasps at the bottom back up. "Man can't live a life wondering if some-one's going drag him back to some place he don't want to be. That's what I told—"

His sentence stayed unfinished as he busied himself resetting the trap in the water.

"Told who?" Elias pressed.

Nick wiped his hands dry on his trousers. "Nobody."

But Elias wondered. Was Stephen going to run? Or Mat? A piece of Elias thrilled at the idea. But another piece worried that Nick was right. That running away was just a lot more pain in the end. How long could Jonah hide down there before he got caught? Before he haunted somebody who wasn't as friendly as Elias or Sarneybrook?

It wasn't like Nick was doing anything wrong, was he? Buying his freedom, all things considered, seemed the most honorable way to get free.

But still. Doctor Croghan owned the cave. And the fish. Did that mean Nick was stealing from him?

But in a flash of clear, quiet thought, Elias understood that he didn't care. He only hoped there were enough fish hiding in these waters to make up what Nick needed.

Chapter Eight

STRANGLE KNOT

L et us say a special prayer on behalf of our departed friend, the widow Patton."

Elias's head yanked up. The widow Patton?

Departed?

Though he'd never met her, having barely even heard her voice while he waited outside during Croghan's rounds only a week or so before, the knowledge that she'd died shuddered through Elias.

Dead. Just like that, he thought. She was alive yesterday, and now she was not. It seemed awfully unfair that she'd put herself down there, stayed in the dark, and did what the doctor said, only to die.

The cave was supposed to be making them better.

Supposed to be giving Croghan time to cure them. But was anybody besides Elias improving?

Maybe the widow had been too old to fight off the consumption, or maybe she hadn't squared up with Doc Croghan's remedies. He reminded himself how important it was that he follow the doctor's prescriptions and avoid the little treats Jonah left, no matter how tempting they were.

But poor widow Patton.

He bowed his head and prayed along with the rest of them that the Lord would speed her along to his side in paradise. "Amen," Pastor Tincher finished. They all sat down to eat. Doctor Croghan had thought it might benefit them all to take Sunday supper together. Stephen and Mat and the others had set up long tables and benches in the space outside Doctor Croghan's office, which blazed with light. It was a stone hut just like so many of the others, but it had a wooden floor, a proper door, and an honest-to-Pete roof.

As they'd walked in, Elias had been teased by the smell of the cooking fire and bacon grease. And through the blessing his stomach had flipped and rolled, his mouth watering at all the food soon to be spread on the table. There was ham sizzling, and Elias was almost sure he could smell potatoes. What he wouldn't give for a mess of potatoes fried up crisp and golden, thick slices of greasy onions mixed in the pile. But when he sat down, Lillian passed him by with her big skillet full of home fries. Hannah acted like she might give him some of that bread she was carrying round before she remembered. Finally Nick brought him a plate of fried eggs, three of them, and his mug of tea. His eyes signaled his apology for Elias's sad plate.

Elias sighed, picked up his fork, and ate dutifully.

After he finished he sat and listened to the adults talking. But they all seemed out of practice with visiting, and none protested as Hannah and Lillian began escorting them back to the huts.

Elias, however, had no intention of wasting another day in his room.

"Hey, Bishop!" Elias whispered when Stephen came close to collect plates. "Nick took me out fishin' yesterday!"

Stephen picked up a teacup. "So I heard."

"What're we gonna do today?" Elias asked Stephen.

Stephen stopped stacking the plates and dropped his voice low. "We can't bring you out today."

Elias's heart sank. "But you said—"

"All of us got things to do."

"But . . . it's Sunday," Elias argued.

"Sunday doesn't mean the same thing for us," Stephen said, his voice curt.

Stung, Elias settled for the next best thing. Stephen had

books, books Elias hadn't read the words off the pages yet. "C'n I have a look at some of your books, then maybe? I was thinking I wouldn't mind seeing them maps—"

If a body hadn't been watching, they'd have thought Stephen dropped the plate that suddenly crashed to the floor out of clumsiness. But Elias had been watching, and he was pretty sure Stephen *threw* the plate he was about to add to the stack in his hand.

The crash and clatter of the clay plate against the rock floor choked off all other sound and conversation. Everyone stopped and stared. More important, it cut off Elias's question.

"Apologies," Stephen said, bending down to collect the shards. Lillian rushed over to help him.

"What'd you do that—" Elias started.

"Not. Another. Word," Stephen said low so only Elias heard, sweeping the slivers aside with his coat sleeve.

Elias stared at Stephen's back. He'd been helpful the other night, hadn't he? What had he done to make Stephen so cross? And who was Stephen to get angry with him, anyway? He had half a mind to ask Doctor Croghan to *make* Stephen take him out, but quickly dismissed the notion. Elias wanted Stephen to *want* to take him, not be saddled with him like his mother did when she used to make him look after Tillie.

Elias fumed, wondering if there were anything he
could say to maybe change Stephen's mind, when a heavy
form settled next to him, the nails in the bench creaking
as they took his weight. Pennyrile.

Elias had managed to avoid him since last night when
he dropped off the letter he had collected at the tree.

The slate tap-tapped on the tabletop. Elias gripped
the side of the bench. Most of the others were gone, but
some were lingering to touch what looked like a bundle
of laundry on a low flat rock behind Croghan's office.

Pennyrile held the slate so Elias could see it. *Gone long
time yesterday just to fetch my letter back and forth.*

Pennyrile was the last person Nick would want to
know about the fish or his plan. "Nick just took me about.
Showed me some gypsum flowers and such." The lie
sounded thin to Elias, but Pennyrile was already writing
again.

You're friendly with them.

Elias read the words and looked at Pennyrile. It was
unmistakable, that look in his eyes. Part disbelief, part
disgust. Like back when Elias still went to school, and
some of the boys found out he'd volunteered to stay
after to empty the ashes out of the woodstove for the
new teacher. Peter and Lawrence and Trumbull couldn't
believe he'd done such a thing, and accused him of being

sweet on her, which he might have been a little, but still.

Elias shifted. "So what?"

Pennyrile twitched his nose like he smelled something foul. But he let it drop and wrote again.

How do the darkies get around out there?

"They do fine," Elias said, wondering what he was after.

More writing. *Blazes on the route? Maps?*

"Mostly they just know where they are and where they want to be," Elias said, "but Stephen's got a good—"

He caught himself. Stephen had dropped that plate on purpose, right as Elias was asking about looking at the maps. And now Pennyrile was asking about the same thing. Had he been watching them? Listening?

And Elias now understood: Stephen didn't want anyone to know about his book.

"Stephen's got a good sense of direction," Elias finished.

After a beat, Pennyrile scribbled, *Have letter. Take tonight.* He waited just long enough to make sure Elias had read it, then erased it quickly.

Elias fought the overwhelming urge to tell him what he could do with his letter, not that it would have mattered as Pennyrile was scribbling away, longer and longer. At last he showed Elias the slate. *Don't want to get your new pals into trouble, do you? Doctor's looser with slaves than he ought to be, but even he would have to take a firm hand with*

*that lot taking advantage of a sickly lad who doesn't know
better.*

Elias's neck grew hot. "Now you know it's not a thing
like that!" He could barely keep himself from shouting.

Pennyrile erased the slate and wrote again. *They'll fool
you blind if you give them half a chance.*

Elias shook his head. "You're wrong."

Pennyrile shrugged. But he didn't have to be right to
get Elias to obey.

Elias set his jaw. "Fine. But I don't know when I'll get
back up there. Stephen said he can't take me out today."

Pennyrile waved dismissively. *You'll work it out,* he
jotted down before he passed another wax-sealed letter
under the table to Elias.

Then began the halting, huffing work of raising himself off the bench. Once Pennyrile was standing again, he
stared at the bundle on the rock. Tincher the preacher
was lingering beside it, head bowed like he was praying.
So Elias asked, "What's that going on over there?"

Pennyrile wrote, *Corpse Rock.*

Elias's breath caught. Corpse Rock.

It wasn't laundry laid out on the stone. It was the widow
Patton. All the others were filing past, paying their last
respects. Elias stared, undone by being so close to the body
this whole time without even knowing it, and undone by

the fact that it all appeared to be so routine to the others.

They must have used it this way many times before for it to have earned the name!

Elias swallowed. *It might be me next, laid out there,* he thought. And if not next, someday.

Pennyrile. Jonah. The exploring. He'd come here for one reason only, and it wasn't to do with any of the those things. He'd come to heal. And he would not be next. Not if he had anything to do with it.

But he didn't want anyone else to be next either. He tore his eyes away from the bundle, and Pennyrile touched his forehead in mock salute, then began to shuffle back up the path.

Elias rose, circled around to the edge of Corpse Rock, and stared at the sheet-bundled body of the widow. He'd never met her, never even seen her face. And he wouldn't. Ever.

How many people will never know me, he wondered. If he died down there?

He closed his eyes then and there and prayed, pleading with God to make him better. To heal him. Promising he'd do what the doctor said and promising to be kind to everyone and promising to not think those dark thoughts about Mama and Granny shipping him off so they wouldn't have to be bothered with him dying anymore.

But he was ashamed that the prayers that came first were for himself. So he screwed his eyes shut tighter and prayed for peace for the widow Patton's soul. But all those other prayers, the ones for himself, kept crowding back in. Finally he gave up, recited the Act of Contrition, and murmured an amen as he made the sign of the cross.

When he lifted his head, he found Nick had drawn near. "All right, son?"

Elias sighed. "I'm all right."

"You see her?" Nick asked. "When you went calling with Croghan?"

Elias said he had not. "Bet she was real nice, though."

Nick's nose twitched. "Naw. Mean, that one."

Elias was surprised to hear Nick talk so. But also relieved somehow. He could always count on Nick.

"But maybe being so sick made her that way. It does that with some folk," Nick continued, eyeing Pennyrile creeping away, stopping every few yards to lean against the wall.

Elias would have to sit there a while if he didn't want to pass him as he made his way back. Maybe Nick was right. Maybe Pennyrile only got so mean after he got sicker, and maybe he was getting meaner by the day, just as he was getting weaker.

"Pennyrile trouble you any?" Nick asked, Elias catching the scent of his tobacco on his words.

Pennyrile had. But Elias couldn't make it Nick's trouble too. "I reckon I'll be all right," Elias said, beginning his own slow march back to his hut. Maybe Jonah would turn up today, he thought. But he doubted even a visit from him could bring his spirits up now.

Chapter Nine

KILLICK HITCH

The next morning after breakfast and Croghan's visit, Jonah returned.

"Hey," he whispered.

"Where you been?" Elias whispered back.

"Around. You the one been out a lot, ain't you? 'Tween fishing with Nick and 'splorin' with the fellas, and the doctor getting y'all out for that supper, you're the real man about town, ain't you?"

"Sorry I missed you them times," Elias said. And he was.

"Gonna be harder to call on than ever, what with Croghan sending you out with the tours now."

"How'd you know about that?" Elias asked. Croghan had only that morning told Elias that he wanted him to join the tour group that would be by later. Since the bit of exercise he'd had so far seemed to be helping, he figured to let him get even more.

"Like I said, I keep up on all y'all," Jonah said. "And you still got the best end of things, you ask me."

"What's he doing to the others now?" Elias knew he should ask about Jonah being a runaway, but was half afraid Jonah might get spooked enough to not come around.

"Tryin' everthing," Jonah said, and Elias could almost hear the glee in his voice. "Been working at bleeding some of them folks."

Elias's skin crawled. "I hate leeches." He'd yanked plenty from his ankles in the freshwater marshes back near Norfolk.

Jonah hissed. "Leeches nothing. Too cold by half down here for them things. And Croghan don't think a knife is civilized at all. Made him some kind of borehole that poke through when he turn a crank."

"You're making that up," Elias said, at once horrified and impressed.

"Naw!" Jonah said. "Does it to a lot of 'em. Don't know if it works any. But I'd say it's a sight better than what he done that Mr. Cherry."

"What's he do to him?"

"Calls it a 'emetic.' You know what that is?"

Elias did not.

"Thing to make a body cast up what he ate. Bad, too. Some mix of raw tobacco and castor oil. I don't hang around much when I hear the doctor call for that one. Sounds is awful enough to make me th'ow up too, and then they'd know I was near."

"'Lias?" Lillian called from the fire. "I see the lights from Mat's tour. You best get down the hill."

"Be right there!" Elias hollered, but he turned quickly back to Jonah. He had to do it now. "You know we called on Sarneybrook."

"Yeah," Jonah said. "I know."

Elias took a deep breath. "You visit him. And he told us about it and even used your name."

Jonah didn't reply.

"Croghan didn't act like your name meant anything to him," Elias went on. "He seemed to think Sarneybrook dreamt you up."

Still Jonah kept quiet.

"They're below, Elias!" Lillian called from outside. "Hurry on!"

"I'm coming!" he yelled, then whispered toward the window. "You're a runaway, aren't you?"

The silence that fell stretched out long and thin. Elias heard Mat's voice in the distance as he addressed his tour.

"Jonah?"

"You got a tour to catch." Jonah sounded grim. Elias wished he could see his face, wished he could read what Jonah might have been feeling.

"I won't tell on you," Elias pressed on, but then he heard Lillian's steps drawing near.

"Now, Elias!" Lillian said, poking through the curtain.

Elias threw one last look at the window, but he knew Jonah would stay hidden or had already gone. "Okay." He scattered extra feed for Bedivere and wrapped his green scarf around his neck. He patted his coat pocket to make sure Pennyrile's letter was still there in case he managed to check the tree.

"Mat's fit to be tied about you coming out," Lillian said to Elias. "You'll only make it worse by holding him up now. Watch yourself."

Elias thanked her for the warning and thumped down the slope. Mat broke off from his little group of tourists to intercept Elias. "Don't get in the way," he growled, then stalked back to the head of the group and snapped at them to come along. A few of the tourists eyed Elias with curiosity, but Mat was moving fast, and no one was keen to be left behind.

Elias was relieved to see that Mat's rough treatment seemed sort of universal.

Elias hung near the back, watching the rest of the folks. There were eight of them. A young couple on honeymoon from Nashville, which he knew because they must have told the other folk on the tour with them a half dozen times. Two other couples, older, one accompanied by a grown daughter. All the ladies were wearing breeches, which Elias could scarcely believe. Finally there was a fat man who seemed to be by himself.

They tracked back through Gothic Avenue, everybody gawking up at the signatures. Mat didn't ask them if they wanted to sign their names. In the Star Chamber, Mat climbed up to show them the stars twinkling overhead, holding the torch high. Then every man on the tour paid for the privilege of throwing a rock up high and making a new star. The quarters clinked in Mat's palm, but he didn't seem any happier for it. Then he led them over Bottomless Pit. When the others hesitated at the bridge, Elias dug up his courage and went first without being asked. Though his legs threatened to turn to jelly, he kept his eyes straight ahead, hoping he looked braver than he felt. Mat didn't appear impressed. Then they wound down to Fat Man's Misery. Elias noticed that the fat man on their tour did seem to be a little more miserable than the others. He thought he saw Mat grinning at that. Elias felt a little sorry for the big man, and hung back and waited as he squeezed himself through the narrow twists. It took a good while, and Elias found himself looking anywhere but at the man, embarrassed for him, embarrassed to have to stand there and wait for him.

Eventually he looked behind him, back up the path. He wouldn't have seen it otherwise.

In a little alcove just to the right of the path lay one of Pennyrile's pigeons.

The fat man was still miserable, trying to unwedge himself, so Elias backtracked to the bird.

The pigeon lay on its side, wings tucked neatly in, tail feathers fanned out behind. It could have died an hour ago or a month ago, Elias guessed, what with the cave vapors doing their magic on the bird's corpse even now.

Elias eyed the little scroll of paper rolled tightly around the pigeon's right leg. How long had it been here?

The fat man had made progress, so Elias didn't have much time. He quickly untied the perfect square knot around the paper scroll and worked it free. He was tempted to read the message then, but Mat shouted, "C'mon, kid!"

He pocketed the scroll and snaked his way through Fat Man's Misery to catch up. He felt awful leaving the pigeon behind, but Mat wouldn't stand for it, he knew.

Mat finished out the tour. When he wasn't telling stories about the cave or pointing out the different formations or grabbing folk by the elbow to make sure they didn't step off the path, he was talking sharp, barking at the visitors for not watching where their feet were going.

But nobody objected. Nobody pointed out that he was only a slave and ought to be minding his manners. In fact, Elias noticed they all seemed to like it. Maybe it made the whole experience of being down in the cave that much more foreign. They would leave here, go home, and tell their friends about Mammoth Cave, where the sun never shone, the fish were blind, and slaves bossed white folk around.

And, why, Mat sure didn't seem to mind everybody obeying him either, for all his acting annoyed. There was a spring in his step, surly or not.

At the end of the tour, Elias followed them back out to the main entrance. As the little group of folk lingered there in the shadows of the arch, asking questions, Elias saw his opportunity. He climbed to the top of the rise, watched Mat and the others edging away from the cave at last. The men were giving Mat money, coins that he took without so much as a nod or a look in their eyes. When they finished, he led them to the rope, and let them all struggle up its length to where Elias sat waiting. Elias did what he could to help a couple of the ladies and the one fat man, who worked up a heck of a lather by the time he gained the top. Poor fellow sat down heavy on a log and handed Elias a dime without even saying thanks, he was heaving so hard. Just as the last person was climbing up, another slave—one Elias had seen in the hospital ward only once or twice—came to lead the group of tourists to the wagons that were waiting there for them. Elias watched them go.

"You comin', runt?" Mat barked from below.

Elias waved a hand at him. "In a minute," he called. He dashed to the tree, cleared wet leaves from the hidey hole, and found, just as before, a letter inside the jar. Whoever this brother Pennyrile was writing to might be, he must live nearby to be writing back and forth so quick.

Elias pulled the letter from his pocket, his fingers brushing the roll of paper he'd taken off the bird. He fished it out too.

"I ain't got all day!" Mat thundered. Elias swapped the letters, then paused, the scroll still in his hand. It wouldn't contain much of use to Pennyrile's brother now, would it? He'd already written since, so the note wouldn't be any count to him.

And what would it hurt, he reasoned, if Elias read just this one?

Only to find out how long the pigeon had been missing, he told himself.

But he hadn't been brought up to read other folks' private business. Then again, he hadn't been brought up to run errands for snakes like Pennyrile, had he?

"Boy, if you make me come up there to fetch you, you won't like it," Mat hollered from below. Elias swapped out the letters, but still held on to the scroll.

Then a queer feeling came over him, and he looked all around the silent woods. If Pennyrile's correspondent was close, could he be watching him now? Elias hopped up and dashed back down the hillside, barely holding on to the rope.

"Slower than molasses in January," Mat griped. "Don't know what Croghan thought to accomplish sending you out with me."

Elias held out the dime. "That fat man give me this," he said. "Figure he meant it for you."

Mat eyed Elias as he snatched the coin. "Small tip for such a big fella."

"They always give you money?"

Mat didn't answer at first, just stalked back into the cave. "Meaner I speak to 'em, the more they think I've saved them from."

Elias smiled, wondering if maybe Mat's meanness wasn't anything more than a habit born of good business. "You gonna use the money to buy your freedom too?"

Mat whirled on Elias. "No concern of yours what I do with money I earn, boy." He was close enough that Elias could see his whiskers were shot through with silver.

"I reckon it's not," Elias agreed quietly. He kept his distance as he followed Mat back into the cave, wondering why the man was so dead set on disliking him and wishing it bothered him less.

Chapter Ten

ANCHOR BEND

How you want 'em, tonight, Elias?" Lillian had an apron full of brown eggs.

"S'prise me," Elias said.

Lillian laughed as she cracked three eggs into the pan. "Yer funny."

He walked past her and tried to ignore the savory broth she had simmering in the kettle. Onions in there, he figured. Potatoes, too. His stomach rumbled at him, but he kept on, straight to Pennyrile's door.

"Mr. Pennyrile?"

The man appeared, waved Elias inside, and snatched the letter from him.

Pennyrile looked a little better today, Elias thought,

though better for the man wasn't much to get excited about. He had a long way to go before he was well. The wrap needed changing, already soaked through with ointment, blood, and serum.

"I can fetch you another one out tomorrow, maybe," Elias said, almost feeling sorry for him. Pennyrile waved him off, popping the wax seal on the letter. Elias saw the little brown bottle with the medicine dropper and recognized the bitter almond scent of laudanum in the air. Pennyrile wouldn't be writing any letters tonight.

Elias considered the scroll. He could—maybe should—tell Pennyrile now what he'd found. But no. He was curious enough. And this was his chance. Besides, the old dog was lucky enough that Elias hadn't just read one of the letters he'd carried back and forth for him. He could have. But that would have been wrong. Well, more wrong. Reading a message he'd found, though? That had been abandoned? Forgotten? Maybe it was wrong too, but not as much.

"I'm goin' then," Elias said. Pennyrile ignored him, already engrossed in his letter.

He passed Lillian carrying a bowl of soup to Nedra. "I put your eggs on the shelf next the stove so that bird won't get at 'em," she said.

"Thanks, Lill," Elias said.

Lillian stopped abruptly, soup sloshing over the rim of the bowl, and studied him. "You welcome," she said, pleased as anything, looking at him like he'd just given her a present.

She shook her head, still smiling.

"What?" Elias asked.

"Nothing," she said, breaking off for Nedra's hut.

Elias watched her go, trying to figure out what he'd done to make Lillian smile. And then it dawned on him. He'd told her thanks.

That was it?

It must have been. And he wondered if he'd ever thanked their house girl back home. Or if he'd ever heard his mother or Granny thank her. He quickly realized they hadn't, that they had done as he always had, mostly acting like she wasn't there unless they gave her an order.

Well.

Bedivere was happy to see him, cooing and warbling and flapping. Elias thought his bad wing was opening up a little better. Maybe he was healing. At least somebody was.

He scattered the corn on the tabletop for Bedivere before wolfing down his eggs. He got through half the tea before he sat back against the headboard to watch the bird eat. Elias felt the worry draining out of him, felt the day's exertion catching up with him, and fell asleep the moment his eyes dropped shut.

He woke an hour or two later, sitting quickly upright in bed.

Pennyrile's note!

Elias fished it out and found it was beginning to unfurl, begging to be read.

He poked his head out the door. Pennyrile's cabin was dark and silent—even his pigeons had settled for the night. Elias snugged the curtain as tight as he could and went back to the table.

He unrolled the little scroll. Each scrape of paper against paper sounded like a scream in the quiet hut. It seemed to take forever just to flatten out the fool thing, and he was clammy with nerves by the time he did. Holding the letter gingerly, rocking it back and forth to catch the light, he read:

My dear brother,

> *Long to be out of this place. Find myself growing weaker. Getting to the entrance to pick up your letters grows more difficult. Don't know how much longer I'll be able to do so. Doctor is a quack. The man in the hut across from mine died*

last week, the doctor unable to cure him in the least. If were the only reason I am here, would go now. But still have hope of finding what we seek. Slaves prove impossible to follow in secret and won't talk free with me. But a new boy has taken the empty bed and I think he may prove useful.

I have not lost heart. I will find the fount, and it will be worth the sacrifice.

Yours truly,
V. Pennyrile

Elias read the letter a second time. The lines about getting sicker, about the new boy, those he understood, but the other parts became no clearer with the second reading.

Following the slaves? Why?

And finding the fount? What on earth was that about?

Bedivere warbled in his sleep, the good wing twitching. Elias read the letter a third time.

He ought to show it to someone. It was too odd and too worrisome to keep to himself. But who? Dr. Croghan? He wouldn't be by until morning. And Elias felt funny about letting it keep. Plus, he'd probably get sideways with Elias for reading the note in the first place, and maybe not even do anything about it.

He emerged from his hut. Lillian was humming softly to herself as she banked up the coals.

"Hey," Elias whispered.

Lillian jumped, hand on her chest. "Lord, Elias. You sure do sneak up on a girl."

"Beg pardon." He glanced at Pennyrile's door. "He sleeping?"

"Gave himself enough of that stuff to sleep to Sunday," she said. "What about you? Why ain't you sleeping? I just sent Stephen off when he came looking—"

Stephen! That's who he should have thought of first. It might even be about him, what with that line about following the slaves.

"Stephen was just here?"

Lillian yawned. "Five, ten minutes ago."

"Where was he going?"

Lillian narrowed her eyes. "Up Black Snake way. Thought you might want to come along but you was dead to the world—"

Elias grabbed the spare lamp sitting by the fire. "I'll see if I can catch him."

Lillian's hand on his arm stopped him, her fingers pinching harder than a blue crab. "You will not!"

"He's only a few minutes ahead, you said yourself," Elias begged.

"You never gone off by yourself but that one time and it didn't go so good."

"Please," Elias begged. The longer he stayed here, the farther Stephen got from him, and the further he'd be from showing him the letter. "I been out there loads more since then. If I don't catch him up in a few minutes, I'll come back directly. And I won't take a single path I haven't been down before."

"Cain't you wait?"

He couldn't. He was *sure* Stephen would understand Pennyrile's letter, and now that he was sure, he couldn't wait a minute longer.

"I'll be careful, Lillian," he said, adding, "I promise. Doc likes me exercising, anyway."

Lillian's grip eased. "You *sure* you know the way? And where to turn off main cave up by Giant's Coffin?"

Giant's Coffin? He wasn't sure of that one, but he took a guess. "Before you come to the Star Chamber?"

"He should be real close to there, but if he's gone, you promise me you'll turn around?"

"I can catch him up," Elias said. "Promise."

Lillian released him. "Don't you dare go past the Camel, or else don't bother coming back at all, y'hear?"

The Camel? Where was *that*? But it didn't matter. Lillian was letting him go. Elias flew down the slope, the oil in his lamp swishing with every step.

Hurrying as fast as he could while still keeping the flame on his lamp burning, he checked off landmarks as he went.

And then he saw it. The Coffin. How could he have missed it before? As big as a double-masted schooner, but shaped perfectly for its name. Wider near the top, narrowing at the feet, sides like they'd been planed down smooth. He wondered why Stephen or the others hadn't pointed it out, all the times he'd been past it. Maybe they hadn't wanted him thinking about coffins, about how the cave itself might as well be one giant coffin for some of them who had come in to heal up. No! He wasn't going to think about that.

He walked on a little farther, picking out landmarks. Just as he started second-guessing himself and his sense of direction, he saw the glow of lamplight from around the bend that told him Stephen was near. And a moment later, there was Stephen.

He was laid out on his belly, reaching under an eave of rock.

Elias hesitated. What was he doing?

Stephen pulled something from the hole and placed it in his knapsack. Then he went back to the hole, reached in, and grabbed something else and loaded that, too, in his pack. He repeated this until his pack was so full that

Elias wasn't sure he could even close it. But he still drew more items from the wall, depositing those in an old grain sack.

What in the world?

Now Stephen was struggling into the heavy pack.

Elias recalled those primers he'd glimpsed in Stephen's pack the other night, how quick Stephen had made up a reason he couldn't take Elias out with him any farther.

And now he was getting—what? More books? And going where?

He let Stephen get a little ahead and then began to follow. Then Stephen did something stranger still. He began to sing.

> *Wade in the water,*
> *Wade in the wa-a-a-ter, children*
> *Wade in the water,*
> *God's a-gonna trouble the water.*

Plenty of the folk whistled in the dark—even Doctor Croghan—to fill up the loneliness. But this was different. Stephen was singing deep and bold, like he was in church.

It made Elias more curious.

And it made Stephen even easier to follow at a distance. So Elias did.

Chapter Eleven

TURLE KNOT

Stephen's song continued, better than a bread crumb trail.

> Who's that yonder dressed in red?
> The Lord's gonna trouble the water.
> Must be the children that Moses led,
> God's a-gonna trouble the water.

Elias followed Stephen through a tunnel and onto a broader avenue he didn't recognize. Then the path dropped sharply as a bigger chamber opened beyond. A narrow track lay at his feet, switchbacking into the darkness. Where was Stephen?

Elias stole a moment to check his bearings. Beside him a curtain of rock spanned from the floor where he stood to the low ceiling overhead. The rock draped and looped, leaving open spaces. The shape looked enough like a camel—all legs and neck and hump—to confirm he'd found the place Lillian had warned him about.

Don't go past the Camel.

But Stephen was there. Lillian would have meant not to go past it *alone*. So he continued.

Elias took one last look at the Camel, committed the shape of the thing to memory, in case he might need it later, then scrambled after Stephen, shale skittering under his boots. The way leveled off, cut to the left and through a wide seam in the cave wall. Elias followed, noting how the path began to rise again. He looked above him briefly to make sure he would not bump his head, and when he looked back down he found his light had cast a wicked-looking shadow in the path before him.

Only it wasn't a shadow.

It was a pit.

His mind slipped instantly back to standing at the edge of Bottomless Pit when Stephen tried to warn him about running around in the cave. He recalled how dizzy he'd felt standing on that rickety wooden bridge.

Only this one . . . didn't have a bridge.

It wasn't as wide as Bottomless, but it ran clear up to the walls on either side, offering no way past but over.

Still, that wasn't the worst of it.

The shape was what set the blood in Elias's veins to ice.

The gash in the floor made the perfect crescent of a smile, gaping like it might gulp up all the light from his lantern, like it might gulp up all the light in the world.

Elias squatted down, grabbed a rock off the floor, and tossed it gently in.

One Mississippi.

Two Mississippi.

Three Mississippi.

He gave up somewhere between his sixth and seventh Mississippis. And when he'd figured it might never hit bottom at all, he heard a faint clatter from somewhere impossibly deep.

While he'd counted, Stephen's song had begun to fade. He must have leaped over it!

Elias pushed down his fear, tried not to think too hard on what he was about to do. He took a few steps back. It was maybe five feet across. He told himself it would be like jumping the creek behind his house in Norfolk.

Only when he fell in the creek, he could swim out. If he fell here . . .

Nothing for it. If Stephen had jumped it, carrying that huge load, Elias figured he surely could. All the same, he tightened his grip on the lamp's handle and whispered a Hail Mary. He checked to make sure he still had the little scroll, then ran. Because of the narrowness of the tunnel and the unevenness of the floor, he didn't have much space to get up to speed, but he did what he could, planted a foot about eight inches before the pit, and leaped. It seemed to Elias that he hurtled through the air forever before landing on the other side.

Luckily, the lamp stayed lit. Elias staggered forward and kept on, not even looking back to see how close he'd been when he landed.

Soon he could hear Stephen again.

If you don't believe I've been redeemed
God's a-gonna trouble the water
Just follow me down to the Jordan's stream
God's a-gonna trouble the water.

A moment later Elias was in another room, two tunnels forking off in different directions. Stephen's lamplight led him left, brighter than it had been before.

And then suddenly Stephen's song broke off.

Now he was talking to someone.

Elias couldn't quite place the other voice. It wasn't Nick or Mat, he was sure.

The voices kept on talking but were moving farther into the tunnel.

Elias pressed on, led as steadily by the need to figure out what Stephen was up to as he was by his need to show him that mysterious note. Soon he emerged in a perfect dome-shaped chamber bisected by a shallow stream. Something about the room made it seem like the kind of place to meet a body.

He ducked down under a low arch—the only way out of the chamber—and continued his pursuit.

The way began to twist on itself, like a maze. When his father had first taught him to tie knots—simple ones like a square or a figure eight—he'd told him to imagine he was as small as an ant, riding the tip of the rope through the twists, trying to find his way out. Elias always liked the notion but hadn't understood the feeling of it until now.

Finally the maze began to open, and Elias found sand beneath his feet.

Sand?

Now he was in a chamber about as big as the Rotunda up in the main cave. And across the sea of sand he saw Stephen's lamp.

He walked side by side with another man who had taken the grain sack. Elias hung back, shielding his light behind him, and watched them disappear into a wide crack in the wall. He waited a few seconds, then, unable to hear Stephen talking or see his light, he dashed across. The path was straightforward, even though the ceiling was low, angling sharply down on both sides and forcing him to hold his head sideways.

It seemed to dead end in a great pile of rock. Elias blinked. What? Had he missed something? He raised his light and saw the pile didn't go all the way to the ceiling. Near the ceiling was a gap of about three or four feet.

Elias put the lamp down. He found the rock easy enough to climb, almost like a ladder, almost like the rocks had been arranged to make it easy to find the way over. A second more and he was peeking over the top.

Another vast chamber, big enough to hold half a dozen triple-masted schooners, Elias judged, appeared before him, full of big lights—No! Cook fires! Burning all over the room. With people—people!—huddled around them, moving between them like shadows.

Lots of people! Dozens! More?

Elias gaped, hardly believing what he was seeing. What were they all doing here? Who were they?

He wanted to get closer. But as soon as he swung a leg over the top, something grabbed him from behind.

Something giant and strong and smelling of smoke and sweat.

Elias yelped.

"Lights-out!" roared a voice as Elias bucked against the arms that held him.

The fires began to go out with alarming speed, and the chamber was plunged into deeper shadow, and then total darkness.

Chapter Twelve

CAT'S PAW

"Hey!" Elias bit and kicked and thrashed against arms that surrounded him like clamps. "Lemme go!" But no matter how hard he fought, he couldn't shake loose. Then he heard another voice, one that made him freeze.

"Elias?" It was Stephen. "Elias, is that you?"

"Stephen!" Stephen! "Somebody's got ahold of me—"

"Oh, Lord," Stephen whispered, then said louder, "Elias, what are you doing down here?" He sounded defeated, not panicked like Elias would have thought.

"Make 'em let me go!" Elias begged. "Put the lanterns back on!"

But the lanterns weren't relit. Whoever held him clamped down tighter. Elias could hear Stephen whispering to someone, though he could not make out the words. Other whispers started up around him.

And the darkness! Ever since he'd come to the cave, he'd never been in full darkness, black as complete as this. Always there was light from somewhere to break it up, but this was different. The blackness made Elias feel somehow disconnected, like his limbs weren't in accord with the rest of him. It all felt tighter and closer, like the big room he'd glimpsed had been drawing in around them, those whispers edging nearer and nearer. . . .

"Elias," Stephen said carefully, "what did you see?"

What did he see? Why was Stephen asking such a thing when someone big enough to snap his spine was holding him prisoner?

"See?"

"Elias," Stephen went on. "What did you see?"

Elias thought. "You. I was looking for you. . . . I needed to show you something . . . and I seen you loading up your pack at that hidey-hole, so I followed you. Then I heard you talking with somebody. Then I came here and seen all those cook fires and a whole bunch of people—"

"Enough." Stephen sounded almost done in. There was more whispering, then Stephen asked. "Why'd you follow me?"

"I . . . I found a dead pigeon, one of Pennyrile's. It had a letter Pennryile must have meant to send out. I—" He hesitated, embarrassed to admit what he'd done. "I read it. And it seemed sort of funny to me, like there was something wrong in it, and I couldn't think of no one else to ask about it except you, so I went out to show you but then I got curious."

"We in it now," a new voice said.

"Who was that?" Elias asked.

Stephen didn't answer right away, sighing. Then he said, "Put him down, Davie."

Suddenly Elias's feet were back on the ground. A tinderbox slid open and soon the lamp was burning again. Stephen held up the light.

"You shouldn't have followed me." But Elias, looking around, was too stunned to reply. So many faces, not one of them familiar, gazed at him. Some were as dark as Nick's; others lighter like Stephen's, but it was plain enough to see now what he had missed when they were all shadowed by the cook fires: they were all Negroes. And not a one looked happy to see him.

Beyond the little circle other lamps flared and the cook fires began to burn again. More people. So many more. Elias saw that near the edges of the chamber, sheets and tarps had been strung up for privacy. They were living down here, Elias marveled. And they were all colored. And if those two things were true . . .

"Runaways," Elias whispered.

"You done it now, Stephen!" another voice called, sounding desperate.

Stephen ignored him. "Give me Pennyrile's letter, Elias."

Elias didn't move, just tried to take it all in. "Runaways!" he repeated. Then he looked sharp at Stephen. "How many are there? How long they been here?"

"Elias, give me the letter." Stephen dropped his chin. There was something pleading in the tone, so Elias handed it over.

Stephen took it, then addressed the one who'd been holding Elias. "Keep an eye on him, Davie." And to Elias he said, "Stay right here, understand?"

"Where you going?"

Stephen gestured toward one of the cook fires. "Just over there. To talk to somebody."

"But—"

"Elias, you've put me in a bind here, so the least you can do is listen to me and wait a minute."

"But—"

"No!" Stephen said, his temper flaring white-hot before he reined it back in. He waved over a boy who was standing nearby, watching silently. "Stay with him."

The boy was a few inches taller than Elias, though

wider and stronger by more than that margin. His hair stuck out in wiry little twists all over his head.

"Whatev' you say, Stephen," the boy said, and Elias instantly recognized the voice.

Jonah!

"You," Elias managed, staring at Jonah.

Jonah took a step nearer Elias and sat down on the sand. Elias did the same, keeping his gaze on Jonah, half afraid that if he blinked, Jonah would disappear.

"You can settle down, Davie," Jonah said to the big man. "He won't go nowhere."

"I didn't know what else to do," Davie rumbled, his voice rich and deep. "I seen him coming over the wall and I just—"

"You did right, Davie," Jonah said. "This all is partly my fault anyhow. I helped Stephen fetch in them supplies. If I'd a stayed my post, Elias wouldn't have got so far."

"Post?" Elias asked. The more he heard, the more confused he felt.

Jonah nodded. "Back up the way, we got a spot we keep watch. Enough room to slip ahead and warn ev'body if someone ain't one of us wanders down."

"Somebody like me," Elias guessed.

"Yep," Jonah said.

All Elias's questions seemed to jockey for position,

demanding to be asked first. *How many are here? How long have they been hiding? Who knows about it? Nick? Mat? Lillian or the others? How do they get by?* But he settled on one he thought might catch him the most information. "What is this place?"

Jonah scooped up a handful of sand and let it drain through his fingers. "Haven? 'Bout what it look like. Mess of fugitives, like me. But we're fair organized. Even got us a school," he said proudly, gesturing toward a corner of the room where a cluster of people were gathered around a man who was writing on a flat piece of the cave wall with a chunk of charred wood.

"But it's nighttime, ain't it?" Elias asked.

Jonah scooped and sifted another handful of sand. "Nolin—he's the teacher—he has classes all times. Folks got to stuff they heads full and got plenty of time to do it down here. Nolin reckons all us can at least learn our letters and how to make our names. He keeps trying to get me to come so he can get me to read, but I ain't got the patience."

A school. Elias watched Nolin trying to wrangle his students back to attention, but they were all too busy staring at Elias. He recalled the books in Stephen's bag that night, understanding at last where he'd been going with them.

Jonah continued. "Stephen and Hughes—"

"Hughes?"

Jonah pointed at the man talking with Stephen across the room. "Hughes in charge. Been here as long as anybody, I think."

"How long's that?"

Jonah picked at his thumbnail. "Almost two years, I expect."

Two years! Elias hadn't even been there for two months.

"Does everybody stay that long?"

Jonah shook his head. "Used to be folks came and went all time. Come for a while to hide, then go when they figure the trackers weren't looking for 'em as keen. When it was safer to get on North, or strike out to the West for one of the free territories."

"Used to be?"

Jonah chucked another handful of sand. "Yeah. There's been trouble."

"What kind of trouble?" Elias asked.

"A boat moored downriver a couple of months ago. Been poking round the spots where river go in and out the cave. Got everybody spooked. And got us pinned down. Cain't get folk in easy, can't hardly get 'em out at all, and moving the water's been near impossible."

"Water?" Elias asked.

"Jonah," the big fellow called Davie warned.

Jonah lifted a hand. "I know, I know. Let Hughes tell him the rest."

Elias studied Hughes. He was swaybacked and held a walking stick. And even though he was seated on a rock, it seemed to Elias like he was somehow still bigger than everyone gathered around him, sort of like King Arthur on a throne.

"What do you suppose they're talking about?" Elias asked.

Jonah looked over at them, then back at Elias. "What to do with you, reckon."

"What to do with me?" Elias yelped. "What's that mean?"

"Means you seen Haven. You know 'bout us. And they can't let that be."

Elias went cold. Was it possible? Would they really . . . "They wouldn't—"

Jonah gaped at him. "What? You think? Naw! We runaways, but we ain't murderers. They're probably figgerin' on keeping you down here, making up some story to tell that doctor about how you went wanderin' and got lost—"

"They can't keep me down here!" Elias started to climb to his feet, but Davie's massive hand clamped back on his shoulder.

"Cain't let you run off telling 'bout what you seen, neither."

"I—"

"Hush, now," Jonah said. "Stephen's ready."

Stephen waved Elias over, and Davie's grip relaxed. "Looks like they ready for you," Davie said.

Elias swallowed. Jonah wouldn't meet Elias's eyes, but he walked with him to where the man sat on the boulder.

"Hughes, this is Elias," Stephen said. "He's a friend."

Chapter Thirteen
CONJURER'S KNOT

Y ou put us in a tight spot, sir," Hughes said. "Real tight
spot. What we want to know now is, can we count on
you? Stephen here says we can."

"Count on me to what?" Elias managed.

"Help," Hughes said simply.

"What kind of help?" Elias asked. If they'd even con-
sider keeping him down here, there was no telling what
they might ask of him. Could he trust them? Stephen,
sure. Jonah, maybe.

But all of them?

Hughes assessed him. Elias wished somebody would
put the lights out again just so he could avoid that stare.
After the moment stretched out long enough to make

Elias even more uneasy, Hughes handed the letter back.

"We read that letter . . . ," Hughes began. "You swear you don't know what it's about?"

Elias shook his head.

"Your Pennyrile come in August," Hughes continued. Elias took plenty of exception to the way Hughes seemed ready to lump him in with Pennyrile, but he kept quiet. Hughes, he could tell, wasn't one to trifle with. Hughes went on, "Few weeks later this flat-bottom boat hid itself up near Cave City."

The fire nearby popped loud and fierce. Elias thought it out. The knots on Pennyrile's wrap, how Croghan told him he was a riverman, that the place the pigeons had been trained to fly home to must be nearby. "You reckon Pennyrile's part of that boat's crew?"

"Timing's a bit too neat for him not to be," Stephen admitted. "But he seemed to be just another patient. And he isn't faking. He's consumptive in his neck. Lillian says she never seen worse. So I didn't think it was important—"

"I decide what's important," Hughes said, but he didn't say it mean. Just stern.

"He's after something," Elias pointed out.

"Seems so," Hughes said. "He ever tell you what?"

"The note mentioned a fount," Elias said. "But no, he never said anything about it to me."

"A fount," Hughes repeated.

Elias grew impatient with having to ask and wished they'd just lay it out. "What's it mean?"

Stephen waited for Hughes to speak, but Hughes nodded to Stephen. "You tell it."

Stephen took a breath. "Not long after it was decided that this place was going to be a permanent sort of station on the road North, we saw we were going to need more supplies and provisions than just what folk came here with when they arrived."

Elias thought about the scraggly shrub planted outside Shem's hut. "Can't grow food down here. And I don't expect those fish Nick's been collecting are enough to feed a body on."

Stephen smiled. "More bone than meat, Nick's fish."

Hughes broke in. "We spent a long time trying to figure out ways to scare up supplies. We pilfered some in the early days, but that was too dangerous. Even a few eggs or a side of bacon go missing from a smokehouse, and folk start asking questions."

"So we knew we had to make a way to get some ready money to buy supplies. We found it not far from where we're standing now. A spring"—Stephen pointed back into the shadows—"other side of th—"

Stephen stopped short, seeing what Elias nearly

missed: a signal, Hughes's sharp shake of the head. But Elias caught it at the last second, like the tail of a snake slipping through dry leaves. And he instantly understood Hughes didn't want Elias to know where it was.

"What's so special about this spring?" Elias asked.

"We settled on using it for drinking water, and going over to the river for bathing and washing. River water is bad over here, but the spring water was clean, even if it had a strong taste to it. Anyway, folks who were in rough shape, or still nursing wounds they'd gotten from masters before they ran, or ones they picked up on the way . . . Well, at any rate, once they got inside, after being on the run for so long, everybody started healing up quick."

Elias thought of what Croghan had said about the cave's effect on people, how the vapors made them feel like they could walk for days. "Quicker than normal," Stephen added.

"Folk started saying maybe the water was special," Hughes explained.

Elias thought back to the medicine shows and elixir sellers who used to set up on the landing back home, the miracle cure men with their little rounded hats and smart vests and smarter talk about whatever magic cordial they were shilling. Granny always said they weren't any count, weren't anything but connivers getting desperate folk to toss good money at the wind, for all the healing they'd bring. Even so, Mama had tried half a dozen of them on Daddy before she quit hoping too. "Y'all think you got tonic water," Elias determined.

Hughes cleared his throat. "What we got is a way to keep this place alive. Something out there that people bought and that would let us get supplies. Leastways, we *did*."

"Does it work, though?" Elias pressed, his mind racing.

Stephen shook his head. "It's more likely just being in the cave and getting rest is what does it."

"Some believe, though," Jonah pointed out. Elias thought Jonah said it like *he* might believe it.

"*Might* it work?" Elias asked, careful not to sound too hopeful. "The water? Might it?"

"We . . . well . . . we've already tried it on you, Elias," Stephen told him.

Elias's eyes went wide as he recalled the metallic taste of the water Nick had given him when they were out that night together, how he'd said it came from a different spring. "And I've been getting better—the doc even said—"

"We've given it to all of them up there," Stephen said softly.

Elias felt the hope that had begun to bloom inside him leak away. "All of them? Lillian's never given it to me up at the ward."

"We don't give it out straight," Stephen explained. "The taste is too recognizable for that. But we cook with it, make the tea with it, even do the baths with it sometimes when we can get away with it."

"Everyone?" Elias asked again.

Stephen sighed. "Even Pennyrile. Nedra, too. And Sarneybrook and the widow Patton . . . and . . . well . . ."

Elias didn't need him to finish. None of the rest were better. Only him.

Hughes took over. "We don't know if it only works for some or doesn't work at all. But selling it has kept this place alive, and the hope it gives people doesn't hurt none."

Elias knew that hope, no matter how dearly paid for, *was* precious. And he wasn't quite ready to surrender it now. If the air of the cave was special like Croghan thought, then it only stood to reason that the water could be too, right?

Then again, even the air didn't seem to work for everyone. The widow Patton had died. Pennyrile and Nedra were both sicker. Old Sarneybrook was slipping. "But why am I better?" He felt almost guilty about it.

"You're younger and stronger," Stephen suggested. "But we don't know. Like I said, some down here will swear by the stuff. And others out there do too. But we've tried,

Elias. We don't know why it seems to work for some and not others, or if it works at all."

"If you told Croghan, maybe then he could try it out. See if there's something to it—"

"He'd have to see the spring for himself. And you can't find the spring without finding Haven."

"But he's smart," Elias argued. "He could maybe figure out why—"

"We can't risk the lives of all my people on *maybe*." Hughes drew himself up to his feet, using all his impressive height to underscore his point. "The doctor having the spring wouldn't accomplish anything more. And it would mean the end for all of us."

It was quiet a second before Stephen spoke. "You see that, don't you, Elias?"

The question shook something loose in him. Were the lives of these runaways more important than the possibility that Croghan could make something of the tonic water?

The boy who'd left Virginia, the boy he was when he arrived . . . that boy might have said no.

But now Elias had explored the cave with Stephen Bishop. Caught blind fish with Nick. Been so impressed by Mat on those tours. Made friends with Jonah.

He wasn't the same boy who'd left Virginia. He wasn't the same boy who would have said no.

"I see," Elias said.

"We don't take it light," Hughes said simply. "But sometimes the hard decisions are the right ones." Elias knew it was true. Knew because it sounded like something his daddy would have said to him.

"But if we don't do something about Pennyrile—and that boat downriver—it's all going to be over one way or another anyway," Stephen said.

"Why?"

Hughes laced his fingers over the knob of the walking stick. "When we first got the idea to sell the water as a cure, it wasn't hardly worth the trouble. Money was slow to come back to us, and them what sold it for us cheated us half blind, but as word got out and folks started wanting it, we figured out which people we could trust to bring the money that was owed us back to us."

"But how do you do it? Without Croghan and everybody catching on?" Elias asked.

"Spring's clear away from anything on the tours or Croghan's paths, so bottling it up's the easy part. Getting it out's a sight trickier," Hughes said.

Stephen took a stick and began drawing in the sand around the fire pit. "The river runs outside, then goes underground and into the cave. It comes up way down here." He made a small mark near the edge of his drawing.

"We used to cobble together rafts or baskets and pack the jars in. Then we'd launch them into the river to be carried downstream and out of the cave. Outside, we had men who know where to look. They picked up the shipments, took the lot to those that sold it for us, along with lists of supplies we needed. The seller kept some of the money and used the rest to buy our provisions. Then he'd send the supplies—along with whatever money was left over—to another friend who knew the spot where the river flowed back into the cave." He tapped the first mark he'd made on the diagram.

"But we ain't had anything coming in for too long," someone in the crowd said.

"What's that mean?"

"It means," Hughes began, "that since that boat come—since Pennyrile come—the river's been more crowded than is strictly heathful for running business."

"Pennyrile's crew found the water y'all sent out?"

Hughes crossed his arms. "Probably. Can't know for sure. We took care to have it sold away from the cave and the river, but he might have worked it out somehow. What we know is, no more runaways have come up the river since that boat arrived. We can't get our water out, and our friends outside are too scared of being seen to send the supplies in the usual way."

"But if you can't get supplies and you can't send people out . . ." Elias did the hard math in his head, afraid to say it out loud.

"Haven's dying," Hughes said, adding, "We're not going to last much longer."

That heavy silence fell again before Stephen spoke. "The last few months, most of what we've been able to get inside has had to be carried down from the main entrance, snuck in by me and Nick."

"But it's not enough," Hughes said.

Stephen swiped his hand through the sand, erasing the map.

"Why don't you just start emptying folk out?" Elias asked.

"We can't, not until we know Pennyrile's crew has cleared off. We're trapped."

Elias thought it over. It was like a siege back in Arthur times—a whole village of people shut up inside a castle's walls, slowly getting starved out. The folk down here in Haven were as desperate as everybody up in Croghan's hospital.

"If anybody tries to get out now, those pirates would just snatch them and make them tell where to get the water themselves," Stephen added.

"Or worse," Hughes said. "He might be after more'n water. He might be after us."

"But he said 'fount,'" Elias pointed out. "That has to be your spring. And he's sick, that's for sure, so I'd bet he'd do all this to get his hands on that spring, even if it's only a chance that it'd work."

Some of the people gathered around murmured in agreement. But others looked to one another and Elias nervously. Elias saw Nick was there, smiling gently at him. the sight of a friend made Elias feel better.

"'Fount' could also mean source," Stephen reasoned. "We don't know what he means for sure. It could be source of the water, or the source of the runaways. Either way, it's . . . Whether he finds the spring and us by mistake, or he's looking for us in the first place . . ."

"Bounty on all of us put together more'n he could ever hope to earn off that spring." Hughes's voice was bitter.

Elias bit the inside of his cheek. He couldn't let that happen to Jonah, not to mention what would happen to Stephen and Nick and Mat when Croghan or the others found out that they had been helping runaways.

"We got to suss out what this Pennyrile knows first," Hughes said.

Finally Nick spoke. "Only way to know which bait the fish'll bite on is to thow a hook in the water." Nick was, as usual, perfectly right. And the murmur of agreement that rippled out confirmed it.

Still, Elias knew how hard it would be. He knew tangling with Pennyrile was trickier than the most complicated of knots.

And then he noticed nearly everyone was watching him, waiting.

He was the only one Pennyrile talked to.

He was the only one Pennyrile trusted.

"Elias?" Hughes asked.

Elias looked at Stephen; his expression was unreadable. Elias took a breath and felt his lungs stretch out farther than they had a few weeks ago. Maybe it was because of the water. Probably it wasn't. But it didn't matter.

Sometimes the hard decision was the right one.

And sometimes it was easy.

"What do you want me to do?"

Chapter Fourteen
PRUSIK KNOT

D*ear Mother,*
I got your letter four days back. Thank you.
I'm sorry I did not write sooner—

Elias stopped. He had not written since he'd learned of Haven. But he couldn't tell his mother why. He could not tell her much of anything, really.

But I have made some new friends and seen a
little of the cave.

True enough, he supposed.

I am glad Tillie caught a fish, and even more
pleased she took it off the hook like I taught her.
Tell her I am proud. Did I tell you yet about the
fish in the cave? They are something else altogether.
They've got no eyes and don't need them on
account of it being dark. They are sort of pretty
once you have got used to them, and Nick says—

Nick. And just like that the page seemed filled up with all the things he couldn't tell his mother. About the runaways, about Nick's plan, about how much he hoped Nick succeeded. Elias groaned in frustration and tossed the letter and pencil onto the quilt.

Before, he'd thought that time couldn't go any slower, but the last three days had seemed the longest of his time so far. It wasn't the boredom that wore away at him now so much as it was the worry. All those people down in Haven, the knowing something had to be done, that he'd be called on to help.

Jonah had made himself scarce, probably assigned extra watch duties since Elias had stumbled into Haven. And Stephen and Nick hadn't been around much either. Nick had passed word that they were all right below and assured Elias they'd fetch him down as soon as it was safe, as soon as Hughes was ready to talk to him again.

But three days? It was torture, the waiting. If Hughes and the others had wanted to punish Elias for nosing about and following Stephen, they couldn't have picked a better means.

Elias glared at his unfinished letter. Then he picked up his tying rope and the piece of twine he'd robbed from the doorframe—the piece that was meant to be used to hold back the quilt. He resumed working on the complicated series of French Prusiks and sheepshanks he'd started earlier.

After Elias had pulled it apart and redone it all three times, the doctor finally looked in for his morning rounds. Immediately, Elias could tell something was wrong.

"Hey, Doc." Elias dropped the twine. Croghan smiled but sank heavily in the chair by the bed. He wore a version of the same stiff suit he always appeared in, but today had a bright blue scarf wrapped around his neck. The stitches were the same smart ones in Elias's own green scarf, and he was sure Nedra had made this one as well.

"Good morning, Elias," he murmured. But he didn't open his bag. He didn't even look at Elias. He just stared at the flame glowing blue at the tip of the wick of the lantern.

"Doctor Croghan?" Elias said, leaning forward.

"Mr. Sarneybrook died in the night." Dr. Croghan

rubbed a hand across his temple. Elias hung his head. Though Elias had met the man only once, the news landed square enough. He was more than sorry for Sarneybrook, and whoever he'd left behind, but he was sad, too. Sad that Sarneybrook's hopes hadn't materialized. Sad that he'd spent all this time underground, given up so much, only to have the rest of it taken away.

"He was so faithful regarding my prescriptions," the doctor said, almost to himself. "He was an active man before he fell ill. Remember how he told us of scurrying up and down Black Mountain one morning before breakfast? Remarkable fellow. But he told me every day that the hardest thing he ever did was remain so immobile." Elias thought of how he himself used to fidget in church, the looks Granny used to toss at him to make him settle down. He couldn't imagine what Sarneybrook endured.

"No one even knew he'd passed until I arrived. Even the night nurse who checked on him didn't notice, so accustomed was she to seeing him so silent and still."

"I'm sorry," Elias said.

"As am I," Croghan said with a sigh. "As am I. And nearly as puzzled. It should have worked, his treatment. But his lungs never improved, no matter what modifications I made." His tone shifted from somebody shocked to somebody trying to work out a mystery. "Really, it should have worked." Croghan paused and looked at Elias directly for the first time. "Perhaps I should have prescribed more of your methods for Old Sarneybrook. Or the other residents."

Elias couldn't meet the doctor's eyes, feeling strangely guilty.

"I should like you to continue your exercise," Croghan said, shaking off his gloom. "And I think we should reintroduce some other foods into your diet. Some bread and greens—just to gauge the effect. If you continue to improve, then I believe we might begin encouraging some of the others to take more activity as well." He drummed his fingers across the handle of his bag.

He didn't seem happy, necessarily, not the way Elias would have thought at the notion that his doctoring had finally made someone better. He seemed concerned, almost, or distrustful.

"You've eaten already?" Doctor Croghan asked.

"Four," Elias reported, "soft-boiled." They'd been awful—goopy and cold.

"Then away with you," Croghan said. "Stephen will be by in a moment with a tour." Croghan started out the door, then turned back. "I almost forgot!" He searched his breast pocket and produced a letter. "Your mother wrote."

His mother had written again! And so quickly! Elias

was too eager to feel badly about having taken so long to reply. He vowed to fill up at least four—no, five!—sheets of paper when he finally wrote back. He'd get the part about Nick's fish just right. Maybe even try to draw a picture of one. He grabbed the letter with a hearty thanks and had already torn it open before the doctor's footfalls faded.

It was a good long one, full of little things about what was happening back in Norfolk, about how the frosts were heavier and the fogs thicker and how Tillie found a sand dollar and Granny's rheumatism was acting up but not so bad as last year. How the parish was planning a potluck supper and one of his friends—did he remember Wendell?—had been made an altar boy. Of course Elias remembered Wendell, and remembered him as the most creative cusser he could name, to boot. But he was glad to hear of it. All of it. He downed the letter at a gulp, reading maybe every third word, letting it all wash over him, catching not so much the meaning and the detail as much as the reassurance that his mother had not forgotten him. And if the length of the letter were not enough, the closing cast out the doubts he hadn't even fully admitted he harbored.

The house is too lonely for you, and so am I. It isn't right that you went so far. And I worry every

*moment that I should not have let you go. But the
doctor was kind enough to write and say that you
appear to be improving and are popular with the
other patients. I am relieved to hear the former,
and not at all surprised to hear the latter. And
though you say you want to come home, part of
me frets that you might become so enamored of
the cave and the people and that pigeon that you
will forget us. Charger still watches the river for
you each morning, as do I.*

Yours ever,
Mama

Elias read it through a second time, then folded it
carefully, blinking back the feeling of missing and being
missed. He slipped the letter under his pillow so Bedivere
couldn't get at it, already looking forward to reading one
more time. But for now, he had a tour to catch.

Elias had done this same tour already with Mat, so he kept
his distance, shimmying up bits of the rock walls when
no one was looking. What struck him was how different Stephen was in this role as guide. He wore his fancy
touring getup—the striped velvet pants, the smart green

jacket, his chocolate-colored cap. His hair was oiled to a shine, curling out beneath the edges of his hat, and he'd shaved that morning. But as fancy as he dressed, and as fancy as he talked, showing off all the books he'd read by quoting out bits of poems here and there when they might echo something he was showing the group walking along with him, Elias couldn't help feeling that he was watching Stephen play a part, like an actor in a play. Stephen didn't lord over them like he did with Elias sometimes. He presented himself as smart and handsome and well-spoken, but he was diminished somehow, like he was holding back.

Curious, Elias thought.

Elias kept hoping he might discover something he could impress Stephen and Nick and Mat with later, but every spot he found had one of their marks scratched onto the wall.

At one cleft, he stuck his head in, held the lamp in as far as he could, and nearly dropped it in fright.

"Hey," whispered a voice, a pair of eyes blinking back at him.

"Frogs and stars!" Elias shrieked, loud enough that Stephen and the others stopped and whirled on him. Jonah was hidden safely, but Elias had to say something.

"Uh," he began, "just spooked myself a tick." His

excuse sounded thin even to Elias's ears, but Stephen easily regained the attention of his little pack.

"Happens all the time down here. And if you follow me, I'll show you the ghost of the lady of the cave and tell you all about how one gentleman nearly scared himself to death when he glimpsed her."

Elias waited long enough for them to be almost out of earshot before stepping away from the crack in the rock. "What are you doing up here?"

Jonah sidled out. "Like to follow the tours," he said. "Watch out with that light or they'll see me if they look back."

Elias put a few feet between them.

"Scared you good."

"Didn't neither," Elias lied.

"Did so," Jonah said. "Even better than I got you in your hut them times."

Elias gestured at Stephen's group. "I gotta keep up."

Jonah stayed with him, always just out of the light, moving so silently that Elias had to check to make sure he was still there.

"Ain't you supposed to be on watch or something?" Elias whispered.

"Not till tonight."

"What about the schooling?" Elias pressed.

"I get bored," he said. "Too much being still."

"If you could read, you wouldn't get so bored, maybe," Elias offered.

"I ain't bored *generally*," he said. "Just with the schooling. Keep myself busy roaming and looking in on Croghan's patients."

"You could nearly do the tours yourself, I guess," Elias offered.

"S'pose. Doctorin' more interesting though. Maybe I'll be the first run'way to become a doctor. Learned me almost enough watching Croghan."

Elias was more eager than he liked to admit to hear more about the gruesome treatments Croghan was attempting on the others. "What's he done lately?"

"Aw, more o' the same, mostly," Jonah began. "That Mozelle got bled again today. Poor girl don't even cry anymore when it's happening. I heard him ordering up another one of them baths. Few days back he was asking Hannah over to the other ward if she could bring him in a wet nurse—"

"A wet nurse?" Elias made a face. "What on earth for?"

"He had a letter from some doctor over in France he said that told him the best cure he'd found was giving grown men and women mother's milk."

Elias was horrified, almost more so than of the bleedings and the baths and the blisterings.

"He were goin' to try something on Old Sarney. . . ." Jonah trailed off.

"I was real sorry to hear on him," Elias said. "Y'all were friends, weren't you?"

"Near 'nough. He was glad of company."

Elias appreciated the simplicity of it, that Jonah didn't have to complicate it. But he knew Jonah had to have been fond of him to risk getting seen when he went to talk with him.

"I called on him last night," Jonah said quietly. "I was too hungry to sleep. So I went up to see him, see if he had any food he didn't want. He always had food he couldn't eat, on account his wife brung stuff down ever' other day or so.

"I whispered hey at him, but it was so quiet. And a body sounds differ'nt when it's sleeping, 'specially him, with all the work he did to breathe. But it was so quiet I knew he was dead before I even peeked in the window."

"I'm sorry," Elias said.

"Me too," Jonah replied.

They followed the tour quietly for a while before Elias worked up enough nerve to change the subject. "How are things in Haven?"

"'Bout the same," Jonah said. "Nobody know what to do yet."

Elias continued on, whispering over his shoulder, "I'm going to do what I can to help."

"I know," Jonah said. "First time I snuck up on you, I knew you wouldn't give nobody up."

Elias straightened. "You couldn't know a thing like that."

"Could," Jonah said. "You get a sense of people when they don't know they're being watched. And being a ghost gives you plenty of chances to watch."

"I never thought you was a ghost," Elias said sharply.

Jonah laughed. "Did too. But no call to feel 'shamed of it. I've had lots of practice. All these folk come through on the tours. Sometimes I sneak up and tap somebody on the shoulder or whisper close on 'em from a good high hiding place."

"You don't!" Elias asked. "Why?"

"'Cause it's fun," Jonah said. "I reckon they like it well enough too, going out and telling people they got tapped by a haint."

"Bet Hughes don't think it's fun. Bet he'd skin you alive if he knew what you got up to." Hughes was clearly so protective of the colony of runaways, Elias knew he wouldn't look warmly on one of them risking exposing them all just to entertain himself.

Jonah fixed his stare on Elias. "You wouldn't tell him, would you?"

"Naw."

They were nearing the end of the tour, the main entrance arcing wide and bright in the distance.

"'Sides," Jonah began. "This place is too big to stay penned up down in Haven. What with all this," he waved an arm around at the cave, "who can stay put when there's so much to see?"

Elias looked about. He felt it too. The urge to see it all, the pull to find the wonders and marvels of the cave. What he'd seen already was enough beauty and mystery to live off for half a lifetime, but he wanted to see even more. More grand arenas like the Rotunda, more haunts like the Devil's Armchair, more magic like the Star Chamber. "I know what you mean," Elias said.

Jonah stopped and pointed toward the rise and the light in the distance. "Far as I go. Can't hide in that."

Elias understood. "See you later then."

Jonah grinned. "Naw, you won't. But I'll be there just the same." And he backed up a few steps, disappearing into the black.

Elias jogged to catch up with the others. The tour folks were giving Stephen coins and shaking his hand as they threw out their last few questions.

Then a little fellow, a man down from Illinois with his wife on one arm and maybe his daughter on the other side, said, "You are a remarkably well-spoken Negro." It sounded to Elias like a question, like Stephen needed to explain why he sounded as intelligent as Doctor Croghan or any other white man.

But Stephen only dropped his eyes. "Thank you, sir."

The wife put her hand to her husband's ear and whispered, like she was afraid to speak to Stephen directly. "How long have you been at the cave?" her husband asked after bobbing his head.

"Seems like my whole life," Stephen said shyly, adding, "but it's been only about four years now."

"I dare say you must know the cave well enough to hide in its depths forever," the man said. "Can you imagine, running away to live underground?"

Stephen's eyes caught Elias's. "I don't think I could," he said finally. "Dr. Croghan is a fair master, but I mean to one day buy my freedom. I shall sail to Liberia or one of the other colonies."

The man's face lit up as he smiled at his wife and daughter. "There you have it," he said. "A noble ambition." He pressed a whole half-dollar piece into Stephen's hand. "A noble ambition."

Stephen thanked him, led them the rest of the way up the path, and then saw them safely up the rope. Elias sat on a tangle of fallen wood. He'd never even heard about anybody buying his way to Africa.

Stephen jogged back down the hill, the coins jingling in his pocket.

"Africa?" Elias whispered fiercely.

Stephen sniffed. "Tourists don't want to hear about how wrong it is to keep slaves. But they don't mind a fellow with plans for his life, especially don't mind a Negro with the aim to leave the country and never come back."

"It ain't true, then?"

Stephen laughed. "No, it isn't. What would I do in Africa? Never laid eyes on the place. Never met a man who has. Might as well be the moon."

"Oh," Elias said, oddly relieved.

Stephen looked up at the ceiling yawning high overhead. "No, this is home. Has been since I first saw it."

"So why you go on like that for the visitors?"

"Safest answer. Mat likes to give them an earful, boss them around, tell them about the injustices he's suffered. And I don't blame him for it. He's had it tougher than some."

"Bet he never got a half-dollar for being so mean," Elias said.

Stephen grinned. "I expect he didn't, but he does all right too."

Elias drank in the sunshine, noting that Old Shem was right: it did have a smell, spiced by the tang in the air from the rotten leaves warming. "It keeps Haven safer too, doesn't it?"

"Hope so. If folks just see a polite Negro with polite ideas about his lot in life, then they've no reason to worry what a man like me might be up to down there." He unstopped his water jug, took a pull, and held it out to Elias.

Elias drank, noting the penny taste of the water. "This is the stuff from the spring, ain't it?"

"Yes," Stephen said.

"You carry it around in your canteen, but you don't believe it does any magic?" Elias pressed.

Stephen didn't blink. "No."

"Think it'd make any difference if you gave it to the rest of them straight, like you did with me? Not cooked into broths or steeped in the teas?"

Stephen shook his head. "I don't, Elias. And if I did, they'd notice the taste, and soon enough it would get round to Croghan and then we'd lose the spring and the way to keep Haven going, and it still wouldn't make any difference anyhow."

"Then why'd you try it on me in the first place? Or give it to the others?"

Stephen took off his hat and scratched his scalp like he was trying to shake the thought loose. "When there isn't much you can do, you want to do whatever you can."

Elias knew that well enough.

Stephen pointed to the ridge. "Get on up that rope and check the tree."

Elias hadn't even thought of the tree since telling Stephen and Hughes about carrying the letters. "Pennyrile ain't given me nothing to carry up."

Stephen rubbed the back of his neck. "Doesn't mean whoever's been writing to him didn't leave another. And having one in hand gives you a good reason to go talk to him when we got a plan worked up."

Elias wasn't even winded when he summited. There was a horse with a fine saddle tethered about twenty yards from the rim, its nose deep in a bag of grain. He wondered who left their mount behind, but he didn't tarry as he ran to the tree. The jar was empty. He raced back down to find that Dr. Croghan had joined Stephen, with Nick hanging behind.

"It really cannot wait," Croghan was saying. "We must have it as soon as possible."

"Yes, Doctor," Stephen said. He held his hands clasped behind his back and cast his eyes down.

"You must see my point," Croghan pressed. "If something were to happen to you—or Nick or Mat—it would be disastrous. You'd take with you knowledge of the routes and byways of the cave that would take others years to re-create. A map is the thing. And as soon as possible."

"Suppose I never thought of it that way," Stephen said.

Elias almost jerked back in surprise. Croghan didn't know about Stephen's maps?

"I want you to begin immediately," Croghan ordered. "I'll reassign some of your duties to the others if it might speed things along."

"Yes, sir," Stephen said. "I'll see what I can muster."

Stephen, Elias reckoned, was as full of secrets as the cave itself.

Chapter Fifteen

BOWLINE

Two mornings later brought another surprise.

"Rise and shine," Nick called out into Elias's hut as he carried in a plate of scrambled eggs, a small pile of fried potatoes, and a couple of tomato slices. The tomatoes weren't fresh, but Elias snatched the plate and crammed one slice whole into his mouth, the juices running down his chin. It tasted better than it had looked—tangy, salty, sweet. And the potatoes were crispy, good and greasy, tasting of the bacon they'd been fried with, the insides soft and warm. Even the eggs tasted better when they weren't the only thing on the plate.

"I'd tell you to eat fast, but don't reckon you could eat any faster," Nick said, clearly happy to see Elias enjoy his cooking so much. He spat a stream through the grate of the stove, and the sizzle and smell of the sweet tobacco bloomed in the hut.

"Why?" Elias asked, running the last few bites of egg across the smear of tomato juice left on his plate. "We got some place to be?"

He meant Haven, and wondered if maybe Hughes had sent for them.

Nick shook his head, reading Elias's thoughts. "Rotunda. Croghan means to walk all y'all. Reckons that's what's making you better, so he best start the others on it before it's too late."

Elias groaned. The walk to the supper that day had plum worn the others out. But then again, they weren't used to it. Maybe Croghan was right, and the exercise would help.

"I'll walk Nedra down there," Elias offered, following Nick out the door.

"Croghan came and took her and Lillian there himself a few minutes ago. I'm meant to get you and Pennyrile over."

Elias slowed at the mention of Pennyrile. He'd avoided him since finding out about Haven. But this could be an opportunity. "I'll walk him," he offered. "Probably ought to talk to him some."

"You sure?" Nick's voice was grave.

Elias was.

"Know the way?"

Elias did.

"I'll catch up after I clean these then." He gestured at the pans. "Tell Croghan I'll be along directly."

Pennyrile was sitting on his bed, already dressed for the walk, finishing up the knot on his neck scarf.

"I'll see you down," Elias said.

Pennyrile pointed at another letter waiting on the desk. "You want me to carry it?" Elias asked.

Pennyrile tapped his nose and pointed at Elias. Even in the silence, Elias was certain the man was mocking him.

"Fine." Elias crammed the letter into his pocket.

Pennyrile remained on the edge of the unmade bed, staring at Elias, his eyes narrowed. He picked up his slate. *You look improved.*

Elias knew he did, but he only said, "S'pose."

Pennyrile waited, as if he wanted Elias to go on. The two pigeons remaining in the loft warbled softly. Pennyrile's silence made Elias uncomfortable enough that he had to fill it with something.

"I'm just doing what Croghan tells me to. Maybe the walking'll do you good too."

Pennyrile's shoulders convulsed in one spasm of silent laughter. Elias remembered how difficult his walk had been on the way back from church. Then he wrote, *They gave it to you.*

The room grew still. Even the pigeons ceased their noises for the span of a breath.

The water, he scratched next.

Elias's heart hammered. He took care with his words, feeling as delicate as stacking cards made into castles.

"Water?" he asked carefully.

Pennyrile huffed and rolled his eyes, wagged a finger at Elias. Elias stood as still as a cornered rabbit.

Finally Pennyrile wrote again. *Negroes. Their miracle water.*

What little air was left in the stuffy hut seemed to rush out. Elias knew his next words were crucial. If he seemed too eager, Pennyrile might smell a rat; if he played dumb, Pennyrile might give up on Elias. He dropped his voice to a whisper. "How'd you know about that?"

Pennyrile erased, then wrote, *I know.*

"I don't know how—"

Pennyrile underlined his last words, the chalk screeching. The birds flapped in protest.

"Then I expect you know more'n I do. And if you'd tell me what you mean, maybe I won't have to waste your time."

Pennyrile scrawled, *Had some outside. Before I came. Want more.*

"They don't give it out. I don't even know how much they've given me."

Pennyrile tapped the slate impatiently.

Elias felt himself start to sweat. "I may be able to talk Stephen into giving you some of it—"

Pennyrile cut him off with a scratch at the slate. *Don't want some. All.*

Elias tried to act surprised, tried to act like he didn't understand. "All?"

Pennyrile circled the word, the chalk screeching.

"I don't know where Stephen gets the water, or how much there even is," Elias admitted, glad that this was the truth. Pennyrile only tapped at the words on the slate.

Elias understood how desperate the man was. How much he needed *something*. He was dying, and he was losing faith in Croghan's remedies, like the rest of them probably were. Pennyrile wanted the miracle water. And if he wanted it bad enough . . .

"I'll talk to Stephen," Elias said.

Pennyrile smiled as if he expected nothing less, and laid the slate aside. Then he leaned heavily on Elias as he walked him out the door and down the slope. Pennyrile huffed and shuffled the whole way, stopping several times to rest, but there was something, Elias thought, something calculated in the way he did so, looking to Elias, making sure Elias took note of how distressed he was, how feeble he was.

All he could think of was what Mat had said about that wounded bear.

Nick caught up to them as they reached the Rotunda. The sight was a sad one.

They were all there, all gathered around Dr. Croghan in a semicircle. The ones who couldn't stand on their own were propped up by nurses and other slaves. Croghan was leading them in lifting their arms over their heads and then back down.

"Ah!" Croghan called out when Elias and Nick led Pennyrile in. "Come here, Elias!"

Elias gave Pennyrile time to transfer his weight fully to Nick, and then slipped to the doctor's side.

"We were just talking about you," the doctor said, sounding madly hopeful. "About your marked improvement, and how the vapors have done such miracles when coupled with your exercise." He positioned Elias in front of the little assembly and stood behind him with his hands on his shoulders.

Elias took them all in. Nedra, looking spent, with Mozelle, flanked by Lillian and Hannah on either side.

Tincher and Shem stood with Stephen. And Mr. Cherry, the lawyer, held up by Dorothy. And Pennyrile, of course.

There were so few of them left.

"Today we'll follow his example and do a short constitutional together," the doctor continued. "I expect over time, many of you will work up to take part of a tour with Mat or Stephen!"

Elias surveyed the faces, all of them drawn and pale. Nedra was staring at Elias with something close to hunger, he thought. He couldn't hold her gaze. Poor Miss Mozelle started coughing in the middle of the doctor's speech, sending his voice louder to be heard. Shem just gazed into the black beyond the top of the doctor's head. Mr. Cherry and Tincher mumbled "amen" or "hear, hear," Elias couldn't tell which.

Pennyrile just smirked.

"Today we'll do a circuit of only the Rotunda. Move at whatever pace seems most comfortable, and stop as often as you find you need to rest."

The residents all stood there hesitantly, each waiting for someone else to move first. And one by one they all looked at Elias. Elias felt their stares, felt their expectation and their envy.

He'd felt sicker before, but he'd *never* felt so rotten for being well. But feeling like a heel wouldn't make anybody else any better. The entire party set out, shuffling up one side of the Rotunda. Doctor Croghan began to whistle. It took a few bars for Elias to recognize the tune to "When the Saints Go Marching In." Elias and Stephen hung back.

"It's the water!" Elias whispered fiercely, telling Stephen in rush about his conversation with Pennyrile.

"He said the water?" Stephen asked, eyes wide.

"Wrote it! Right on that slate! My eyes near bugged out of my skull!"

Stephen rubbed the back of his neck.

"But that's good, ain't it?" Elias asked. "At least he's not after runaways."

Stephen wasn't convinced. "Seems too easy. Nothing ought to be easy with a man like that."

They watched Pennyrile trudge away. It seemed to Elias that every time Pennyrile stopped, he made sure Stephen and Elias were watching.

"He's dreadful sick," Elias said, watching Pennyrile pause to lean on the wall, Nick hovering close. "If we're careful, we might be able to get him to take the water and just go."

"We'll wait and see what Hughes says. Did Pennyrile give you another letter?"

"Yeah."

"Good," Stephen said. "We'll read it and then take it up night after next before we go see Hughes."

"That long?" Elias asked.

Stephen kicked a rock. "It can't be helped. Croghan wants us up at the hotel tonight for a party."

"What about Pennyrile? In the meantime?"

"Keep clear of him if you can. We've got to work out what we're going to do first. Now, run on up there and catch up to them," Stephen said. "It's your fault they're all down here parading around, anyhow."

Chapter Sixteen

LIGHTERMAN'S HITCH

Two nights later Elias had really, finally, finished his letter home. The reply he composed read to him like a retread of the letter written earlier, save for the fact that this time his assurances that he was improving, that he felt better, were more than just an attempt to ease his mother's mind. They were the truth.

He managed to fill two pages with descriptions of the things he'd seen, as well as reports on Bedivere's wing, which seemed to be healing almost as rapidly as Elias was. Maybe he'd give him some of the water and see how it worked on pigeons. He was just rereading his last few lines, realizing he'd not spent them pleading to come home. That's how he'd always closed his letters. But this time, he'd merely said he missed Mama and Granny and Tillie.

Funny, he thought.

A rapping at the doorframe made his pencil jump.

"Elias?" Nick called.

"Yeah, Nick?" Elias whispered.

He poked his head inside. "You eat yet?"

Elias put the paper and pencil aside. "Lillian gave me some biscuits," Elias said. He was enjoying the food— even the eggs—more than he imagined he could. Before he'd started healing, he'd clean forgotten what it even felt like to be hungry. Now he felt it nearly all the time.

"Wanna take a walk?"

Elias ran the back of a finger down Bedivere's throat, then hopped up. They were heading to Haven, he could tell! He followed Nick out, noticing that Pennyrile's curtains were shut tight. But Elias imagined he was listening, that he was noting the fact that Nick was leading him into the cave again.

Halfway to the entrance Nick dropped his satchel and pulled out a thin knife. "Stephen and Hughes said we was to read that letter 'fore you dropped it."

Elias handed the letter to Nick, who moved the plug of tobacco to the side of his jaw. The letter was a thin one, maybe a single sheet of paper folded on itself. Nick heated the blade of his knife in the lantern's flame, then laid it flat along the paper, slicing neatly under the wax seal.

Elias wondered why he hadn't thought to try the same thing before.

The letter popped open, Nick gingerly unfolding it the rest of the way. He held it to the lamp and screwed his eyes up. "Short, anyhow," he muttered, handing the letter to Elias. Elias wondered if Nick could read like Stephen. He read the two words printed in the middle of the page, Pennyrile's signature slithering underneath.

Stand ready.

"Won't have no trouble remembering that to tell Hughes and Stephen, will you?"

Elias shook his head and folded the letter. Nick used his knife to chunk off a blob of the wax around the edge of the seal. Then he balanced it on the tip of the blade, holding the knife above the flame of the lamp until the wax melted enough to smear it on the folded letter, resealing it nearly enough to pass muster.

"Press that good, and it'll set up right." Nick lifted his pack and led the way back to the entrance.

They took care of dropping off Pennyrile's letter, but their hopes for a revealing reply they could sneak a look at were unrealized when Elias found the jar empty again.

Elias thought back to when Pennyrile first rooked him into all this, how he'd said he used the birds because they were faster. He also knew not to expect letters unless he had first sent one, which made the use of the birds make more sense. And the fact that Pennyrile was up to something half-explained why his correspondent did not want to be seen.

Elias and Nick then made the long descent down to Haven. Upon arriving at the pit, Nick was good enough not to notice Elias's hesitation, and was even kinder to break the silence. "We named it Smiley."

Once they were across, Nick began to sing.

> *Wade in the water,*
> *Wade in the water, children*
> *Wade in the water,*
> *God's a-gonna trouble the water.*

"Why you singing?" Elias asked.

"Code," Nick explained. "So they know we're coming in and we're safe. Singin's been code for folks on the path for years. Slaves sing about when to go and when to stay, where to go, who to trust, the route to take."

"So what's the song you're singing mean?"

"Like it? Old spiritual like th'others. Means to take to the river and walk in the shallows so the dogs cain't track. We use it here to signify a friendly person heading for Haven."

Who that yonder dressed in red?
The Lord gonna trouble the water.
Must be the children that Moses led—

But before he got to the last line of the verse, another voice, sweet and clear, came sailing in.

God's a-gonna trouble the water.

It was a beautiful voice, shaking high at the start of the line before tumbling down for the last note. And then a figure moved from inside the cleft they were heading for and called out, "H'lo, Nick." Elias could see her face now. She was a pretty girl, maybe his age. Skinny as a wet cat, but her eyes gleamed bright in the lantern light, and her smile was wide.

"Evening, Josie," Nick said. "All quiet?"

"Like white folk at church," she said, smile dropping as she leveled her gaze hard at Elias.

"You met Elias yet?" Nick asked.

"Saw him last time he come," Josie said. "He don't say much."

"Maybe that's why we get 'long so good," Nick said, then spat.

Elias studied Josie. Despite being so grim, she was even prettier than Nedra might have been once. He tore his eyes away from her face and saw she was holding something in her hands. It was a doll, fashioned out of corn husks. Tillie had some just like it. This one looked well made, the head good and round, features drawn on in charcoal. The dress swooped out into a full skirt like fancy ladies wore. "Ain't you a little old for dolls?"

Josie ignored Elias, handing the doll over to Nick. "Would you give it to Mat? For his little girl? I keep thinking he might visit, but if you wouldn't mind—"

"Pleased to," Nick said.

Josie smiled, quick and shy, before setting her face again. "See y'all on the way out."

"I'll fetch back coffee," Nick said as he and Elias resumed walking.

"Don't bother. Grounds reused too many times. Tastes worse than dirt."

"I'll do m'best to sneak some down next time," Nick promised.

"Sugar, too," she called back, her voice growing faint. Nick laughed softly.

"She's got no light," Elias said, staring into the dark behind him. "Jonah never did either."

Nick led him through the little tunnel. "All scouts trained to know routes without light. Can walk 'em by feel. And silent, too. That way, if they have to run ahead of somebody nosing in who got no business coming, they won't be seen."

"Can you do it?" Elias asked. "Down here, I mean?"

"Go without the light? When it suits me."

Elias thought about that—they were like bats, sailing around in the dark, not smashing themselves into walls. Or homing pigeons, knowing the right way to fly home. And then he thought about the danger of it—the fact that one misplaced foot could mean the end. His stomach tightened up like a figure eight knot.

Elias followed Nick over the wall. Things looked just as they had been when he arrived the first time. There were people at the school, folk laughing as they stooped over cook fires, a few dipping bottles and jars into a big kettle of boiling water, still others stretched out on bedrolls here and there.

"What are they doing?" Elias asked as they passed by the people with the kettle and the bottles.

"Washing up. We boil 'em good before they're refilled. Got that notion off Doctor Croghan. He has Lillian and me and th'others cook all his tools and bleeding things before he uses them on y'all."

"They really moved all those bottles in and out on the river?" There must have been fifty or sixty awaiting a dip in the kettle.

"Mmhm. Backing up now, like the travelers. But folk we move in mostly through the main entrance."

"You'd never!"

Nick grinned slyly. "Most runaways cain't find the river entrances, only know that Haven is here. So they come through the main opening like everybody else. Getting 'crost the road and by the hotel risky, but if they can manage that, we bring 'em in when it's safe. Mat brung Josie in," he explained, spitting again before adding, "I reckon the doll's her thanks."

"Don't anybody recognize the strangers?" Elias asked.

"Naw," Nick said. "Only ones around here permanent are Croghan's slaves and Croghan himself. Th'other hands don't say nothing, and Croghan's got enough to occupy him. Most guests don't pay enough mind to even notice we're different from one another."

Elias knew it was true. Knew it because of the way he'd not paid attention at first. Knew it because of the way even now he had a hard time picturing the features of the girl who served them back home. He felt a twinge of shame.

Nick didn't seem to notice. "See them?" He pointed to a young man and a girl about eighteen cozied up next to the light of a fire as they shared a book.

"What about 'em?" Elias asked.

"Got married two weeks ago. Met down here."

"Y'all got a minister?" Elias asked, staring at the pair.

"Hughes does it. Ain't a bad preacher, neither."

"Hughes does it all," Elias said. "You think he's got a plan cooked up yet?"

"We'll see." As they made their way to Hughes, a few hands rose in greeting to Nick. When folks set eyes on Elias, men touched their caps and women whispered blessings.

"Why they doing that?"

"Thankful."

It made Elias feel funny. "But I didn't do anything."

"Like I tol' Josie—you don't say much. That's a whole lot to us and them."

Hughes was perched on his rock, eating a bowl of steaming mash and talking to Stephen. He lifted his chin toward Nick and Elias as they approached.

"I told them what Pennyrile said to you," Stephen explained. "Did you read the letter?"

Nick nodded to Elias. "He did."

"It only said 'Stand ready,'" Elias reported.

Stephen and the others let it settle. Elias knew they

understood what he'd worked out since reading the note: Pennyrile was confident that he'd get what he came for soon.

Elias waited as Hughes scooped a lump of porridge with a wedge of corn cake. The man took a long pull from a glass bottle like the ones Elias saw the others washing earlier. Then he wiped his mouth on a red handkerchief and began carefully, "I've been thinking . . ."

A small crowd began to gather around them. Soon Jonah was at his side.

"I've been thinking about our problem," Hughes continued after he took another drink of the water. "And the more I think on it, the more delicate I find it becomes."

"Not if we do what we ought to," one man cried, edging forward. "He's an old man. He's a criminal, and he's consumptive to boot. He ain't bound to live long either way. And if we just move him along—"

"Daniel!" Hughes said, the smoke and thunder back in his voice. "Killing him, no matter how rotten the man may be, won't do."

Elias sat spellbound. They were talking about killing someone! A peculiar thought flitted through his mind—the knights and Arthur had to go around killing monsters and villains and giants all the time. He expected they wouldn't have lost any sleep over someone like Pennyrile. But Elias was with Hughes: killing Pennyrile still sounded wrong.

Stephen chimed in. "If you kill him, it doesn't mean somebody else won't come looking. Doesn't mean his crew will just give up on him. Or on finding the spring."

"Exactly right," Hughes said. "Exactly right."

Jonah whispered to Elias, "Could use us a glamour right 'bout now, wouldn't you say?" A glamour would have been just the thing. When Merlin had a problem, or needed things to go a certain way, he used his magic. A dose of magic at the moment would be a whole lot neater and raise a lot fewer questions than a dead pirate.

"Wouldn't even have to last long," Elias offered.

And the possibility struck him. A wonderful possibility.

A glamour didn't have to last.

Only long enough to fool somebody.

Elias looked wide-eyed at Jonah. Jonah must have had the same thought, for he whispered, "We ain't got to *kill* Pennyrile. We jes' got to trick him."

"Right!" Elias said excitedly, loudly. Too loudly. He sensed all eyes upon him. Even Hughes stared at him.

"Something to say?" Hughes leaned forward.

"The best thing to do is to give him what he wants so he'll go away," Elias blurted out.

Some of the men crowded in on him. Elias and Jonah sprang to their feet.

Daniel stepped so close, he could have bumped chests

with Elias. "Stephen may be fool enough to trust this boy, but it don't mean we all are! We got no reason to believe he ain't working with Pennyrile already."

Jonah made himself a wall between Elias and Daniel. "We didn't mean—"

Elias drew himself up as tall as he could go. "I'd never!"

"Simmer down, the pack of you," Hughes rumbled.

"I meant we could trick him!" Elias fumed, not caring a whit that Hughes told him to be quiet.

"Go on," Hughes said.

"You tell 'em, Jonah." Elias didn't trust his words to come out right. He felt the way he had on the day he'd punched Theodore Coates in the school yard. That feeling of running out of words, something else taking over.

Jonah rubbed the back of his neck with one hand. "Elias and me was talking about Merlin and how he used his magic, made one person look like another when it suited him. And there's this other story Merlin ain't in but a green knight—"

"Merlin? Green knights?" Daniel barked. He swung round to face Hughes. "We ain't got time for fairy tales—"

"What Jonah's sayin'," Elias broke in, "is that all we got to do is lead Pennyrile to some other spring or pool or something and make him think it's the one y'all get your tonic from. He's sick enough to believe what you give him. And he believes it works, thinks that's why I'm better. He's known about it the whole time he's been down here, so he ought to be ready to believe what you show him."

"It's a kind of *glamour*," Jonah put in, sounding proud to impress somebody with the word.

No one spoke. Even Daniel seemed stuck dumb. Elias wasn't sure if it was because they all thought the notion was so foolish, or so brilliant. Finally Stephen broke the silence. "It'd have to be near one of the river exits," he said. "Pennyrile probably already knows we move most of it out on the river."

"And it'd have to be off the main runs we use," Hughes added. "So they won't see anything we don't want them to."

"There's that pool, just up from Lake Lethe," Nick said excitedly. "Got a bit of that funny taste too. Might serve."

"Far enough away," Hughes said at last as he began drawing crosshatch patterns in the sand with his cane.

Even Daniel warmed to the notion. "That'd put him on the River Styx, which we don't even use—"

"Meaning the way out on the Echo and upstream would be safe for us," Hughes supplied.

The prospect of the way North opening again, of Haven finally exhaling after having held its breath for so long, seemed to brighten every eye.

"Still . . . Pennyrile's smart," Hughes went on, somewhat

reluctantly. "He may be desperate, but he's too smart not to be suspicious. He'll wonder why you're willing to help him now."

Stephen was grim. "I thought the same thing. And I think I got a plan."

Stephen's plan was the last thing Elias ever expected him to say.

"I'm going to tell him he has to take me North."

Everyone froze.

"Stephen—" Hughes began.

"I've worked it over a thousand different ways. He won't believe me unless he thinks I'm getting something out of it. And there can't be anything I'd want from him except that."

The fire popped and hissed in the gloom. There they stood, surrounded by dozens of runaways who wanted to escape, biding their time until it was safe enough to continue on their way. And then there was Stephen, perhaps the only one who wanted to *stay*. The cave was his home, he'd said. He was as happy as he figured he could be.

But he would give it all up. Run. So others could do the same.

"You can't . . . ," Elias began, not sure what else to say.

"I have to," Stephen said, though there was no joy in saying it. "You all know it too. Plus, if he and his crew are busy smuggling me North, then they'll be off the river for a spell, and give you all a clear shot out."

Nick laid a hand on Stephen's shoulder. "You're sure?"

Stephen clenched his jaw and nodded once.

Hughes seemed unable to speak for a good long while. Finally he said, "You've kept us going. And now you'll give us a chance. We can't ever make good on that debt."

Stephen just gazed at the sand beneath his feet. Elias was proud and sad and disbelieving all at once. Stephen was in every path and route and nook of this cave. He *was* this cave. His leaving was like . . . like . . . Arthur without Excalibur.

But even Arthur's time ended.

Chapter Seventeen

JUG SLING

After supper Stephen and Elias approached Pennyrile's hut. "You don't think we ought to give it a day?" Elias whispered.

"It has to be now," Stephen insisted, sloshing the jug of the special water they'd brought along in case Pennyrile required proof. "Before he has time to learn more."

At the door, Pennyrile pulled back the curtain. His boots were laced up tight and his neck wrap had been freshly changed, almost as if he'd been waiting for them to arrive.

"Evenin', sir," Stephen whispered, looking round as if somebody was going to pop out of the shadows. Pennyrile held his slate in one hand and his chalk in the other, but his arms were crossed.

"There was no new letter," Elias offered without being asked.

Pennyrile shrugged without taking his eyes off Stephen.

Stephen stepped forward. "I reckon we should talk."

Elias made to go back to his hut, but Pennyrile slapped his hand against the slate.

"I figure you two—" Elias began, but Pennyrile pointed at the ground at his feet. He wanted Elias to stay.

"Elias tells me you're looking for something." Stephen kept his voice low, but the two remaining pigeons in the loft still shied away.

Pennyrile didn't move. So Stephen went on.

"How'd you know the water came from in here?" Stephen asked him.

Pennyrile simply stared. He had no intention of giving up what he knew or how he knew it. Elias found it maddening, the waiting and guessing and wondering if this was going to work at all.

"Look," Stephen said, Pennyrile's stony silence beginning to unnerve him as well. "I'll take you to the water, but I'm not doing it out of kindness."

Pennyrile's eyebrow lifted a hair. Stephen's tone had drawn him out. It figured to Elias. Kindness didn't seem to be in Pennyrile's wheelhouse. Manipulation. Bargains. Skullduggery. Those were languages he spoke.

The man lifted the slate and wrote hurriedly. *I have money.*

"Don't want money . . . ," Stephen began, sounding more confident now that he'd moved Pennyrile to words. "I heard about a rough crew aboard a boat out on the Green. I wonder if they're anything to do with you?"

Pennyrile's mustache quirked at the mention of the riverboat.

"I wondered if with the pigeons and all, if that might be who'd you'd been writing to—"

At this, Pennyrile began to scrawl frantically. Elias glanced at the birds. He was surprised to see that one had a little bit of paper wrapped around its leg.

Curious, he thought. He'd figured Pennyrile had given up on the pigeons. How long had it been there?

The chalk screeched across the slate as Pennyrile finished writing. *No more nonsense. What do you want?*

Stephen took off his hat and rubbed his head. "Safe passage," he said. "You and your crew will carry me up to the Illinois territory."

Pennyrile tilted his head to one side. *Running?* he wrote.

"You and your boat may be my best chance."

When?

Stephen put his hat back on. "I'll show you the spring tonight," he said. "There's a new moon night after next. That'll be the best time for me to slip away."

Water tonight? Pennyrile wrote, his eyes gleaming.

"Sooner you get it, the sooner you start feeling stronger. And there's nobody about to wonder what we're up to but Lillian, and she'll hold her tongue."

Pennyrile tapped his chalk against the slate, thinking. Then he hung the slate around his neck with a leather cord and gestured toward the door.

Elias felt himself exhale. It might work. It just might.

Stephen led them out. "Go on to bed, Elias—"

Pennyrile rapped on the slate.

"What now?" Stephen said.

Pennyrile wrote, *The boy comes.*

This had not been part of the plan. Stephen was supposed to go with Pennyrile alone. Elias was meant to stay behind.

"I don't—" Stephen began, but Pennyrile was writing again.

Witness.

It took Elias a second to figure out what he meant. His eyes flashed back and forth between the word and Pennyrile's eyes. Then it dawned on him: Pennyrile didn't trust Stephen, but he still saw Elias as an ally.

"Fine," Stephen relented, handing the water jug to Elias to carry. "But the both of you stay close and keep quiet."

They passed Lillian sitting by the fire. Her back was

squared to them, and she was staring straight ahead, shaking her head stiffly from side to side. Elias could tell she was mad enough to walk right through that fire, but figured she'd done all her hollering at him when Stephen explained the plan to her beforehand.

But someone was watching them go. Nedra stood at her window, a candle in her hand. She seemed about to cry out, but fell to coughing instead, and Lillian jumped from her seat and ran to Nedra's window, blocking her from view.

"Elias!" Stephen whispered sharply. "Move!"

Elias hurried to catch up and soon was near enough to smell the sour stink coming off those wraps on Pennyrile's neck. He expected that if they lost Pennyrile, they could always hunt him down by scent. Not that that seemed likely. Pennyrile was already working hard, chest heaving, face glistening with sweat.

At the path, Stephen handed Pennyrile a lantern. "We're going deep down, sir," Stephen said. "Farther than even Croghan knows about. Stay right on my heel. But we got to move if we're going to get you two back before morning rounds."

Pennyrile waved his hands impatiently. He didn't need to write the words out for them to know that he meant for Stephen to get on with it.

They worked their way down the passage, three

lights bouncing off the walls, three pairs of feet shuffling softly down the corridors. They filed past Giant's Coffin, descended into Wooden Bowl, and back up to cross Bottomless Pit. Pennyrile crossed over the narrow foot-bridge without a moment's hesitation. He had gumption, Elias had to give him that. But then again, he figured a body didn't come to be a river pirate without a little bit of fire in the belly. Still, Elias was worried—more worried than he had been even before. If Pennyrile had that kind of steel in him, and was cagey enough to insist Elias came along so Stephen couldn't pull something, would their plan be enough to trick him after all?

Then again, the farther they went, the more often Pennyrile stopped to rest. He was sick. Bad sick.

From the pit they wound down deeper, through the sideways squeeze of Fat Man's Misery, into the vastness of River Hall, where Elias's heart leaped a little at the pros-pect of finally seeing the river. He smelled it before he saw it, the heavy misting scent of river water, the whisper of the flow growing louder as they drew closer. But the joy sucked right out of him when he finally glimpsed it. The dark water lagged by slowly at their feet, as if it were con-fused at having found itself flowing underground, as if it were giving up. He wasn't sure a river belonged under-ground.

A little boat tethered up near the edge bounced against the rocks.

"Help me cast off," Stephen said as he nimbly stepped into the boat. Elias set the jug in the boat and steadied the bow while Pennyrile climbed in. Stephen then grabbed a long pole laid up inside the dory and stood in the stern while Elias slipped the loop of rope from the rock it was tied around, bringing it to the boat as he hopped in. Stephen dipped the pole into the water and pushed off.

Pennyrile picked up the jug and tipped it up to drink, loosening his scarf. Elias tried and failed not to gape at what he saw there.

It was no wonder Dr. Croghan called it the King's Evil. It *looked* evil, like fruit rotting from the inside out, great bruising shades of purple rimmed with yellow, swollen out to the size of crabapples, up and down the side of his neck, smeared in the ointment and crusting at the edges.

"It's a tricky approach from here." Stephen's voice was almost apologetic. "But from outside, you can start where the Nolin forks off. You know that place?"

Pennyrile indicated he did, but Elias could see he wasn't listening. Not really. He was staring at Stephen's pocket. Elias followed his eyes and saw the shape of the little notebook outlined against the worn fabric.

Something passed through Elias, like a ghost shuddering by.

This something was trouble. Elias knew it deep, but there was no way he could say. Not now. Not until they'd seen it through.

They slipped off the river, across a shallow channel and into a wide body of still water. Ever the tour guide, Stephen announced, "Lake Lethe."

He poled across the surface, sending the water rippling out to the edges of the cave, where it slapped against the shores, echoing like the chiming of tiny bells. Eerie and beautiful, the chorus grew stronger and fuller as they crossed the lake, but in the silence of the boat, in the worry that seemed to chant inside Elias's head, the bells seemed to toll out a warning. And if he listened closer, they almost sounded like voices whispering. He'd not have been surprised at all to see the Lady of the Lake staring up at him from the other side of the mirrored surface.

Stephen docked alongside a tunnel whose bottom edge sat a few feet above the lake's surface, a trickle of water spilling over the lip. Elias tied the boat off to a handy spire as Stephen stepped up into the tunnel. Pennyrile followed, with Elias coming last. They climbed up the chute, feet sloshing in the water, then they ducked through a tunnel so low that they had to crawl. Pennyrile was struggling now, his breath growing ever more labored, sweating heavily.

Then, all of a sudden, they could stand again. They had arrived.

The pool was no more than four feet across, still as glass except when a drop fell from the rock above. "Water drips in all the time, but it's spring-fed from below," Stephen explained, anticipating their question. "And it's as full as it was the day we found it. We been drawing off it near two years, but it never reduces."

Pennyrile frowned. He seemed to be waiting for something more.

"Go on, drink," Stephen said. "Sweeter water you won't find. Folks paying near a dollar a bottle for a little one, but reckon you can set whatever price you want when word gets out what it can do."

Pennyrile sighed, screwed up his mouth like he wanted to say something, but then wrote.

We? Who else?

Stephen realized his mistake, but he recovered. "Me and Nick and Mat. We're the only ones that know about it. I heard about it from a man who was here before me, who heard about it from a fellow before him, who was brought here by an old Shawnee."

Pennyrile rubbed his thumb over the edge of the slate.

"But Nick and Mat won't be any trouble. There's enough water for them to take a little and keep selling on the sly."

Pennyrile then pointed at the shaft beyond, raised his eyebrows in question.

"Dead end," Stephen explained, digging into his pack and producing a bottle for Pennyrile to fill.

But instead of taking it, Pennyrile lowered himself, scooped up some water in his palms, and drank it noisily. Then he removed his scarf, soaked a section of it in the cold water, and wrapped it back around his neck. Elias caught Stephen's eye, trying to figure out if Pennyrile believed that this was indeed the pool.

Elias almost felt bad for Pennyrile. Despite how awful he was, he was also awfully sick, no question. Elias felt terrible giving him false hope.

Pennyrile breathed deep and smiled like it was the best water he'd ever drunk in all his life. He pointed at the jug in Elias's hand and motioned for him to dump it out. Elias caught his meaning.

"Go on, Elias," Stephen said. Elias stepped aside and emptied the jug, the water sloshing onto the floor. Then he submerged the jug in the spring, the chill near freezing his hand. He lifted it out when the last bubble rose to the surface, stopped up the jug, and handed it to Pennyrile.

Only it must have slipped from Pennyrile's grasp, because the next thing Elias knew, it was crashing to the stone floor and busting all to pieces.

Stephen had lunged forward to try to catch it, but he was too slow, stumbling onto his hands and knees. "Blast it, Elias," he said.

"I'm sorry," Elias said. But Pennyrile didn't seem to mind. He even grabbed Stephen about the waist and one shoulder, and helped him to his feet.

"We can fetch you more jugs," Stephen told Pennyrile. Pennyrile wrote.

We can manage.

Stephen and Elias exchanged looks.

"Then we're square?" Stephen asked. "You got what you came for? And you'll take me North?"

Pennyrile nodded emphatically.

"I guess that's it then," Elias said, maybe a little too excited. "We ought to head back."

Pennyrile tapped his nose and pointed at Elias, winking. Then he ducked down with his light and crawled back through the passage without even waiting for Stephen to lead them through. As Pennyrile's light faded, Elias whispered, "Think it worked?"

Stephen closed his eyes. "Hope so. Lord, I hope so."

At the boat, Stephen took up the pole and made to

shove off, but Pennyrile held up a hand and stood, sure as sure on legs that had spent plenty of time on boats. With his chalk he made a small white *x* on the wall above the passage, and sat back down. Elias almost collapsed with relief.

Pennyrile was marking the way.

And if he was marking the way, it meant he'd come back.

It meant he believed them.

Even Stephen seemed to relax as they made their way back to the main cave. He asked Pennyrile if he needed any markers from the place where the Echo came out, where Pennyrile's crew could come in and make their way to the false spring, but Pennyrile tapped his temple. He knew the spot.

When they were close enough to the huts to smell the smoke from the fires, Pennyrile took up his slate. *Can find my way from here.*

"I'll see you back," Stephen offered.

Pennyrile waved him off, wrote *Night is young for a spry pair like you. Expect you have another adventure waiting?*

Elias and Stephen exchanged a look. "Well . . ." Stephen began. It was past midnight, Elias figured, but he was too keyed up to sleep anyway. Plus, if they hurried they could get down to Haven and tell Hughes and everyone that Pennyrile had taken the bait.

"'Member that spot you meant to show me?" Elias asked.

Stephen took a beat, then nodded. "Mummy Ledge, right. I suppose we have time." He turned to Pennyrile. "You sure you'll be all right?"

Pennyrile saluted with the hand still holding his chalk, and gave what Elias guessed must pass for a smile. Then he tromped up the path and back into the camp. He already seemed to be moving better, a little quicker. The thought of the healing water was already doing its work.

When he was good and gone, Stephen said in a low voice, "I don't know about this, Elias."

"Why? He seems pleased as punch. Notice how much quicker we got back up here? Like he thinks the water is already working or something!"

"A fellow like Pennyrile is most dangerous when he seems pleased about something," Stephen said carefully. "C'mon. Let's go tell Hughes it's done."

They were nearly to Haven, already past Smiley and quickening their steps. Elias was too busy watching his feet as they hurried when he should have been looking up. His head glanced against a sharp edge of rock jutting down from the ceiling of the maze.

"Bells and bibles!" Elias said, hand flying to his temple,

actual stars dancing across his eyes. He felt the blood seeping at his fingers.

"Watch yourself, Elias!" Stephen slowed and reached into his pocket for a kerchief. "We don't have time for—"

Then he stopped.

He thrust his hand into his other pocket. His eyes went round as marbles. Then he ripped off his coat and turned it inside out.

"Stephen?" Elias asked, no longer worrying about the scrape, mopping up the blood with the tail of his green scarf.

"It's gone." Stephen voice was a whisper.

"What's gone?" Elias asked, touching his forehead and then looking at his fingers. The bleeding had already stopped.

"My book!"

His book? "Your notebook? The one with—"

"The maps."

Elias's heart started thudding. "Maybe you dropped it on the path?"

"I keep the pocket buttoned. Always. It's never fallen out."

Suddenly it felt like the rock was giving way under their feet. "Pennyrile." Elias gasped. He recalled the way he'd stared at Stephen's pocket as he poled the boat. And he'd admired the knots Pennyrile had conjured up in his scarves, knew those fingers were nimble. Nimble enough to undo a button and lift the notebook when . . .

"When he helped me up," Stephen said at the same moment Elias was thinking it. He jammed his arms into his coat sleeves. "He filched it. C'mon!"

Neither of them spoke as they raced back up to the ward. Neither of them said what they knew now to be true. They'd been wrong about what Pennyrile was after. Marking the tunnel had been his own bit of skullduggery, pretending they were giving him what he was after, when all the while he'd taken it for himself. They'd bet on him being after either the water or Haven. They hadn't dreamed he was after both.

They made it to the ward faster than Elias thought possible, but it was still too late. Lillian was slumped on the floor. Stephen ran to her side and helped her up. "Lillian?"

She stirred, rubbing the back of her neck. "Something hit me."

"Where's Pennyrile?" Stephen demanded, holding her head in his hands.

She winced. "He came back a good while ago. Went in his room and then a little later—"

Stephen looked at Elias, fear in his eyes. "Check his hut!"

Elias bolted across the courtyard and threw back the curtain.

"Gone!" Elias yelled. His eyes fell on the pigeon loft.

There was only one bird left inside.

He stepped closer.

The big one, the one with the message tied on, was missing.

Missing along with the one last message Pennyrile had ready, Elias supposed. Elias imagined the message tied to that pigeon's leg must have been a simple one. One telling someone to come and fetch him. And he'd probably carried it aboveground himself.

His heart sank as he tore out of the hut, racing for the entrance to the cave, Stephen at his heels.

Chapter Eighteen

TURK'S HEAD

Elias grew winded as they hiked to the entrance. Neither he nor Stephen said out loud how hopeless it was to chase Pennyrile—he had nearly an hour on them, what with how long they'd taken to realize he'd swiped the book. Once he got himself out of the cave, there was no telling where he'd go.

They burst into the open air, the gray light of dawn pouring softly over the edge of the ridge above them. Elias ran ahead to the steps but found the rope piled in a heap, five or six yards down slope from where its end usually hung.

"Sliced the rope." Stephen cursed as they began to climb. It slowed them down, not having the rope to steady themselves, but they made it to the top faster than Elias would have thought possible.

Still, Pennyrile was nowhere in sight.

"They must have had it planned from the beginning!" Elias reasoned. "And then he let the pigeon go when he got up here."

"Sending word ahead to his crew," Stephen added. He threw his hat against the ground and half growled, half bellowed. "We should have known! We should have figured on him knowing about all of us."

"Can he use the maps to get around?" Elias asked, stooping to pick up the hat, dusting it off.

The birds were starting to wake up, chits and calls from all corners of the wood.

"You saw it yourself," Stephen said. "That night when you asked me why all the routes seemed to bend around that hollow place on the main map. You didn't know what you were looking at then, but that was Haven."

"Just an empty space on the map?"

"Only way I knew to make sure that if anybody ever found my notes they wouldn't see it—"

"But if a fella knew to look for it in the first place, and then figured on you maybe hiding it, even in your own maps—"

"It'd be proof enough," Stephen admitted.

Elias watched the crimson of the sun creep up over

the ridge. He couldn't remember the last time he'd seen a sunrise. But it didn't feel hopeful, not at all.

"Maybe . . . maybe he *won't* know what to make of it," Elias ventured.

Stephen grabbed up a twig, broke it in half, and then into halves again.

"We've been fools," he said bitterly. "He knew what to make of it as soon as he came down here."

"But how could he?"

Stephen let all the broken pieces of the twig fall from his fingers. "Bounty hunters been looking for a while. Trackers have tried for years to connect the railroad with the cave. Everybody figured since slaves have been hiding all over the countryside, why wouldn't a place as big as Mammoth be better than a barn or under the floorboards of a house?"

"Seems like a lot of trouble," Elias said. "Getting himself sick, holing up in a cave, training all those pigeons . . . for what? How much could all of 'em be worth?"

Stephen's glare was dark. For the first time since he'd been there, Elias felt as young as he truly was. Stephen and the others had been treating him as a friend, an equal. But he wasn't, and not because of his color only. But because in truth, he was just a kid. A pretty dumb one at the moment. One who let himself ask dumb questions. He stared at the ground, too ashamed to meet Stephen's eyes.

Stephen threw his head back. "Hard question."

"I meant—"

"I know what you meant," Stephen said, his tone a little kinder. "Hard to answer, though. Some of them know what they were worth on their masters' inventories. Others don't. But usually the bounty for bringing back a runaway is more than the price of a slave."

"Why?"

"A master can't have slaves running off. Can't have a tracker catch one just to find the nearest convenient market or farm to sell him off to. If the owner pays above price, the slave is likelier to end up back where he started. Back where the master can make an example of him for anyone else who might get notions about taking off."

Elias didn't know what to say.

"I expect if Pennyrile even got half the people in that cave out for himself, he and his crew profit somewhere north of five thousand dollars," Stephen said.

Elias's jaw fell open. It was a powerful sum of money. He knew for a fact that the house in Virginia cost less than five hundred dollars and it was built brand-new.

"We got to do something!" Elias clambered to his feet, pounding his fist against his thigh.

"We got to do something, indeed." Stephen stood. "We have to tell Hughes."

★   ★   ★

"You mean he'll be coming here?" Hughes loomed over Stephen, furious.

"We all wanted him to be after the water. How could I—"

Hughes's grip tightened on the shaft of his cane. "How could you make a map to this place?"

Elias stared, stunned. Even Hughes hadn't known about the notebook!

But Stephen wasn't fazed. "I didn't! I left the area where Haven is on the map marked unexplored. Nick and Mat and me even marked all the paths leading in as dead ends in case anybody ever wandered this far. But to someone who knows to look—"

"We have guards," Hughes interrupted, thinking ahead. "Sentries. And we can draw back farther from the river—"

"Too dangerous," Stephen said. "If he means to catch runaways, the exits will be unsafe. And if he finds this place . . . If they somehow slip past the sentries—"

"Don't suppose you were kind enough to write up all about our security in your little map book, were you?" Hughes snapped.

Stephen fought to keep his voice steady. "'Course not. But if he comes here with weapons, with enough men—"

Hughes waved a hand. "We can't slip but one or two

people in here at a time. He can't get a whole gang down here at once."

"Either way," Stephen said, "we must get folk ready to leave."

"I decide when we leave!" Hughes roared. Silence fell heavy around them.

When Elias and Stephen had come in, life in Haven had been just stirring, breakfast over cook fires, folks still huddling under blankets. But now Elias saw that a small crowd had gathered round, eyes wide with fear, mouths set tight as they listened to Hughes and Stephen argue.

Hughes collected himself. "We start leaving. Tonight."

"But they could still be up on the river—"

"We'll send scouts to find a good route. Three or four will go out and then double back to say if it's safe. If they don't come back, we'll know it ain't—"

"But . . . the scouts might get caught!" Elias protested.

"That's all we can do!" Hughes said. "If it's clear, we'll keep going every night until we're all out. But in the meantime we'll shift to a better hiding place."

"There's no other place big enough and hidden enough for everyone," Stephen said. "I don't know how we'll get supplies in—"

"You'll have to," Hughes said, daring Stephen to say more. Stephen started to, then bit back his words.

"I'll go tonight," Davie offered, stepping into the ring.

Elias looked at Davie in awe.

"Thank you, Davie," Stephen said.

Elias couldn't stay quiet any longer. This was all partly his fault. Pennyrile hadn't gotten close until he'd crooked Elias into carrying letters for him. And now this. It made him want to bury himself in some hole deeper than where they stood now, the shame he felt at the danger he'd put them in. Elias swallowed hard. "How long do you think you'll have before he comes?"

Stephen and Hughes exchanged looks. "There's no way to know," Stephen said. "But I can't imagine he'd wait long. Not having left me behind to warn everyone."

He was right. They had to be ready. Soon.

"Get some extra bodies on the river watches," Hughes ordered.

Men began to stir into action. But something troubled Elias.

"Who says he'll only try the river?"

Stephen frowned. "He's a river pirate, Elias. And that's the clearest way through the middle of the ball of nothing on my map. It's what I'd do."

Elias saw the reason, but Pennyrile and Stephen couldn't be more different. How did any of them know what he would do?

Chapter Nineteen

ANGLER'S LOOP

Ncave on its head. There were search parties above
and belowground. Croghan suspended his rounds to
direct and participate in the searches. He called all the
slaves off the tours and had them join the hunt. And
though Elias was confined to his hut and spoke precious
little to Stephen or Nick, he expected Haven was just as
panicked.

But after two days with no signs of Pennyrile, and with
no news of his appearance at any of the towns nearby, the
uproar finally began to ebb. Croghan could neglect his
patients no longer, so he resumed his examinations.

The doctor, of course, continued to worry, as did Elias,

though for different reasons. Two days Pennyrile had been gone. Two days to prepare. But for what?

And Davie had not returned from his scouting mission.

"You gonna send out another search party later?" Elias asked, cautious, as the doctor examined him.

"After the tours are finished for the day, I'll have Stephen and Nick and Mat go out again. I'm still flummoxed by how he slipped off in the first place. Lillian really should have kept a closer watch."

Lillian had fibbed to the doctor, forced to say that she'd gone in to sit with Nedra and that Pennyrile must have snuck off then. Croghan had been fit to be tied. Elias wondered how much Croghan would worry about Pennyrile if he knew that the rogue had hit poor Lillian in the back of the head like a coward.

Elias burned with wanting to tell him.

For his part, the doctor didn't quite know what to do with himself. He'd listened to Elias's chest three times. "I sent Stephen to look again today. Nick is out as well. I can't afford to delay the tours any longer, so Mat will be taking a group this morning. I've a couple of other men who mostly work up at the hotel out looking in the forest and along the river, but—" He broke off, looking past Elias. "I can't deny I fear the worst."

Elias stayed quiet. Doctor Croghan had no idea that the

truth was much more awful than what he was probably imagining.

"The growth on his neck was spreading," Croghan said, sounding so sorry about it that it was hard for Elias to keep back what he knew about Pennyrile. "My treatments weren't doing much for the poor man. I shouldn't have admitted him in the first place, but he was so persistent. And so devoted to my treatments after he arrived."

Elias dug his fingernails into his palms. It rankled him something fierce, having to go on letting the doctor think Pennyrile was some poor lost lamb.

Elias still wondered if they should—*could*—trust the doctor. But Croghan, in the end, *owned* Stephen and Nick and all the others. Maybe he treated his slaves better than some, but how would he react to learning that those slaves he trusted so much were hiding runaways right under his nose, in his own cave?

It was a big leap to go from being decent to your own slaves to wishing others could get free. And helping runaways was a crime.

Bedivere flutter-hopped from the table to the quilt, curving his neck down toward Elias's hand to see if he had any feed hidden in his palm.

Croghan eyed the bird. "We noticed one of the pigeons he kept was missing, so that makes me think he might have been going toward the entrance to release it, though I thought he'd abandoned the practice weeks ago. He could have gotten lost on the way there or back . . . or fallen or . . ." He trailed off, still watching the bird. He tilted his head, looking oddly like Bedivere. "You two had become friendly, hadn't you?"

Elias's face grew hot. *Friendly.* The word made his flesh goose up. But he only said, "We visited a little. When I fetched food for Bedivere."

"Did he say anything? Anything odd?"

Elias coaxed Bedivere onto his wrist. "Odd?"

"About things inside the cave?"

Elias was careful not to react at all. "Not to my recollection—"

"It's just that"—the doctor checked Elias's eyes—"he once asked me about springs in the cave."

Elias focused on Bedivere, the way the feathers on his wings nestled neatly into each other, the knobs on his toes. Anything but the doctor and his question. "We didn't talk much about the cave," Elias said.

"I think he'd gotten into his head there was some fountain of youth in there somewhere," the doctor said sadly, feeling around Elias's neck. "He asked about it only once, but—" He stopped himself, fingertips going to the scab that had formed at Elias's temple.

"What happened here?" the doctor asked.

Elias shied away, the scrape still stinging, the skin bruised and sore around it. "Just knocked my head. Being careless."

The doctor seemed dissatisfied, but Elias was saved from telling further half truths when Nick appeared at the door.

"Sir?" Nick was breathing fast, the top of his pack spotted with rain.

Croghan stirred. "What is it, Nick?"

"Titus up at the hotel just tol' me somethin'. . . ." Nick stole a look at Elias before he continued. "Horse missing from the stables. Belonged to that painter fella who'd come round to draw. Titus figured the painter hadn't shut the stall good, but they still ain't found it wandering."

"Why is this the first I'm hearing of it?" Croghan's voice grew sharp. Elias noticed his trousers had a new tear at the hem.

"Titus weren't keen to bother you with Mr. Pennyrile missin', but then he seen a saddle was gone too and he reckoned—"

Croghan sounded not quite relieved, but at least calmer. "That might be the best news of all," he said.

To Elias, the fact that Pennyrile had likely stolen the horse wasn't exactly welcome, but it did explain how the man had disappeared so completely and so quickly.

Croghan ran his hands through his hair, causing it to stick up at odd angles. "I must say, the possibility is better than the alternative. I was beginning to fear that one of the tours would happen upon him. Go back up top and send riders toward Cave City and Bowling Green," he ordered Nick. "Maybe someone saw him. Even on horseback, Pennyrile couldn't have gotten far in his state."

Nick withdrew, leaving Elias and Croghan alone again. Croghan stared at Bedivere.

"I shouldn't have let him stay," Croghan said to himself, almost forgetting Elias was there. "Not when his mind seemed to be slipping."

Elias felt bad for him. "You did all you could for him, Doctor."

Croghan swallowed hard. "But it wasn't enough, was it? None of it is enough." He was more broken down than Elias imagined he could be. Croghan was so low, so despairing. Elias realized that while there were all those runaways down below whose world had just been blown apart, Croghan's had too. His last chance at medical success seemed to be dying with the lot of his patients.

"But at least we've had one bright spot." The doctor forced a smile. "I wrote your mother," he explained. "Sharing news of your recovery."

"Really? When?" Elias asked.

Croghan narrowed his eyes, thinking. "Before all this happened, Pennyrile vanishing, I mean. Thursday, perhaps? She'll have the letter soon if not already. I told her there was nothing left for me to do for you. I thought about asking if I could keep you at the hotel for a while, just to see if your recovery lasted, to make sure the consumption didn't recur. If I'm perfectly forthright, I'd love to have more time to figure out why you're better and everyone else . . ."

He trailed off, listening to Nedra coughing weakly from across the ward.

"But it wouldn't be right to keep you from your family."

"You mean . . ."

Croghan snapped his bag shut and sat forward on the chair. "Yes, young man," he said. "I'm sending you home. As soon as I have your mother's reply, you'll be on your way. Possibly within the week."

His first reaction was joy. A week! He'd get to go home! He'd run with Charger on the beach, maybe even go back to school. It seemed almost too good to believe—even the part about school. Most of all, it confirmed what he'd been too afraid to admit to even himself all this time. He *was* better. He wasn't going to die.

And yet another thought struck him. *A week.* Haven! He couldn't leave. Not when Haven was in danger.

"Are you all right, Elias?" the doctor asked. "I should have thought you'd be much happier at such news."

"I am happy," Elias managed. "Just surprised a little. I miss home terrible, but I might miss this place a little too."

Croghan stood. "It does grow on people, I think. And it certainly has on you. Go and soak it up while you may," he said, sliding his watch from his waistcoat. "Mat's tour should be along soon. You ought to be able to catch it up at Broadway. Maybe he'll have a new tale to tell today. Maybe he'll show you something you haven't seen before."

Elias buttoned up his shirt and wrapped the green scarf about his neck. But Croghan didn't go. Instead he stood there, looking at Elias. Then he stuck out his hand. Elias shook it, like men do when they're finished doing business. And by the look of Croghan, they were finished. The doctor was, at any rate.

Elias laid out food for Bedivere.

Bedivere.

What would he do with the pigeon? He supposed he'd figure out a way to fetch him home. Tillie would love him. Granny would hate him. The notion made him smile. Maybe Nick could help fashion some kind of cage to transport him in.

The wondering of it carried him down the slope, but

as he made his way up to Giant's Coffin, his worries all climbed back up as well. He wasn't in the mood to take the tour. But he wasn't keen on sitting on his hands back in the ward, either.

The tour was already past the coffin. Elias usually loved to hear Mat give the tourists a bad time, but today it didn't appeal the same way. Plus the group was duller than usual. Elias did a quick count. Eight men, no ladies among them. That was peculiar. There was almost always a wife or a sister or a mother in the group. *Pity,* Elias mused. The ladies' reactions and carryings-on were often the best part. They scared the best.

Odder still was the way the men didn't seem to care a whit about what Mat pointed out. Most folk spent all their time with their heads thrown back, swiveling around like owls trying to take it all in. But these men seemed more interested in Mat himself.

Mat was off too. He wasn't lashing out and talking roughly. He kept his voice low, only giving out the most necessary of details.

Why, Mat seemed nervous!

Elias started to move closer to see what was so odd about this group, when he felt a presence at his elbow.

Jonah. Hands on his hips, eyes were narrowed at Mat.

"H'lo, Jonah," Elias whispered.

"Mornin'," Jonah offered.

Mat's group slipped around a bend. The two boys followed.

"Doc means to send me home. Reckons I'm better."

"That's good. Real good."

"Davie come back yet?"

Jonah acted as if he didn't hear. "Give me that lamp," he said, reaching for it. He stowed it in a cleft in the wall, and it glowed bright enough to guide them back, but not bright enough to show them off.

"What're you doin?" Elias asked.

"Teachin' you to go in the dark." He took hold of Elias's wrist and led him toward the others. "Want to get a closer look."

"You seen it too?" Elias whispered. "How odd that group Mat's leading is?"

"Somethin's peculiar," Jonah said.

Elias found the walking got easier as they went on, but he couldn't imagine doing it without Jonah leading him. Not in a million years. He felt Jonah yank hard on his wrist, pulling him to the left, away from the group, and felt the path slope sharply down. Jonah moved like a fish through a stream. "Here."

Soon Elias could see light breaking up ahead.

Jonah explained, in a voice two steps below a whisper,

"We're coming up from Indian Avenue. Get a better look this way and they won't see us."

Sure enough, they reached a short wall of rock and peeked over, finding themselves at eye level with the floor of the Star Chamber.

Mat stood on a rise above the tour group twenty yards off, facing Elias and Jonah's hiding spot. Mat had set the torch for the stars to start twinkling, but even this did not seem to impress the men. Mat had fallen silent.

The sight of Mat struck dumb was strange enough, but there was something stranger.

Elias counted the group again. Ten.

Ten?

Ten men surrounded Mat.

Ten where there had been only eight before.

And then Elias heard it: the sound of chalk against a slate.

Elias's lungs tightened up all of a sudden, as if the wheeze that had been gone for so long was now creeping back. He panicked, ducked back, and flattened himself against the wall.

Elias felt Jonah's fingernails dig into his wrist: a silent message. He'd seen it too.

They'd already come!

Pennyrile and this other fellow must have been waiting

down in the Star Chamber for Mat to bring the group there.

Pennyrile's river pirates had walked right in the front door.

One of the men said something.

"Look here, somebody told—" Mat began before a rap on the slate cut him off.

Elias screwed up his courage and peeked over again. Pennyrile was scrawling on his slate. Mat stared, wide-eyed, looking from man to man and shaking his head. "I don't know what you're on about," he said. "There's nothing down there!"

"Quit your lying!" the man beside Pennyrile growled. "We know. We have that other one's maps!" He waved Stephen's book in the air, his thumb marking the place where the big map spread across the two pages in the middle. The two sides of the book flapped like a pigeon's wings.

He signaled to the man to his left, a giant, big as Davie at least, who hauled Mat roughly off the rock and threw a fist into his gut. Elias winced as Mat doubled over.

The same man spoke again. "We'll pay you well. My brother says you're the least loyal of the whole lot down here."

Brother! The man was Pennyrile's brother! But Elias didn't have time to think on it long.

Mat still was half hunkered over, sputtering. Elias and Jonah stood stock-still.

They both knew Mat didn't have much to do with Haven. Mat merely put up with Croghan, and he had more reason than anybody to try to take what he could and get himself gone. However, Mat raised himself fully up, still struggling to catch his breath. "Thank your brother for the kindness," he said, breathing heavily. "But seeing how I don't have a notion of any underground colony, I'm afraid I must disappoint him."

Pennyrile was writing again. "Yes, Victor," the man said, after glancing at the slate. Then he addressed Mat, handing Stephen's book over to Pennyrile. "My brother expected you might set yourself stubborn against us."

He pulled something from inside the folds of his long traveling coat and held it out so Mat could get a good look.

Mat changed in a second. Fire leaped back into his eyes. "Where'd you get that?"

Elias felt sick.

It was the doll Josie had made for Mat's little girl.

"Where?" Mat demanded.

"Same place we found your two little brats this morning," Pennyrile's brother said. "Over by your place, near the river. Your wife—Parthena, ain't it? She'll be sore worried over 'em by now—"

"Those're my children!" Mat pleaded.

Pennyrile's brother waggled the doll in front of Mat. "Well, by the letter of the law, they belong to Parthena's master, don't they? But either way, we've got 'em now. And whether they end up back at home safe with you and your pretty wife, or carried off downriver with us, where we'll sell 'em off to the worst, low-down—"

"All right!" Mat roared. "All right."

Pennyrile's brother chuckled. "See, boys? Their kind do feel attachments after all."

As the others laughed, Elias wanted to scream. He found his hand clutching up a fist-size rock, and he ached to throw it.

"I—" Mat began before catching himself.

Mat was looking right at them. Past the shoulders of the ring of men surrounding him straight at the spot where Elias and Jonah were hiding.

Though it was dark, though they hadn't made a sound or a movement, Mat somehow knew they were there.

"I'll show you the way."

Elias couldn't breathe.

"It's a long way," Mat said, nearly shouting, much louder than he'd been talking before. "From here it's quickest to head on down Main Cave, then through the Rotunda, and the Cataracts down to Echo River. Then we got to go upriver, 'crost Lake Lethe, work up through Fat Man's, cross Bottomless, then over t'the Wooden Bowl, and then sideways before we cross Smiley Pit."

What now? Elias pictured the route in his head, thought of all the walks he'd made down to Haven. Fat Man's wasn't on the line at all. And the route Mat just laid out would take double the time it needed to, what with getting that pack of men up the river and then across Lethe.

"I don't see that on the map," Pennyrile's brother said.

Mat laughed. "'Course you don't see it on the map!" He sounded more like the old Mat than before. "Bishop ain't stupid enough to lay it all out in the map. The map just works around it."

"How far?" one asked.

"Couple of hours," Mat said. "But the river will be a trick. We ain't got a boat big enough for all y'all. We'll have to ferry across in batches."

"What's Smiley Pit?" another of the men asked, sounding almost like he didn't want to know.

"Smiley isn't on the regular tour, no way," Mat said. "Too dangerous. No bridge like Bottomless. It ain't so wide, but it's double deep and the ground's uneven." He gave the men a proper Mat Bransford glare. "The best way to protect things is to put them out of reach."

And then Elias knew what Mat was doing. Why he was

shouting so loud, why he was taking the pirates the long way round to Haven.

He was giving Elias and Jonah time. Time to get Stephen or Nick or Croghan or anybody. Time to get to Haven and warn everyone.

Jonah must have had the same thought at the same moment. His hand found Elias's arm and started to steer him back down the tunnel.

"Move, then," Pennyrile's brother was barking. "And look lively, men." But he was already an echo.

Elias and Jonah backtracked steady and quick to the main stretch of cave. When they were far enough away, Elias asked in a rush, "How you think Mat knew we were there?"

Jonah was nearly running. "Mat always knows when I'm lurking. And he'd have seen your light before."

"I'll go find Stephen or Nick or somebody," Elias offered.

"And I'll go to Haven and let 'em know. Then let's meet back at Smiley. If we got to make a stand, I don't think there's a better spot."

Chapter Twenty

MAGNUS HITCH

Elias sprinted up the hill back into the ward, lamp swinging wildly. He saw two shapes bent over the fire. Nick was back! "Nick!" he called out. Nick glanced up from the pan he was helping Lillian scrub out. "Where's Stephen?" Elias shouted.

"Down Gothic way—"

"We got to find him!"

Nick straightened up. "What—"

"Is that Elias?" Nedra called from her window.

Elias glanced at the window, then back at Lillian. "She all right?"

"No worse. She was sleeping 'til you came in hollerin'—"

"*He's* back!" Elias fought to keep his voice from going shrill.

Lillian's eyes grew wide.

"How many with him?" Nick asked quietly.

"Ten all together. One of 'em's his brother. We have to go!"

"Get!" Lillian ordered, shooing them off and then scurrying over to check on Nedra.

Nick grabbed his pack. "Where we going?"

Elias's eyes fell on a length of rope coiled near the fire, and he snatched it up. "Smiley," he whispered.

As they barreled down the slope, Elias quickly told Nick what he and Jonah had seen.

"You sure it was Pennyrile?"

"Using that slate to talk. Can't be many who do that."

They found Stephen at Gothic. "Croghan send you out to look again?"

"No need," Nick said, leaving it to Elias to explain.

"Pennyrile's here." The story tumbled out of Elias as the three of them ran past the Camel, dropped down the rocky slope, and hurried through the passage that led to Smiley Pit.

They stared at the jagged half-moon carved into the rock. It seemed to laugh at them now. It didn't look nearly as wide or as terrifying as Elias recalled. The room around it was barely bigger than Elias's hut. Not much of a place to make a stand. But it would have to serve.

"You sure ten of them?" Nick asked.

"I'm sure," Elias said.

"I saw Parthena before I come down. She rode over with Mat today to work in the kitchens. Left the children at home. If they've been took, Parthena likely don't know yet," Nick offered.

"Pennyrile's men didn't see you two?" Stephen asked.

"They'd have run us down if they had."

Nick rubbed the back of his neck and shifted the twist of tobacco to his other cheek. "River'll slow 'em some, but they'll get here eventually. Mat cain't run 'em round forever."

Stephen agreed. "Then we'll have to be ready, won't we?"

"They got guns?" Nick asked.

Elias hadn't seen any, but then the sight of the husk doll had been enough to gain Mat's compliance. "More'n likely."

It was grim. Ten armed men against four, or five if Mat could get free. And those ten probably with weapons, probably with plenty of experience fighting and brawling.

"Should we bring some folks up from Haven to help?" Elias asked.

Stephen shook his head. "They'll hide, which they

ought to anyhow. And there's not enough room in here to move free. Jonah knows it. He'll keep them down below."

"What are we gonna do?"

"Can't shoot if they can't see," Nick said simply. "How many lanterns they got, Elias?" He crossed to the wall, crouched, and rubbed at a spot near the floor.

Elias pictured the men in the Star Chamber. "Two," he recalled. "Mat had one, and one of the fellas had th'other."

"We can get them lights out," Nick said, shedding his pack. "They'll be blind. Ever'body knows a blind fish is the easiest of all to trap."

Trap? Elias felt like they were speaking in code.

But Stephen was catching on. "You got your drill, Nick?"

Nick already had it out. Stephen fumbled out of his pack straps and rummaged inside until he found his own drill and a pair of eyebolts.

"What're you doing?" Elias asked.

Nick was already at work, spinning the drill's hand crank furiously. Stephen went to the opposite side of the chamber and got to work. "We'll put a couple of bolts in here," he said, and then pointed over to Nick. "And there. Then we can set up a trip wire."

"How long's it take to drill the holes?" Elias asked.

"Maybe quarter hour each," Stephen answered. "Stone's plenty soft down here."

"What should I do?" Elias asked, desperate to help.

Stephen didn't look up. "I seem to recall you're handy with a rope, Elias."

The rope.

Elias dropped the rope from his shoulder and began to pay out the line, laying it across the floor of the chamber end to end. "We'll have to be on the other side," he said, looking at a big boulder they could hide behind, perfect cover for springing the trap. He jumped Smiley and then saw quickly that they wouldn't have enough length.

"Bells!" he hissed. "Too short!"

"Check my pack!" Stephen whispered. They were all too aware that the gang of men might any moment draw near enough to hear them.

Elias hopped back over, too scared now of Pennyrile's crew reaching them first to worry about falling in the pit. He found another rope in Stephen's kit.

"Got it!" He crouched down, setting to work splicing the lines together. Then he leaped back over and checked the length of the rope. Plenty long—they could even let it drape down inside Smiley so maybe the pirates wouldn't notice it when they came into the chamber.

Jonah appeared behind him. "What y'all doing?"

Elias hurriedly sketched out the plan for the snare. "Are they all set down below?"

"As can be," Jonah said. "I met Josie on the watch, and she ran in the rest of the way. They gonna make 'emselves scarce but send a handful out to hide in the maze so they can get a drop on the pirates if they make it past us."

Elias knew none of them had weapons to match the ones Pennyrile's crew might be carrying. Even if they managed to surprise the pirates before they could get their guns firing, he wasn't sure they'd be able to overpower them all.

The trap had to work. If it didn't . . .

Anxious with waiting, he jumped back across, hovering over Nick's shoulder as he worked.

"Hold the lamp up, 'lias," Nick said as the drill's gears ground and whirred, the bit making powder of the stone. The limey smell of dust filled the chamber. Every dozen turns or so, Nick had to stop and blow a great puff of breath into the hole to clear out the powder. Then he'd check the depth with his finger and start drilling once again.

The whole thing went faster than Elias thought it possibly could. Still, he worried it was taking too long. How long had they been at it? How much longer did they have? How long could Mat stretch out the journey? Each minute that passed seemed a day.

By the time Nick had the hole as deep as his second knuckle, Elias felt frantic.

"Bolt!" Nick said, looking around.

"Here!" Stephen said, digging one from his pocket. Elias scurried over and passed it to Nick.

Nick fit the tip into the hole, and twisted and wiggled it as far as it would go by hand. Then he grabbed the hammer, hands trembling, the shaft slipping in his sweat-slicked palm. "I'm spent, Elias," Nick said, huffing. "C'you drive a nail?"

Elias snatched up the hammer and crowded past Nick.

"Wait!" Nick said. He snatched Elias's scarf and laid it across the top of the bolt to muffle the sound. Elias went to work, hammering away. It was still louder than he would have liked, and the scarf slowed the work some, but Elias got it done. Nick gave the bolt a tug.

"Solid!" he cried out to Stephen.

Jonah was already helping Stephen drive the other bolt in the rest of the way. "Nearly there!" Stephen said, chest heaving, dripping sweat.

Elias tossed the hammer in Nick's pack and grabbed the end of the rope. He threaded it through the eye of the bolt and anchored it off with a strong bowline. It would hold. Then he bear-crawled to the other side, where Jonah was already feeding the rope through Stephen's bolt.

"We'll have to get 'em back out of here once they're

blinded," Stephen said, packing up. "I'm going to have to go up and find Croghan and get some men from the hotel, send somebody over to Cave City for the marshal."

"They'll come, you think?" Elias lay on his belly, carefully drooping the line just inside the pit so it would be out of sight.

"They'll come when they hear Mat's kids got took," Nick said, tossing his knapsack over the pit. "They belong to Parthena's master. Nobody looks kindly on somebody else's slaves getting thieved."

Elias didn't have time to feel angry at that. None of them did. Satisfied the rope was as hidden as it could be, he jumped to the other side of Smiley. Nick followed, hiding his pack behind the rock and picking up the end of the rope.

"I'm goin' with you, Stephen," Jonah said. No one objected. "I'll see if I can catch up to Mat and them. See how far along they are, how much time we've got."

But no one moved just yet. Nick and Elias stood on the far side of Smiley; Stephen and Jonah stood on the other.

"Check it," Stephen ordered. Elias and Nick both grabbed the end of the rope, gave it a hard tug. The rope snapped up, zinging through the bolts and snapping taut between them on the opposite side of the pit. The bolts and knots held true.

It didn't look like much, but Elias prayed it was enough.

"Good," Stephen said as Jonah tucked the rope back over the edge of Smiley. Stephen scanned the floor to make sure they hadn't left anything behind. Then he and Jonah started off. At the edge of the chamber, Stephen whispered, "Elias?"

A wave of panic crashed through Elias. Had they come already? "What?" he whispered from behind the rock.

"Thank you."

"Huh?"

"Whatever happens now, you and Jonah did good," Stephen went on. Then he ducked out before Elias could respond.

Nick cocked an eyebrow at Elias, then he doused their light.

In the darkness, Elias whispered, "Don't know what Stephen was thanking me for. All I did was tie some knots."

Nick huffed. "You give us a chance," he said. "Thinking quick like you and Jonah did—that's worth heaps more'n a knot or two."

Chapter Twenty-One

FINGER TRAP

Elias fiddled with the end of the rope, tying and retying it, barely finishing one knot before starting the next, all neater and easier to work out than the knot in his stomach.

It was awful, the waiting. The dark pressing in from every side Elias had grown used to. The waiting and the worrying that the plan might fail, the wishing something would go ahead and happen, those feelings were new. And unbearable.

He thought of all the runaways down in Haven. The months they'd spent waiting, worrying that they might be discovered or that they wouldn't ever get away. He wondered how they could hold up under the constant gnawing, expectant feeling that ate at him now.

And now maybe it would all be for nothing. But no! That couldn't happen. Still, the hoping and the worrying and the fretting set his leg to bouncing, and he couldn't have stopped it even if he'd tried.

Nick, however, seemed as still and quiet as dead seas. "Settle down, 'lias," Nick whispered, resting a hand on his knee.

"Sorry." Elias tried, but the leg wouldn't obey. "Maybe I should stay on the other side," he offered. "Round up the lanterns when they drop them."

Nick was resolute. "If they don't break or roll into the pit, Mat or Jonah'll kick 'em in. And you can't go in the dark like them. 'Sides, I need your strength here on the rope."

Nick was three times as strong as Elias, and they both knew it, but Elias let it pass.

"It'll work, won't it, Nick?"

Nick lifted his hand off Elias's knee. "Don't know," he said honestly. "Hope so."

Elias hugged both knees to his chest to try and quiet that jittery leg. "I—"

"Shh!"

Elias's hands grew clammy. He listened. And then he heard the soft pattering footfall.

Jonah.

"They're a few minutes behind, maybe less," he whispered breathlessly. "Y'all ready?"

Elias said they were. "They seen you?" Nick asked.

"No," Jonah said. "They're keeping the lights in front and staying bunched up tight."

"That's good, ain't it?" Elias said. "If they're up there together, we can likely get 'em at the same go!"

"Can you hide o'er that side?" Nick asked Jonah.

"Reckon," Jonah said. "Got a little spot I can tuck myself."

"Get in it and get ready. Mat may need you when the lights go out," Nick ordered. Jonah complied without another word, and the silence settled back in. Just as it began to be unbearable again, the sound of a cough echoed toward them.

"Look sharp," Nick warned.

Elias made himself smaller behind the boulder and peeked out through the little crack between the rock and the wall. He tightened his grip on the rope, his heart pounding so loud that he was sure it must be echoing across Smiley. Light began to dance off the ceiling and the walls.

The two men holding the lamps came into the clearing first. Elias saw them take in the pit, saw their eyes grow wide. The men behind them began to crowd the passage, edging forward, but the first two weren't coming closer.

Mat was in the middle of the group, glancing around like he was looking for someone, but even Elias could tell Mat didn't notice the rope or see them hiding.

So far so good.

"Careful now, pit's up there," Mat said halfheartedly, like he didn't care if they fell in or not.

"Hold it," a voice called out. It was the same one that had done most of the talking earlier. Elias could see the speaker now in the light; he was a healthier version of Pennyrile. His brother, for sure. That explained the seal on the letter at least.

Then came the telltale scratching on the slate. "He says to send the lights ahead, to show the way over and what's on the other side," Pennyrile's brother said. Elias's grip tightened on the rope to the point that it felt like his knuckles were fit to split out of his skin.

The two with the lamps edged slowly forward, side by side.

Bells! They were going too slowly. The rope wouldn't trip them up if they were creeping that way.

"Hurry it up, you Lily-livers!" Pennyrile's brother barked. Luckily, the two men seemed to be more afraid of Pennyrile and his brother than they were of falling into Smiley, because they quickened their steps just enough. Elias watched as they drew nearer and nearer . . . one more step . . .

"Now!" Nick whispered. Elias and Nick heaved, leaning back as the rope sang through the bolts, drew taut, and held.

And then Elias felt it. The rope quivered and shook. He braced his feet against the rock as the rope took the weight of the two men getting snagged up in the lines.

"What—" one of the men cried out as he fell, the other making a noise that was almost a scream. They both began to tumble forward, arms windmilling. Almost falling, but not quite. The men were used to the pitch and roll of a boat, and would have better balance than average, but their arms still spun, they still faltered. Elias saw both of them staring in horror at the pit, and the fear of falling in made the difference. One of them let his lamp fly out of his hand in order to steady himself. It sailed up, crashed against the ceiling, and then dropped like an ember into Smiley's gaping maw. Elias almost whooped with joy. Then the second man gave up fighting his fall, deciding it would be better to drop hard short of the pit than risk rolling in. As he went over, he hugged the lamp to his chest, trying to protect it. But unable to twist in time, he landed belly first on top of the lantern, snuffing it out.

The tiniest spell of silence followed. No breath, no noise—nothing but the quiet. But it was long enough for

the fear and the understanding of what had just happened
to swell up and crash over the pirates.

"Hey!"

"What—"

"The devil!"

"Tarnation!"

There were other words, saltier ones that Elias had
heard, and plenty he hadn't. Elias himself was near
enough to panicking, near enough to forgetting where
he was, even though he knew he was secure beside Nick.
Jonah called above the roar. "Up and out, Mat!" And Elias
knew that already they were making their way along the
walls out of the passage. Then there was more scrabbling,
the soft thudding sound of a kick or a punch landing, and
the sharp cry of pain that followed, and then the shouts
swelled up again.

"Grab him!"

"Get back here!"

The volley of foul words and awful curses that flew up
brought a small smile to Elias's face.

Then Pennyrile's brother bellowed, "Quiet!"

And then a voice that sounded like it was carving the
words with a rusty knife broke in. "Easy, men," it said.
There was only one man who could sound that crooked,
that out of practice with the art of speaking.

"Grab on to the man next to you," Pennyrile said. "I expect we'll find our guide has slipped us." Elias let the line go slack. He hadn't thought that Pennyrile could frighten him more, but that *voice*. And if anyone was crafty enough to figure a way out of the mess they were in, it would be Pennyrile.

And they had no more traps to spring.

Then came the sound of a match striking. Of course Pennyrile would remember matches! Pennyrile's mean smile appeared in the light. "Porter?" he called out.

"M'lamp's busted," Porter—apparently—answered, holding the crumpled tin up to catch the match light.

"The oil?" Pennyrile leaned close.

Porter shrank back. "Spilt. Most on the rock, but m'coat's soaked."

"Dawkins?" Pennyrile asked.

"Lost mine. Could be on the other side. Or down that hole."

Elias could almost see the wheels spinning in Pennyrile's mind. He had to remind himself to breathe. The match sputtered, burning right down to Pennyrile's fingertips. The darkness closed back in.

A few of the men began to work themselves up again.

"The light!"

"Please, boss!"

"Stop your caterwauling!" Pennyrile rasped. He waited, almost as if he wanted the men to obey him before he struck the next match. Finally a white burst of the phosphorous flared from Pennyrile's hand like a conjurer's trick. "Give me the coat, Porter."

Elias felt Nick, tense, lean across him to look through the crack in the rock as the light moved closer to the edge of the pit, closer to their hiding place.

"We're not finished yet," Pennyrile said. "One of you dogs find me something long enough to make a torch."

A torch? But how?

Elias's heart sank. The coat. Soaked in oil.

Pennyrile could use it to make a torch.

Bells! The devil himself might have hunkered down and waited for rescue, but not Pennyrile.

The men stared at Pennyrile. "Well? A stick, anything!" he demanded. The pirates stayed put, but they cast about halfheartedly. Stephen had swept the area clean. There was nothing on the other side to help them.

"Someone has to have *something*!" Pennyrile was losing patience, the match nearing its end. How many did he have?

"I got my Bowie," said a ratlike little fellow on the left, his eyes wet with worry. He drew a knife that was not quite a sword from a scabbard inside his coat. The Bowie blade shone wickedly as the man flipped it in his hand to extend the grip to Pennyrile. Pennyrile dropped his match, then struck another.

"We have to go back, boss!" whimpered the big fellow who'd slugged Mat.

Pennyrile didn't respond; he simply passed the knife to his brother. He took the coat from Porter and hurled it at another of his crew, a man with lank black hair hanging like seaweed around his face who began wrapping the coat tightly around the blade Pennyrile's brother held.

"Back?" Pennyrile sneered. "No."

"We ain't got no guide!" another voice called out.

"The guide we had led us on a fool's chase. But I've been on Gothic Avenue before, and I know the way from there," Pennyrile said. "No, we won't go back. Not now."

The completed torch came forward to Pennyrile. Pennyrile kissed the match to its surface in several places. Elias prayed that it wouldn't light, his hopes growing each time Pennyrile had to try another spot, but they sank when the flame caught, tongues of orange and blue licking up the sides of the coat.

Elias noticed Nick's lips were moving silently, but his eyes were on Pennyrile.

"What *can* we do, Victor?" his brother asked. The pirates around him seemed emboldened by the success of the torch. Elias knew it would burn itself out soon enough, but it might give them the time they needed.

"We press on. Find the colony ourselves."

An uneasy silence followed as the pirates looked from one to another, each one thinking the same thing, each afraid to say it. Finally a voice from the back asked, "But how we gonna find our way out?"

"Fools! We have a map," Pennyrile said, holding up Stephen's book.

"I ain't goin' near that hole!" The biggest one, his face pocked with scars, pointed at Smiley.

Pennyrile sniffed and edged nearer. "You can clear it in a stride, Jones. We're going."

Elias almost bolted up from his hiding place, but Nick's firm hand on his shoulder kept him anchored. Pennyrile seemed to sense the movement, for he stalled, his eyes flickering across the pit. When no other noise or movement came, he went on, one step closer. Now he was less than a foot from the edge. "It can't be far from here if they bothered with a trap. And if need be, we'll rook one of the runaways into leading us out in exchange for his freedom once we've found the colony."

"We don't know that! It could be miles from here!" the rat-faced one said. "And that torch won't hold us long."

Pennyrile was clearly fuming but didn't bother to

respond. His eyes were drawn to something else. He took a step closer to the pit. "We may not need the torch much longer after all," he said, looking over the edge.

The next thing Elias knew, the rope moved in his hands. He watched in horror as Pennyrile pulled it slowly until it was drooping from his grip, exposed. Pennyrile traced the rope to the bolt anchored in the wall. "Well, well," he said as he spied the other bolt on the opposite wall. Pennyrile gazed across the pit, following the rope to the point where it disappeared behind the rock Elias and Nick hid behind.

"Not long at all," Pennyrile said, taking a step nearer the edge.

"I don't reckon I'd keep walking," Nick called out without preamble. Surprised silence fell again.

Then Pennyrile gave what might have been a laugh. "See, boys? They're even closer than I expected."

"Best stay put and wait for Stephen and Mat to fetch the law. That's th'only way you lot are walking out of this cave alive," Nick said.

"That's Nick, isn't it?" Pennyrile sounded almost cheerful. "Well, Nick, I'm a fair cardplayer, no mistake. And I can hear a bluff as easy as I can spot one with my eyes. And I'd lay money on something else: you'll not have stranded yourself without light."

The torch flared hot for a moment, the edges of the coat peeling outward. A chunk of the fabric burned off and floated down into the pit.

"Show yourself now, Nick, and maybe we won't tell Croghan you knew about this little batch of runaways."

"Tell Croghan what you want," Nick fired back. "But wait till he come down here with the law and haul you out himself."

Pennyrile stared at the rock, his eye twitching. Elias could see the grease and fat smeared at his neck sores glistening in the torchlight, the wrapping soaked through. He looked stronger than when he'd last been in the cave with them. He'd come all through the cave with Mat, and still seemed fresher than he had that day Croghan had forced them all to exercise. It dawned on Elias that Pennyrile's feebleness had been part of his trickery. He'd been sick, but not as sick as he let on. It was the only thing that would have accounted for him being able to escape the cave with Stephen's book so quickly that night.

"No, boy, I don't think I will," Pennyrile said. "Men, show the Negro why we won't be turning back."

Elias watched as the pack of men rearranged itself, many of the men drawing pistols of all varieties into view. The barrels glinted in the torchlight as they pointed at the rock Elias and Nick hid behind.

Elias drew back. "You see, we've come prepared," Pennyrile explained. "And all it will take is one of us to come across. We'll have your lantern and be on our way, and won't think twice about leaving a few neat holes in you for our trouble if you have any more tricks planned."

Pistols. Six of them. But the men continued glancing nervously at the pit, none ready to be the first across. Elias knew how they felt. Still, it wouldn't hold them long.

"So," Pennyrile said, taking a step forward, the toe of his boot only inches from the edge. "Will you do the wise thing and help us outright?"

Nick said nothing.

"Well, then," Pennyrile rasped, sounding more impatient. "Your kind are simple, I know. I'll give you to the count of three before we come and get you."

He began to count. "One."

Nick made no sound.

"Two."

The torch popped, another ember breaking free.

"Three." Pennyrile almost sounded disappointed. "Very well," he said. "Jones, you—" Pennyrile twisted to address the men, but maybe too quickly. Because as he did, another chunk of the torch burned free, broke off, and caught in the draft of Pennyrile's movement. It dropped straight down onto his shoulder.

"Damnation!" Pennyrile cried, moving to brush it off, but it was already too late.

All that bear fat. All that whale oil. All of it smeared on his neck, all of it soaking his neck scarf, all of it rubbing off on his own coat.

Pennyrile was halfway to being a torch himself.

It happened almost too quickly for Elias to believe. Pennyrile's deft fingers scrabbled at the knot with his free hand, undoing it and sending the scarf fluttering down into the pit. But the flames had spread to the coat, and now Pennyrile panicked and tried to slip his arms from the sleeves, only to fumble his grip on the torch. As he lunged for it, he lost his balance.

His men began to scream, began to understand what was happening, but by then it was too late. Pennyrile's feet danced beneath him, his whole body teetering at the edge of the drop. He was too close for any of his men to try and tackle him to put out the flames. None were *that* loyal, save his brother, who took a step forward. "Victor!" he yelped.

Pennyrile fell. It seemed to Elias that the time between realizing the pirate would fall and the time he actually did was impossibly long. Long enough for Pennyrile to look across the pit, toward the darkness of Elias and Nick's hiding place.

Elias would never forget the sight or the man's eyes or the smell of grease and oil and smoke and fear as Pennyrile tumbled over the edge, the chamber descending again into black.

A second later Elias felt the line in his hand go taut. Instinctively, he held on, the full weight slamming him and Nick into each other and into the rock. It took him a moment to realize what it was.

Pennyrile had caught the rope!

A faint glow from six or seven feet below the pit's lip confirmed it. Elias held fast, the men on the other side were shouting, horrified. Pennyrile's brother wailed along with the others.

"Nick?" Elias managed.

"I know!" Nick grunted back.

But all at once, the line went slack. Elias tumbled back, knocking his head hard against the rock.

Pennyrile had let go.

"Victor!" Pennyrile's brother screamed.

But there was no answer. Only the faint sound of the draft created by the falling weight of Pennyrile, and then the sickening thud that came impossibly later.

And no more.

A sob erupted from the dark. Pennyrile's brother began to call, "Victor! Victor?"

When no reply came, Nick sighed. "Tol' him not to move."

"You've killed him, you low-down—"

"Afore you start your jabberin', let's get something squared."

The men began to shout and scream and curse again, each word fouler than the last until Nick had had enough. "Pipe down!" he thundered.

Elias had never heard him so angry. He'd never heard him angry at all. But it worked. "Till I hear the sound of six pistols getting tossed into that pit, I ain't lightin' m'lamp, and I ain't sending word back up to my crew to come down and fetch you," Nick growled.

"Never!"

"No!"

"We'll whip you till yer bones are showin'!"

The rest of the insults and hate were swallowed up by the roar of all the men shouting and screaming at once.

When the men finally began to lose steam, finally ran out of different ways to insult and threaten Nick without getting a rise out of him, the anger gave way to panic.

"Is he gone?" one whispered.

"He wouldn't leave us—" another said back.

"We're gonna die down here in the dark!"

"Get back here, you dirty low-down—"

"Hush up," Nick called over to them. Then he muttered to Elias, "Lord. What a bunch. Gonna whip me one second and want me to hold they hands the next."

"I ain't getting rid of my pistol!" one of them shouted out.

"Suit yourself," Nick said lightly. "But you can't eat no bullets when you start to get hungry. Can't use 'em for light, neither. And it don't matter how many matches you got between you; it ain't enough to find a way to this side, or to get yourselves out. But I wouldn't figure on that, 'less one of you was dropping breadcrumbs 'long the way. There's near a hundred miles of passages we know of down here, and even more we don't know."

"Yer lying!"

"Don't think I am. Cave's mighty big. Big enough nobody ever gonna find a mess of dead pirates. So if you want to live, chuck them pistols. If you don't, then you might as well follow your friend Pennyrile down that hole. Bad way to go, down Smiley, but I 'spect it's a sight better than waiting in the dark for death to find you in its own sweet time."

Elias smiled. Nick's words were surely finding their mark on the other side. He heard whispers across the chamber.

Something clattered across the floor and into the pit.

Nick remained calm. "C'mon, now. I know the sound of a rock getting throwed when I hear it."

More cursing.

"Don't be trying to fool old Nick. I'm a heap smarter than I look. Which you'd know if you had any light to see me by."

Elias almost whooped with laughter.

A second later he heard the first sound of something heavy whistling through air, clattering against the walls of the pit as it spun down.

"That's one," Nick said. "Old Pennyrile—devil rest him— he liked countin', didn't he?"

A bellow, half rage, half anguish, came in reply, but Pennyrile's brother didn't say any more.

Then Elias heard another pistol go over. Nick was right: they didn't sound a thing like rocks.

"Two," Nick said. "Now you gettin' the hang of it."

And then a shower of guns, one after another, some thrown so hard that they landed on the side where Elias and Nick hid. After the last pistol had been thrown, a voice shouted, "Now the light!" Elias recognized the rat-faced one's voice.

"Not quite," Nick replied. "I think I'd like to hear some knives going down too. They sound altogether differ'nt, I expect."

Elias listened as coats shifted, knives were tossed. Nick was right again. They did sound different. Some whistled. The blades clanged like broken bells.

"That's all," the big one pleaded. "We got no more weapons. Just give us the light and let us go!"

"Go?" Nick sounded offended, spitting a great stream of tobacco off into the black. "Y'all just got here. No hurry."

The men began to shout and curse and volley insults again.

"Naw," Nick said in a voice that gave up his smile. "Cave's a good place. Good place to sit and think. 'Sides, no good ever come of rushing through nothing. Make yourself at home. I think we'll sit a spell."

Chapter Twenty-Two

CLOVE HITCH

Funny thing, sitting in the dark. Real, complete darkness. The kind where no light from anywhere showed.
The kind where a body could wave a hand in front of his
own face and only know it's there because he felt the
breeze from the movement of it.

Full dark like that did a number on a man. If Elias hadn't
been in it before, hadn't been sitting right next to Nick,
hadn't spent the last month buried down there under tons
of rock where it threatened dark all the time, he wasn't
sure what he would have done while they waited for Mat
and Stephen to return.

One thing he was certain of, he would *not* have been
carrying on like Pennyrile's crew.

Those fellows were whimpering and begging. After a while Elias tossed little pebbles over their way, just to see what they'd do. But the men got so spooked every time he did it, wondering aloud what kind of thing might be creeping there in the dark, that Nick whispered to Elias to stop unless he wanted to send another one of 'em down the pit.

In the end, it was sitting in the dark like that that made them downright gentle as lambs when Mat and Stephen showed up—an hour or three later, who could tell—with lanterns and a way out. Even if they still had weapons, the sight of Mat Bransford with a double-barreled shotgun was enough to take the starch out of any man. Mat and Stephen weren't alone, either. They'd rounded up half a dozen men from the hotel, all of them armed with pistols.

Mat marched straight up to Pennyrile's brother, jabbing him in the belly with the shotgun. "Where're my girls?"

"Get this animal away from me," Pennyrile's brother gestured at Mat but looked to one of the white men who had come down with him from the hotel. "He's got no right to a gun, much less one aimed at me!"

The man stepped forward to stand beside Mat. "Those kids're owned by Mat's wife's master. And when you go stealing another man's property, you're inclined to have all kinds of folk pointing guns yer way."

"Tell me where my children are." Mat buried the barrels deeper in Pennyrile's brother's gut.

"Boat's half a mile upriver. They're on board."

"How many guards?" the deputy asked.

"One," the other Pennyrile admitted. "We brought all the hands we had down here."

Mat kept the shotgun in place, but rummaged inside the man's coat, rescuing the little husk doll from within. He gave one last jab with the barrel, spat quick down at the man's feet, and bolted from the chamber.

"Hey!" the deputy called, but Mat was already gone. He addressed one of the other men. "Go with him, Harlan. We'll catch up after we get this lot out of here."

And faster than Elias thought possible, Stephen and the others had Pennyrile's men trussed up like a stringer of catfish. Hands bound and connected to each other, they began the long slow shuffle up and out of the cave.

"You all right, Nick?" Stephen called.

Nick struck a match and lit his lamp. "Never better."

Elias found his legs and shook out the stiffness from sitting on the cave floor.

"Can't help noticing Pennyrile isn't here," Stephen said, thumbing back toward the column of men.

"He's here, all right," Nick said, pointing down into the pit. "But he ain't leaving."

Stephen looked over the rim, his expression blank. Elias couldn't tell if it meant he was sorry to think of anybody—even Pennyrile—dying like that, or if he was just annoyed that he'd fallen in such a place where he'd be impossible to get out.

Elias suspected it was the latter. Stephen coiled the rope while Nick jumped across to help. Elias lingered. He'd just gotten over his fear of Smiley Pit, and now it was not only a terrifying hole in the ground, it was also a *grave*. Back in Virginia, he and the other boys used to dare one another to walk over a fresh grave in the churchyard.

He bet none of them would have taken this dare. He didn't even want to, but there was nothing for it. So he mustered his courage, took his little run, and sailed across.

"Where's Jonah?" Elias asked as he landed on the other side.

Stephen snorted. "Slipped off. He doesn't cotton to getting seen by a bunch of strangers. He's too clever for that."

"Long as he made it okay," Elias said.

"He's all right," Nick said. "Probably found hisself a good perch to watch the parade."

Elias loved the notion of Jonah hiding, watching, like always.

"C'mon," Stephen said. "We'd better catch up. There's gonna be plenty of questions."

The three dashed up the path and caught up to the column of men near Giant's Coffin. One pirate at the back of the line muttered something about the Negro having found himself a heck of a shortcut all of a sudden, but they shut up when Stephen hushed them.

Minutes later as they hooked into Broadway, another set of lights began moving toward them fast. "What's going on?" Doctor Croghan cried out. He held his lamp high, his eyes wide with confusion at the sight of the deputy leading the band of men under heavy guard.

"We got it in hand," the deputy called back. "Coming your way."

Croghan, watching in disbelief as the prisoners filed past him, thundered, "Where is Stephen?"

"Here, sir," Stephen said. "We tried to find you, but there wasn't time—"

"Explain this at once!" Croghan said. "Lillian told me there was trouble, and then I saw Mat running with a shotgun—"

"Seems the morning tour was really a band of pirates," Stephen said quietly.

"We ain't no pirates! We're bounty hunters," one of the men said indignantly. "Came down here to collect runaways."

Croghan made a face. "Runaways? These men are not—"

"Not them," Pennyrile's brother said. "The ones down deep in the cave. The colony—"

"Colony?" Croghan looked from him to Stephen. Elias caught something in that look, a slight narrowing of the doctor's eyes, a moment of recognition, before he recovered and asked, "What nonsense is this?"

"My brother, Victor—"

"Pennyrile?" Croghan stepped closer, peering at the man. "Extraordinary, the likeness . . . Do you know where he is? He is gravely ill and—"

"They killed him," Pennyrile's brother choked out. And Elias almost felt bad for him.

"Killed?"

"Your boys set a trap and we lost our lights, and now my brother's dead in the bottom of some hole down there."

"Tol' him not to move," Nick said calmly.

Croghan's mouth opened and shut like he was trying to find the right question to ask next. "Explain!"

Nick hitched his pack up on his shoulder. "We penned 'em up, blinded 'em without light. And I told 'em to stay put till Stephen came back with the law. They'd been safe as eggs under a hen, but Pennyrile had his own mind about it. Got himself tripped up and fell down Smiley."

Croghan's eyes darkened. "And Smiley is . . ." He

waited. He didn't know about Smiley. Stephen and the others hadn't mentioned it to him.

"Good and deep," Nick confirmed.

Croghan let out a sharp breath like he'd been slammed in the belly. "Oh, dear. Poor soul—"

"He knew," Pennyrile's brother insisted. "He'd been here months, and he knew of the colony. Got himself in here to look for it."

"But . . . your brother . . . He was terribly sick . . . His scrofula," Croghan said, still not comprehending. Elias tensed, looked back and forth from Nick to Stephen. For all his high ideas and for the way he had his head in the clouds all the time, talking about frontiers and his cures, Croghan was no fool.

Pennyrile's brother charged on. "'Course he was sick. Had that King's Evil for near three years. It didn't pain him much, so we figgered on using it to get him down here, get him looking for that tonic water and that den of runaways we heard—"

Croghan held up a hand and raised his voice over Pennyrile's brother. "First," he began, "I'm sorry for your brother's death, no matter what kind of man he was, or what kind of man you are." Croghan stole a look at Stephen and chose his words with care. "But tonic water and runaways . . . I'm afraid that the disease had begun to affect his mind."

Elias gave Nick a sidelong glance, but his face was as blank as ever.

"That's a stinking lie!" the brother said.

Croghan's voice was gentle. "I'm very sorry, but it's true. He was losing his faculties. And when he disappeared, I feared the worst."

"We have proof!" Pennyrile's brother shouted. "Maps he stole," he said, whirling around to look for Stephen. "Off that one there!"

Croghan cut his eyes toward Stephen. "Maps?" he asked, the question sharper than a whittling knife.

Oh no! Croghan had pestered Stephen about the maps, and Stephen had said he'd get around to them, never owning to the notebook he kept.

"I don't have any maps," Stephen said evenly and, Elias realized, technically, honestly.

Croghan waited for Stephen to say more. When he didn't, he addressed himself to Pennyrile's brother. "Produce this proof," he said, holding out a hand. "Show me these maps."

A murmur went through the column of men. Then Pennyrile's brother cursed softly. "My brother had them when he . . . fell."

Croghan kept his eyes fixed on Stephen, studying him for some reaction. But Stephen might as well have been carved from the walls of the cave for all he gave up.

"How convenient," the doctor said.

"It's true!" Pennyrile's brother shouted. "We all saw them!"

"But you never saw him take them from my man Bishop, did you?" Croghan pressed.

The brother gaped, furious, but had to shake his head.

"So . . . ," Croghan began, sounding like he was puzzling out a diagnosis. "Under the command of an invalid with an addled mind, a band of pirates first kidnapped inno-cent children belonging to a neighboring farm, then came into the cave under pretenses that they wanted a tour. They then proceeded to blackmail the father of those children—*my* man Mat Bransford—into leading them to some mythical underground colony of runaway slaves?"

"I'm tellin' you—" Pennyrile's brother began.

Croghan held up a hand. "But I'm still unclear how Mat sent out the cry for help. How did Nick know to lay the trap?"

Elias swallowed and stepped out from behind Stephen. "That'd be me, Doctor."

"Elias," Croghan said like he wished he were wrong. Before he could scold him, Elias spilled out the nearest version to the truth he could without giving up Jonah or Haven. He told him how he'd caught Mat's tour, hung back and saw the trouble he was in, and heard the pirates say they'd taken Mat's kids. How he rounded up Nick and Stephen, and they made to bail out Mat.

"I daresay this is more activity than I prescribed when I sent you out this morning," Croghan said, almost smiling now.

"Reckon so." Elias hung his head, trying to look good and ashamed of himself.

"Well," Croghan said, "I believe you men have completed your tour. Nick, please escort the deputy and the rest out to the main entrance. I suppose the marshal will be along directly. I'll come up and wait with all of you." Nick started walking, yanking hard on the rope that led to the first man in the column.

Stephen and Elias made to follow them, but Croghan held up his hand. "A moment."

Out of the frying pan . . . , Elias thought. Croghan waited until the men had moved off, then he slowly followed, motioning to Elias and Stephen to join him. "A strange turn of events, wouldn't you say so, boys?"

"Yes, Doctor Croghan," Stephen said.

He gave them each a look. "Funny that Pennyrile managed to convince them of the existence of a whole hidden colony of runaway slaves."

Neither Stephen nor Elias responded.

"But if they've heard doings of some sort of haven—"

He paused and looked at them both pointedly. Stephen's jaw twitched. Elias felt his face go white. After all they'd been through, after managing to stop Pennyrile's gang, what if it still wasn't enough? What if Croghan knew?

And then Croghan did the darndest thing. He grinned. Just for a second. But it was enough. "Then I'm certain others of their ilk might be looking as well."

"You could be right," Stephen said, his voice trembling high.

Adrenaline raced through Elias's limbs. Was the doctor going to help them?

"So we must set the world at ease that such a mythical place does not exist. And what better way than with you finally completing your maps."

"Yes, sir," Stephen squeaked out.

"I think it's high time you took a sojourn to work on those maps," he said, motioning for them to follow as he started back up the path. "I should think a fortnight cloistered at my father's estate in Louisville will afford you enough time to complete the work?"

"Should," Stephen said.

"You can ride out with Elias when he goes," Croghan added.

"Goes?" Elias asked.

"There was a letter from your mother waiting at the

hotel this morning. She's sent the money for your fare. There's a stage tomorrow from Cave City. You'll both be on it."

"Tomorrow?" Elias croaked.

"Tomorrow," the doctor confirmed. "Unless you've other business in the cave I should know about?"

"No, sir!" Haven was safe.

At the entrance, Nick and the deputy and his posse spurred the pirates up the slope. On the ridge, more men waited, hands on their hips, staring down. Elias could make out a six-pointed star glinting from the shirtfront of one of them.

"I'll go on from here without you," Croghan said, waving to the marshal. "I must ask if I can do anything to see Mat's children recovered"—he caught himself—"for the sake of Parthena's master, of course." He headed off, leaving Stephen and Elias stunned. Croghan glanced back and found them still gaping. "Go on, then," Croghan said, almost smiling. "You both have packing to do."

"Yes, sir," Elias and Stephen chorused.

"And, Stephen?" Doctor Croghan said over his shoulder as he climbed up. "Do take care with your mapping. We wouldn't want anyone stumbling anyplace they didn't belong, now would we?"

Stephen smiled broadly. "No, sir, we wouldn't."

"I didn't think so," the doctor said, springing up the slope.

Elias watched him go, marveling that, for the ways the cave had awed and surprised him since he arrived, he could never recall feeling quite as dumbstruck as he did now.

Chapter Twenty-Three

SQUARE KNOT

Stephen and Elias weren't the first ones to leave. Elias, exhausted, had forgone his packing to take a short nap, and woke to find it late afternoon.

He looked around his room again, the room that had been his home for . . . how long? He checked the marks on the wall, even though he'd stopped tracking them days ago. Forty-three. So, around two months, he guessed. Two months he'd lived in this narrow hut, slept in this bed, watched the fire at the grate.

And he would go home tomorrow.

He heard Nedra cough across the way. Maybe it was the guilt that he was leaving, or the guilt of having not sat with her more, but he walked over to look in on her.

"Squire," she said when he appeared at her door.

She sat on the edge of her bed, wrapped up in a traveling coat and hat. Her trunk, packed and wrapped with twine, waited on the floor next to her.

"You're going?" Elias was stunned.

She didn't respond at first. "Squire Elias," she repeated. "Can you feel the spring coming?"

Elias felt awful. Awful that Croghan hadn't been able to help her.

"Will Brandstrom know me?" she asked him before she fell to coughing, holding a linen handkerchief to her mouth. *Brandstrom?* Elias wondered. He guessed he must be the fiancé. Nedra reached for a bottle of water sitting beside her on the table. Elias uncorked the top and held it out to her. She let the handkerchief fall to her lap. Elias saw the blood sprayed there like cinnamon scattered on a pudding.

"Nobody could forget you, ma'am," he said as she drank deeply.

The bottle trembled as she passed it back to Elias. "Pennies," she said.

Elias fitted the cork back in. Pennies? Nedra was given to odd talk, but usually he could follow the thread. "Miss?"

"Tastes of pennies," she said, still not looking anywhere in particular.

Elias's eyes fell on the bottle in his hands. *Tastes like pennies.*

"Who brought this?" he asked, looking around for the pitcher and cup that was usually here. They were already gone.

Nedra smiled at him. "You wore your scarf."

Elias noticed two other bottles of water waiting on top of her trunk.

"Did Lill give you these?" he persisted.

"Brave Squire Elias," she went on. He was too pleased to see the bottles to care that he couldn't keep up with her talk. Stephen and Nick and Mat had given the water out, pure and strong, to all of them. *When there isn't much you can do, you want to do what you can.* Wasn't that what Stephen had said?

There was something Elias could do too.

He slid the chair over. "You know those stories we both like, Miss Nedra? 'Bout Arthur and Lancelot?"

Her eyes seemed to clear briefly.

"Remember what they were after in the end? Their greatest quest?" Elias leaned in, clutching the bottle tighter.

"The Holy Grail," she whispered, the flash of the beauty that had been hers, that still was there, Elias decided, almost startling.

"Remember what the Grail could do?" He found

himself whispering too, like they were sharing a secret. "If you drunk from it? It made you well, didn't it, Miss Nedra? It healed anything, made a body whole again. That's why they searched so hard and so long for it, didn't they?"

"Through kingdoms and ages," she murmured.

"Yes!" Elias could barely keep his seat. "But this," he said, holding up the bottle, "this would have launched a thousand more quests! This water's magic, miss. And if you'll drink it, and you'll believe—"

She studied the bottle, the water almost cloudy as it sloshed inside.

"Pennies," she repeated.

"*Hope,*" Elias insisted. "Promise you'll drink it all?"

She took the bottle, cradled it in her arms. "Promise."

Lillian cleared her throat. Elias wondered how long she'd been standing there. "Mat's here to fetch your trunk up. And Doc Croghan's had the sedan chair sent down. They ready for you."

"Ready," Nedra repeated.

Stranger things had happened down there than people taking miracle cures, Elias figured. And Stephen and Hughes and the others were right—a little extra hope never hurt.

Overcome, Elias stooped and kissed the back of Nedra's hand, just like Lancelot might have.

Nedra gave one short, girlish laugh. *Gosh, she is young,*

Elias thought, probably not more than eighteen. Elias wondered why he hadn't noticed before.

Mat appeared, and though Elias couldn't swear to it in the lamplight, he was almost sure the man winked at him. Either way, it was the nearest to happy Elias'd ever seen Mat look. But Elias wasn't fool enough to smile back. Instead he bent down to help him lift the trunk. Once Mat had it on his shoulders, he waved Elias off.

Elias helped Nedra into the sedan chair waiting outside. "Take care with her," he said to the men who'd carried it down, adding, "Please."

"They will, Elias," Lillian said gently, helping Nedra settle in, tucking the bottles of water in around her feet.

Elias scanned the empty room and saw Nedra's knitting basket peeking out from under her bed. "Wait!" he scooped it up. "You're forgetting this!"

Nedra's eyes flicked from the basket to Elias. "No more knitting. No more."

"But—"

Nedra held up a hand. *"She left the web, she left the loom, / she made three paces through the room."*

And though Elias still didn't understand the words, he'd read Nedra's favorite poem enough times to at least recognize the lines. So he didn't press; instead he held the basket to his chest. "Yes, ma'am."

"Good-bye, Squire. Don't forget your scarf." The men lifted the chair.

Elias smiled, but his eyes stung. "Good luck, Miss Nedra."

She bobbed her head, just like a queen in an Arthur tale might do, and was carried away.

After Elias finished his own packing and ate his supper (with no eggs in sight, thank you very much), he heard Stephen outside his hut.

"Hey," he said, poking his head inside.

"Hey," Elias replied.

"Brought you something," Stephen said, carrying an object that was roughly square and made of slats woven loosely together.

"What is it?"

"One of Nick's old traps," Stephen said, passing it off. "He modified it. To be a bird cage."

"It's perfect," Elias moved to where Bedivere was pecking up grain.

The pigeon side-hopped to get out of the way and inspected the cage, neck craning to take it in. He cooed.

"Reckon he likes it," Elias said. "Think it's big enough for two?"

Stephen smiled. "You planning to take the bird Pennyrile left behind in the hut?"

Elias shrugged. "Shouldn't leave it here. That way Bedivere'll have a pal."

"I think it'll serve them both fine," Stephen said. "You can build a better loft when you're off the road."

"Thanks." They watched Bedivere peck at the slats, testing to see if he could eat them before he settled for his corn.

"Davie's all right," Stephen said.

Elias whirled on him. "What?"

"They found him on board Pennyrile's boat, chained up."

"Oh no," Elias said.

"Croghan claimed he was one of his. Acted good and angry at how those pirates had taken one of his men."

Elias gaped. "That means . . ."

"The doctor knew." Stephen nodded. "I don't know how he knew, or how long he knew it, but he knew something. Knew enough to make it look like Davie belonged here with us and the pirates had kidnapped him. Only we'll all have to call him Phillip for a while."

"Phillip?"

Stephen laughed. "I guess it was the first name that came to Croghan's head. We all had to play along so the marshal and the others didn't suspect anything."

"How's Dav—I mean, Phillip like it?" Elias asked, grinning.

Stephen shook his head. "Well enough. Brought him back with us. He's up at the hotel now, splitting wood. He'll slip down to Haven in a couple of days when things settle again."

"Haven's staying put? Even with Croghan knowing?"

Stephen shook his head. "Only to move folks out slow. Safer that way," he said. "Even Hughes'll go when there's no one left. Croghan is right: others might come looking."

"It's over, then?" Elias asked.

Stephen nodded. "All in one fell swoop. Hospital and Haven together. But it's right, I suppose. A body can't live forever underground. Not even Hughes. Not even you."

"Maybe you," Elias suggested.

Stephen considered, then shrugged. "Glad I don't have to find out. But in the meantime, you feel like taking a walk?"

"Sure," Elias said. "Where to?"

"Just to Smiley," he said, looking round. "Nick and Mat and Jonah got something we need to do before you and I go in the morning."

"Do?" Elias asked. "'Nother tight spot only I'll fit into?"

"Something like that," Stephen said, but he smiled when he said it. "Come on."

Elias held up a finger. "Hang on." He scooped up Nedra's basket. He knew just who might want it. Then he flipped open his trunk, fetched out the book, and tucked it with the yarn and needles. Nedra wasn't wrong about leaving some things behind, he'd decided.

Stephen eyed the basket. "What's that for?"

Elias shrugged. "Just some stuff to pass on."

When they were a few minutes away from the ward, Stephen asked softly, "Miss Nedra seem all right when she went?"

"Lillian gave her some of the water, fresh," Elias said.

Stephen took off his cap and dusted the brim. "Even if it's nothing but snake oil, it can't hurt. Probably just getting out of this place will heal 'em up."

"What's going to happen to the spring?" Elias asked.

Stephen sighed. "Nothing, I don't suppose. Served its purpose. Just like Croghan's hospital."

"Will the doctor be all right?" Elias asked. They owed him plenty. And he was the one whose hospital and schemes for the cave had failed.

Stephen hitched his pack up higher. "I think so. Already he has plans to expand the tours when I get back. And he means to build a hotel down here next, up there in the Rotunda. Thinks he can get a road laid so folks can ride all the way up to the door by wagon."

"That'd be something to see," Elias said. A road and a hotel. Somehow it seemed even more spectacular and far-fetched than the hospital and its promise of a cure. "Make sure he gets better beds than we had."

"Come back and try one for yourself then," Stephen said. "When it's finished."

"You'll still be here?" Elias asked.

"Wouldn't want to be anywhere else," Stephen said without hesitation.

They walked on, Elias taking in the cave. "You might think me peculiar, but I'm going to miss it. Being here."

Stephen didn't seem the least bit surprised. "I expect so. You took to this place quick. And it took to you almost as quick."

"There's nothing like this back in Norfolk," Elias said, thinking of the docks and the sand and the marsh and the sea and the sunshine. And he was amazed to realize that he didn't know what he was going to do with himself back home.

"You'll find something to do. And you can write me and tell me about it," Stephen suggested.

"Yeah?" Elias asked.

"I might even write back. That all right with you?"

Elias flashed back to that evening in the tunnel, Stephen asking if it were all right with Elias that he could read. Funny how different the question felt now. "I'd like it," Elias said.

They arrived at Smiley and found the room bathed in light.

Nick, Mat, and Jonah were waiting. They had two lamps, one on top of the rock Elias and Nick had hidden behind, the other on the floor just beside it.

"What's going on?" Elias asked, looking to each of them.

Mat leaped across Smiley's grinning mouth with the ease of a deer jumping a stream. He locked eyes with Elias. Then he put out his hand. "I'm obliged to you, Eli," he said, his voice breaking. Elias was too stunned to do anything but shake his hand. "You stuck your neck out for me and mine, and all them folk down at Haven," he said. "And you didn't have to."

"'Course I did," Elias told him.

Mat swallowed hard. "Even so," he said, but didn't go on.

"Y'all want to move this along? I'm 'posed to be on watch," Jonah said.

Stephen groaned. "If I had a nickel for every time you were meant to be on watch—"

"Just get over here," Jonah said.

"C'mon," Stephen said to Elias, jumping the pit. Elias tossed the basket over to Jonah, took a couple of good running steps, and leaped. He couldn't quite shake the sight of Pennyrile falling in, or imagining him down there.

"You bring us a picnic?" Jonah asked, peeking inside the basket.

Elias took it from him. "Nedra left her knitting things. I was hoping you might take it to Josie. That doll she made turned out a treat, and I bet she could use the yarn and the needles."

"Bet she could," Nick said, grinning, and spat into the corner of Smiley.

Elias rummaged inside. "And this," he said to Jonah, "this is for you."

He handed the book over. Jonah's mouth fell open as he held the book up to the light. The gold letters flashed brilliantly. "What's it say?"

"It's my Arthur stories," Elias explained. "Thought you might want to read the rest, after you learn and all."

Jonah held the book as if it were made of glass. "I'm obliged," he whispered.

Elias took in Mat and Stephen and Nick, and wished he had something to leave with them as well. "That's all," he said, embarrassed.

"Not quite," Stephen said, setting down his lantern so he could dig in his bag. He produced a stubby little awl. He handed it to Elias, guiding him around to the back of the rock until he was standing where he and Nick had hidden.

"What's this?" Elias asked.

"*This,*" Stephen began, "is explorer's right."

Elias studied at the awl in his hand, the tip glinting in the lamplight.

They meant him to write his name.

He'd seen the names all over Gothic Avenue, and other places, too, crowding together. But those were just the tourists.

He'd seen Stephen's, Nick's, and Mat's all over as well, but hidden, in the byways and corners of the cave others didn't see. And Elias knew what it meant. A marker that they'd been first, that they'd been the ones to find the way. He remembered Stephen, Nick, and Mat arguing the night they first took him out, when he shimmied into the dead end they couldn't fit inside. How Stephen had asked if he could write his name. And the time Nick asked him if he wanted to put his name up next to those of the other visitors in Gothic. How he'd felt like he passed some kind of test when he'd declined.

But now.

Here.

There were no marks past the Camel. No marks down here at Smiley, all on account of keeping Haven safe. "But—"

"Make your mark," Mat growled. The friendliest growl Elias had ever heard from him. They were paying him the highest compliment they knew how. This time he wasn't going to refuse them. So he crouched and dug the point of the awl into the limestone.

As trim and neat as he could, he carved his full name: ELIAS JEFFERSON HARRIGAN. It took a while, but the others didn't seem to mind. When he finished, he straightened up. Nick took the awl and wrote his own name next to Elias's. Then he passed the awl to Mat, who did the same, and then Stephen. Finally Jonah took it, scratched out a letter *J*, and handed the awl back to Stephen.

"I'll come back and do the rest," Jonah said, meeting Elias's eye. "That's all I know so far." Elias studied the carved names, thinking he was sure he'd never been prouder in his whole life.

"That'll do," Nick said, patting Elias on the shoulder. "Best get back."

Stephen lifted his pack and light. The others made ready to go.

Jonah shook Elias's hand and disappeared down the passage toward Haven, carrying a light this time, and keeping an eye on his new book. Elias and his friends cleared Smiley one by one. They began the hike back up to the huts clustered in the ward, to Gothic Avenue, and finally to the world waiting beyond the craggy opening of Mammoth Cave.

March 15, 1843

*Y*oung Elias Harrigan will be home by month's end, I should think. As pleased as I am to have him leaving stronger and more spirited, I cannot but feel melancholy at his departure. He was in more ways than I can tell a light in the dark. The other patients and I are encouraged at his improvement, and I count on the hope that he provided delivering them as they go as well.

Oddly, I have but Elias's recovery I can boast of. One healing alone is not enough to publish my work on my treatment of the disease. But there are dozens of other lives spared and improved that I will never speak of, many of which owe a debt to young Elias as well. As it reads in the Gospel of Matthew, "Let not thy left hand know what thy right hand doeth. . . ."

Respectfully submitted,
Dr. John Croghan

FURTHER READING

I grew up in Owensboro, Kentucky, not far from Mammoth Cave. I earned my degree in English at Western Kentucky University in Bowling Green—which is even closer. I visited the cave with my family as a child and again as a student as part of a geography class, and was always impressed by its grandeur, the otherworldliness of it, and the feeling of being so small in something so vast.

It wasn't until our extended family had a reunion there in 2011 that I knew I wanted to write a book set in the cave. While on one of the shorter tours (in between bouts of carrying my kids), I looked at the map they gave us when we entered, wishing I could keep going, exploring the far reaches of the cave. A photo inset on the map showed a stone hut and bore a caption that read *One of the buildings used in Dr. John Croghan's experimental tuberculosis hospital.* My husband (who was probably carrying both our children at this point) saw the mad gleam in my eye, sighed, and said, "You're about to write another book, aren't you?"

Sometimes, I love it when my husband is right.

While this story is fictional, the place, circumstances, and some of the people who inspired it were very real. As an author, the fun of writing for me often comes in muddling around in the spaces between the facts, inventing things that might have been, while staying relatively faithful to the established record. If you'd like to learn more about what's real and made up, you can do your own digging.

My first recommendation would be to visit Mammoth Cave. There you can see firsthand the wonders of the largest cave system in the world; speak with the amazing, dedicated park rangers and historians; and walk paths forged by Stephen Bishop, Mat Bransford, and Nick Bransford. But if traveling there in person isn't possible, reading provides excellent alternatives. Any of the following resources offer wonderful insights into the cave itself; people like Dr. Croghan and others who waged the battle against consumption; or the extraordinary lives of Stephen, Nick, and Mat.

Happy adventuring.

Farrell, Jeannette. *Invisible Enemies, Revised Edition: Stories of Infectious Diseases.* New York: Farrar, Straus and Giroux, 2005.

This is a wonderful book about the history of infectious diseases. The chapter on tuberculosis (also called "consumption" or "phthisis" at the time of the book's setting) includes a fantastically gruesome listing of the treatments various doctors attempted to cure the disease.

Hovey, H. C. *One Hundred Miles in Mammoth Cave—In 1880.* Vistabooks, 2000.

H. C. Hovey was the state geologist of Kentucky. He wrote this lengthy article describing explorations in the cave for *Scribner's Monthly* magazine. Wonderful illustrations accompany the text, and it does an excellent job of recreating what the original tours in the cave (which have been offered since 1816) might have been like.

Lyons, Joy Medley. *Making Their Mark: The Signature of Slavery at Mammoth Cave.* Fort Washington, PA: Eastern National, 2006.

Writing about real people in a fictional story is always a bit tricky, particularly when those people are as unique and brave as Stephen Bishop, Nick Bransford, and Mat Bransford. All three are integral parts of the rich history and exploration of Mammoth Cave. All three remained at Mammoth Cave until their deaths—even after they'd been freed. While I made up some details about their personalities, I did my best to honor their stories and build on what we do know about them. This was my favorite resource in that regard. Beautiful and insightful, it offers a riveting account of the African-American experience at the cave predating that of Nick and Stephen and Mat, all the way up to the present day, when an actual descendent of Mat Bransford works as a ranger (and yes, guide) at Mammoth Cave National Park.

Mammoth Cave National Park. http://www.nps.gov/maca/index.html. National Park Service. 2010–2014.

An excellent resource for anyone wishing to learn about the cave. There is wonderful information about the cave, its history, and exploration, as well as articles about many of the main characters in the story.

Murphy, Jim, and Allison Blank. *Invincible Microbe: Tuberculosis and the Never-ending Search for a Cure.* New York: Clarion Books, 2012.

Tuberculosis has been around for centuries, and Murphy and Blank's book does a phenomenal job of chronicling the history of this devastating illness. At the time of Croghan's experimental hospital in the cave, they had no idea the disease was transmissible and had no real understanding regarding its treatment. This meant that Dr. Croghan did indeed allow visitors on the tour to interact with patients, and sadly this also meant that both Dr. Croghan and Stephen Bishop later died as a result of having contracted tuberculosis at some point. The book is an engaging, revealing account for those interested in learning why some were able to recover from the disease while others were not, and how modern medicine eventually began to win the battle against the illness.

O'Connor Olson, Colleen, and Charles Hanion. *Scary Stories of Mammoth Cave.* Dayton, OH: Cave Books, 2002.

This book was one of my favorites. It speaks to the spookiness and mystery of the cave, recounting the many legends of ghosts and hauntings that visitors are drawn to, as well as the dangers and perils faced by some early explorers. There is a brief chapter about the hospital as well, which informed my story and set me imagining what it might have been like to live underground, desperate to get well.

O'Connor Olson, Colleen. *Mammoth Cave by Lantern Light: Visiting America's Most Famous Cave in the 1800s.* Dayton, OH: Cave Books, 2010.

O'Connor Olson is a ranger and historian at Mammoth Cave. This book is indispensable for learning more about the cave at the time of the novel's setting, the hospital experiment, and the celebrated guides. It also recounts many of the cave's famous visitors and anecdotes that could inspire entire novels of their own.

ACKNOWLEDGMENTS

I am grateful to many, many people for their support and interest in this book. To Angie Wright . . . just because. Jacqueline and Josh Hawkins, for your friendship and reading of the manuscript at just the right moment. Stephanie Guerra, thank you for reading this book countless times, and for always finding the right ways to challenge me. To the ladies of the Sunday writing group, thanks for hearing those early chapters and asking for more. Thanks to my mom for asking when I was going to write a Kentucky book, and for reading repeatedly without complaint when I did. To Ron Spoelstra for teaching me about carrier pigeons and sharing your story with me.

This book would not exist (or at least the historical portions would be far less rich!) without the help of the many talented National Park rangers and historians who were kind enough to respond to my e-mails and phone calls. Special thanks to Joe Williams and Gabe Esters for the tour and for letting me hang back and furiously scribble notes. Thanks to Joy Medley Lyons—both for her beautiful book and for answering my questions about Nick, Mat, and Stephen. Many, many thanks to Colleen O'Connor Olson for answering my e-mails, for the chance to talk and walk the cave with you, and for offering such helpful feedback on the innumerable details of the cave, the history, and this story.

And I'm so thankful to the many people who helped this story become a real live book. Thanks to Rick Britton for the painstakingly created map, to Grady McFerrin for the just-right cover, and to Michael McCartney for making this book (and all the others) so beautiful. A whole cave full of thanks to Beth Miller and Robin Rue—there's no other team I'd rather be on this adventure with. And, of course, to Caitlyn Dlouhy, for being the best guide a writer could hope for.

Most of all, thanks to Evie and Arun for your patience when the writing was hard and your encouragement when it was working. Your stories are still my favorites to tell. And finally to Jimmy, for taking all those tours with me, for never minding when I asked you to read it again, and for always being the light that led me back home.

The story of one girl's unrelenting quest for freedom.

NATIONAL BOOK AWARD FINALIST

WINNER OF THE SCOTT O'DELL AWARD FOR HISTORICAL FICTION

* "Startlingly provocative . . . nuanced and evenhanded . . . a fast-moving, emotionally involving plot."
—*Publishers Weekly*, starred review

* "Anderson explores elemental themes of power, freedom, and the sources of human strength in this searing, fascinating story."
—*Booklist*, starred review

A
atheneum books for young readers
Published by Simon & Schuster   KIDS.SimonandSchuster.com

Don't miss any of these amazing novels from the winner of the National Book Award and the Newbery Medal,

CYNTHIA KADOHATA:

cynthia kadohata

kira-kira

Weedflower

CYNTHIA KADOHATA

Outside beauty

Cynthia Kadohata

CYNTHIA KADOHATA

A Million Shades of Gray

NATIONAL BOOK AWARD WINNER

THE THING ABOUT LUCK

CYNTHIA KADOHATA

CYNTHIA KADOHATA
AUTHOR OF THE NATIONAL BOOK AWARD WINNER THE THING ABOUT LUCK

Half a World Away

Atheneum

IRRESISTIBLE FICTION
from Edgar Award–winning author
FRANCES O'ROARK DOWELL!

ANYBODY SHINING

THE SECRET LANGUAGE OF GIRLS

THE KIND OF FRIENDS WE USED TO BE

THE SOUND OF YOUR VOICE . . . ONLY REALLY FAR AWAY

THE SECOND LIFE OF ABIGAIL WALKER

FALLING IN

DOVEY COE

WHERE I'D LIKE TO BE

CHICKEN BOY

SHOOTING THE MOON

Atheneum

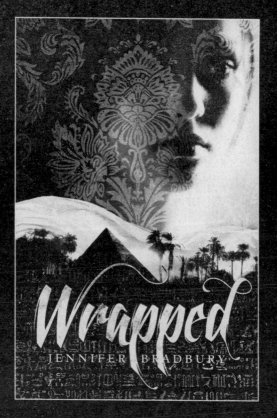

Get wrapped up in this exotic adventure from Jennifer Bradbury!